Rushed

Brian Harmon

Rushed

ISBN: 1481882902
ISBN-13: 978-1481882903

For Guinevere

Chapter One

Eric Fortrell lived a perfectly unremarkable life until he happened to have a very extraordinary dream. It wasn't that it was an especially meaningful dream. In fact, he could remember nothing about the dream except that there was something about a bird, and even that vague detail was so far lost to his waking mind that only the word itself remained. "Bird." It was not any particular kind of bird, no bird of any particular color or size. It was nothing more significant than *something about a bird.* And yet this dream filled him with such a profound sense of urgency and foreboding that he immediately left his bed, dressed himself and fled his home in the middle of the night. By the time he came to his senses and realized that there was nowhere for him to go, he was already standing in his driveway with the door of his silver PT Cruiser wide open, ready to climb in and drive away.

He was confused, of course, and a little unnerved. After all, he wasn't exactly known for being impulsive. It wasn't like him to do anything without a reasonable amount of thought, much less jump up in the middle of the night and go running out to his car, inexplicably convinced that he desperately needed to be somewhere. But more than that, he was embarrassed. He closed the vehicle's door as quietly as he could and gazed around at the darkened windows of his neighbors' houses, very nearly convinced that at least one of them must be watching him, wondering where he thought he was going at a quarter past one in the morning, laughing at his ridiculous antics.

He was a reasonable enough man to know that this was utter nonsense. Even if someone *was* up and wandering around in their unlit home at this hour *and* just happened to be looking out the window as he hurried out the door, they'd have no reason to suspect that he was behaving strangely. Perhaps he'd lost something, his wallet, maybe, and was checking to see if he'd left it in his vehicle.

Still, he hesitated to lock the car for fear that the brief sounding of the horn would alert every nosy neighbor on the block to his presence and somehow instantly let them know that he was acting as if he'd utterly lost his mind.

He left the PT Cruiser unlocked in the driveway and returned to his house and his bed.

He was not crazy. He did not have a history of insanity in his family. He had no excessive mental or emotional stress in his life. He was also intelligent. He'd earned a Masters Degree in education and literature. With honors. He was a respected high school English teacher and he had never in his life poisoned his mind with drugs. He didn't even drink that much. Only seldom in his life had he drank enough to qualify him as being drunk, and never so much that he couldn't remember what he did the next morning.

And yet here he was.

Karen was waiting for him when he returned to bed. She was

concerned, of course, and wanted to know what had happened, why he had risen and dressed, where he had gone. He told her the truth. He always told his wife the truth. And of course she laughed at him and told him how silly he was because she was always equally as honest with him and it was, after all, a funny and silly thing that he had done.

But long after Karen had drifted off to sleep again, Eric remained awake, staring up at the ceiling in the faint glow of the street light that filtered through the curtains and the nightlight that shined through the open bathroom door. He kept thinking of the dream he couldn't remember and the odd compulsion that had driven him out of his bed and into the cool August night.

The following day was no better. He couldn't stop thinking about the dream (something about a bird...) and that feeling of desperately needing to be somewhere (*now*). In fact, he still felt this compulsion. It gnawed stubbornly at him. His eyes kept drifting to the windows and doors. His thoughts kept returning to the parked PT Cruiser in the driveway. It was like an itch.

He very much wanted to get in the vehicle and drive down the road. Yet he remained unable to say *where* it was he wanted so badly to go.

That night, the dream returned. Like the first time, he recalled nothing but a bird (or birds, or something bird-like...he simply couldn't remember) and like the first time, he awoke utterly convinced that there was somewhere he very much needed to be, that he was, in fact, desperately *late*.

He did not make it all the way to his car this time. When Karen switched on her bedside lamp, he stood frozen and bewildered, his pants only halfway on, squinting into the blinding glare and trying to remember where it was he thought he was going.

Soon after, he was back in bed, the lights back off. Karen did not laugh at him this night. She did not tell him he was silly. She urged him back into bed and he came willingly, ashamed of the concern he saw in her sleepy face. The desperation he had felt was overpowered by the simple logic that he *did not have anywhere to be*. He returned to his pillow without a word and she snuggled against him as if determined to anchor him to the bed until morning.

Again, he lay awake, that feeling of being late still stubbornly refusing to release him and let him rest.

The next day was much like the one before it. He remained constantly distracted, his thoughts and eyes inexorably drawn to the parked PT Cruiser and the unknown roads it promised to carry him down.

Each time he forced his eyes away from the windows and doors he caught Karen watching him. She was no fool. No matter how many times he told her he was fine, she knew something was troubling him, and he felt terrible for worrying her. But still he could not shake the urge to get up and go.

The third night inevitably arrived and Eric awoke once more from the same mysterious dream with the same maddening desire to rush out of the house.

This time, he did not bother returning to bed. When Karen came downstairs and switched on the kitchen light at a little before three in the morning, she found him sitting at the table, fully dressed, a steaming cup of coffee in his hands and his car keys sitting in front of him.

For a moment she stood watching him and for that moment he

watched her back, admiring her. She was considerably heavier than she had been ten years ago when he married her, but still as lovely as the day they met. In fact, he rather preferred her a little plumper. She'd been too skinny back when they dated, far too preoccupied with her weight. Now that she'd accepted that there was nothing wrong with being larger than a size zero, she'd filled out her figure with magnificently sexy curves. His eyes washed over her bare legs as she stood leaning against the doorjamb, clothed in only her favorite pajama top, her arms crossed over her chest as if chilled.

"You know," she said finally, "there's bound to be an easier way to sneak off and see your mistress."

Eric smiled up at her. "I know. She told me to stop waking her up at two in the morning."

"No girl's horny at that hour."

Still smiling, still admiring her lovely shape, he sipped quietly at his coffee.

"How far did you get this time?"

"Pretty well right here."

"Same dream?"

"Far as I know. Still can't remember it."

She stared at him and said nothing.

He kept smiling. "It's just a stupid recurring dream."

She was silent for a moment longer. She would not admit that she was worried about him. That simply wasn't her way. But he could see it in her eyes. And he didn't blame her for feeling at least a little concerned. These dreams were troubling. They were interfering with his life. Neither of them had ever dealt with anything like this before.

Finally, she spoke: "What are we going to do?"

"I'm going to go," Eric replied.

This surprised her. She stood up straight, her pajama shirt falling open a little at the bottom, where she'd left it unbuttoned. There was no force on earth that could stop his eyes from being drawn there. "Go where?"

Eric shrugged. "I'll just drive. See where it takes me."

"Okay…but there's nowhere to go. It's just a stupid dream. You said so yourself just now."

"I know. *Believe me*, I know. But this is the third night in a row I've had it and for some reason it's really getting to me. I've been so distracted. I *constantly* feel like there's somewhere I need to be."

"But there's not. You know that."

"I *do* know that," he assured her. "But apparently some part of my brain *doesn't*. That's why I'm going. I'll open myself up to it, do what it wants me to do. I'll just get in the car and drive. After a while, I'll prove to myself that there really isn't anywhere for me to go. Then I can come home and finally sleep. I mean, why not? I'm already awake."

She stared at him, studying him, considering what he'd said. He didn't know what else to say to her, so he took another sip of his coffee and let his eyes slide down her naked legs while he waited for her to speak.

"I guess that makes sense," she replied at last.

"*I* thought so."

"Show that messed up little brain of yours it doesn't know what it's talking about."

"Put it back in its place, right? That's what I'm saying."

She shifted her weight and continued to stare at him. He could almost see the thoughts swirling behind her lovely eyes.

"I'll be fine," he assured her. "And I can finally get this weirdness out of my system."

"But what if it doesn't work?"

"Then it doesn't work. At least I'll have tried, right? If I'm still having the dreams after this, I'll call the doctor."

Karen nodded. She knew there was no reason to be concerned. It was only a dream. It was irrational. So why not embrace the irrational and see what happened? Maybe then he'd at least be able to sleep through the night again.

And even if it didn't work, he wouldn't be any worse off for trying.

"I guess gas *is* cheaper than therapy," she reasoned.

"Just a little, I think."

"Just a little."

Eric took another sip of his coffee and found his eyes drifting to the door again. He felt impatient to go, but he refused to simply rush out the door.

"It'll be a fun little adventure for you."

Eric returned his eyes to his wife and smiled again. "I'll bet it will."

"No picking up sexy hitchhikers."

"But those are the best kind."

"I keep telling you, you don't know where they've been."

"If my adventure has a serious lack of romance, it'll be your fault."

"I'll just have to live with the consequences. How long will you be gone?"

Eric shrugged. "Long as it takes, I guess."

She didn't like this answer. She chewed thoughtfully at her lower lip. He loved it when she did that.

"Probably only a couple hours. I mean, really, where am I going to go? I'll be fine."

"Do you have your cell phone?"

Eric pulled the phone from the front pocket of his khaki pants and showed her. He hated cell phones, saw no value in them whatsoever, but she insisted that he carry one in case of emergencies. She was utterly unwavering about it. She'd even wanted to get him a high-dollar one with more functions than his laptop, like the one she carried, but he'd put his foot down. He carried nothing fancier than a cheap, pre-paid model from Wal-Mart. Even so, it had an obnoxious amount of extras built into it that he had no idea how to use. He didn't even know how to add minutes to the ridiculous thing. Karen took care of that for him.

He returned the annoying device to his pocket, finished his coffee and then stood up and rinsed out his cup in the sink. When he turned back around, Karen was right next to him, slipping her arms around him.

"It's okay," he promised her. "I'm just driving around. I *can* drive at night, you know."

"I just don't like being left alone. You know that. You won't fall asleep, will you?"

"I'll stay caffeinated," he promised. "Just go back to sleep. I'll be home before you know it."

"I won't be able to sleep. I never sleep well when you're not here."

"Try."

"You and your convoluted schemes to sneak off with your women."

"I like to keep it interesting. I'll tell your sister you said hi."

She gave his arm a gentle smack. "Pushing it," she warned him with an amused grin.

Eric smiled and kissed her again. "What've you got going on today?"

"Birthday cake for Joss."

"Oh yeah."

Karen was a talented baker and a freelance cake decorator. She'd earned an impressive reputation here in her home town and regularly earned fairly decent spending money.

"Toni's coming by to pick it up this afternoon." Toni was Karen's cousin. Joss was Toni's son, whose first birthday was tomorrow. He was an exceptionally adorable baby.

"That'll be fun for you."

"I know. Also, I'll probably get started on those pies for Lana." Lana was one of Karen's oldest friends. They went to grade school together. Lana often organized social events for the church, a responsibility she inherited from her mother when she was diagnosed with cancer several years ago. Karen made various pies, cakes, cookies, whatever recipes she wanted to try out, and Lana regularly earned her new customers.

Eric had tried to talk her into starting her own website, but she wasn't interested in expanding her hobby into an actual business. She was convinced it would take all the fun out of it.

"Maybe I should just get started now," she said, glancing at the clock on the stove.

"I think you should at least *try* to get more sleep. You don't want to be too exhausted when you're decorating that cake."

"I guess so."

"Go back to bed. I'll see you in a little while."

"Okay."

"Love you."

"Love you too."

Eric kissed her one last time and then collected his keys and walked out of the house.

Karen watched him from the doorway as he climbed into the PT Cruiser and backed out of the driveway.

Now he had only to convince *himself* that this wasn't completely insane.

He settled back into the seat and again tried to remember the dream. But like always, all that came back to him was the bird. It wasn't even an image of a bird. It was just the *idea* of a bird. As if that made any sort of sense.

He drove away with no idea where he was going, confident that he would find nothing waiting for him in the great open world and hoped to soon return home satisfied and back to normal.

Chapter Two

At this time of morning, Creek Bend, Wisconsin was peaceful and still. It was difficult to imagine that almost nine thousand people lived in the city when only a handful of vehicles roamed the quiet streets.

Most of the time, Eric liked being out when it was like this, but today there was a peculiar eeriness to the silent city. Something about the empty sidewalks and darkened buildings made him uneasy. It was as if he were walking through a graveyard instead of driving beneath bright streetlamps.

Although he told Karen that he might be gone a couple hours, he'd expected to be home in no more than fifteen or twenty minutes. He thought that he might merely circle the block a few times, or at most make his way across town to the shopping center and turn around. Unable to find whatever his troubled mind was seeking, he assumed he would quickly be resigned to return unfulfilled, though hopefully much less obsessed with traveling. Instead, being behind the wheel felt remarkably *right*. And soon he found himself driving south on the highway, leaving Creek Bend behind him.

He assumed the feeling would simply dissipate as he drove, that it would fizzle out as mysteriously as it had come to him, and then he'd be able to return to his home and his wife and be done with it. But the urge to drive only grew stronger as he made his way south, passing one town after another, until he came to the interstate. There, he felt compelled to take the onramp and proceed west.

It was about now that he began to wonder what he would do if this strange compulsion to drive overcame him to such a degree that he found himself irresistibly drawn right out of Wisconsin and into Illinois or Iowa or Minnesota. What if the approaching day found him cruising through Missouri or Nebraska or Indiana? What if wherever his subconscious mind was trying to take him wasn't even in the Midwest? Or what if it didn't exist at all?

A chill raced through him as he imagined himself helplessly driving on and on and on. He supposed that, eventually, Karen would kill his credit cards and he'd run out of money for gas. But would he then simply get out of the car and walk?

It was an eerie thought, and one he promptly pushed out of his head.

He was *not* crazy.

It was just a damn dream. That was all.

It was probably something psychological, something that he'd forgotten, perhaps, bubbling up to the surface through vivid dreams that were too complex for him to remember upon waking. The result was an irrational compulsion to seek something that wasn't really there.

That sounded reasonable. He guessed. He was no psychologist, but it seemed like a fairly sound explanation. It was at least *something*. It was better than crazy.

One exit sign after another passed by in his headlights as he made his way ever farther from home. Even long after he made up his mind to forget this ridiculous nonsense and turn around, he kept passing perfectly good exits. On and on he drove until, more than three hours after leaving Karen and Creek Bend behind, with the sun peeking over the eastern horizon, he at last switched on his turn signal and drifted into the exit lane.

Yet he still did not turn around. Instead, he cruised on down a little two-lane road that wove through countless acres of cornfields and cow pastures, ever farther from home.

After a while, he turned off this road, onto a narrow strip of blacktop that was far overdue for resurfacing, and drove for several more miles before turning onto yet another two-lane country road.

A loud buzzing rose from his lap as his cell phone began to vibrate enthusiastically in his front-left pocket. He didn't often get calls on his phone, and as such, the vibration usually surprised him, sometimes provoking him into using some of his favorite expletives. But it did not startle him this time, as he was just thinking that Karen should be calling to find out exactly where the hell he'd gone. Instead, it was the physical act of wrestling the phone from his pocket as the seatbelt fought to hold it in place that made him curse.

Like countless times before, he swore that one of these days he was simply going to throw the stupid thing away.

"You need to wrap up this booty call and get your ass back home," Karen said when he'd finally freed it from his pocket and pressed it to his ear.

"Sorry. You know how I like to snuggle after."

"No, you like to *snore* after."

19

"Right. I always get those two mixed up."

"Where are you?"

"Not sure, to be honest."

"You're not sure?"

"I'm not sure," he said again. "I see cornfields and a lot of cows."

"Quaint. Did you get lost?"

"Nope. I know the way home." Or he *thought* he knew the way home, at least. "I just don't know where I am, exactly. I'm pretty sure I'm still in Wisconsin."

"*Pretty* sure?"

"Yeah. *Pretty* sure."

Eric checked his mirrors to be sure he was still alone on the road. He didn't like using the cell phone any time, but least of all while driving. It pissed him off when he saw other drivers using theirs. But there was no shoulder and he had no intention of parking in somebody's driveway just to talk to his wife.

"You do know you're acting like a complete nut job, don't you?"

"Yes I do."

"You know a lesser woman would be really freaked out by now."

"I know she would. I'm so lucky."

"Yes you are."

"I'm probably just having the world's weirdest mid-life crisis or something."

"You're too young to have a mid-life crisis."

"Third-life crisis?"

"Besides, aren't you supposed to buy a motorcycle or an expensive sports car or something? I was looking forward to shopping for the car."

"We still can. We can *both* have mid-life crises."

"Don't be ridiculous. You know the women in my family stop aging at twenty-nine."

"Oh yeah. I keep forgetting about that. Funny math in your genes."

"It's called 'aging gracefully.'"

"My mistake."

"So are you coming home anytime soon?"

"I hope so."

"When?"

"When I'm done. Just trust me, okay?"

"You know I do."

"Good."

"But I warn you, if I have to eat lunch by myself I'm ordering delivery."

"Knock yourself out."

"Ooh. Fun."

"I can't explain it, but this feels right somehow. I think it may be working."

"'Nut job crazy' is working?"

"I think it is."

"Cool."

But if he were to be *completely* honest, he had no idea if this was really working or not. He'd assumed that he'd find himself with no idea where he wanted to go and therefore the compulsion would fade, but the farther he drove, the more it seemed to pull at him. He was beginning to wonder if there might be some specific place he was being drawn, though he could not fathom why he'd have any kind of subconscious desire to come here. He'd never been in this part of Wisconsin before.

"If nothing else, maybe it's the road that's good for me. Maybe I'm just overdue to take a nice long drive to clear my head."

"If you say so."

"I do. Did you start the cake?"

"I did. It's cooling. I'm starting my pies while I wait."

"What kind?"

"Strawberry."

"Yum."

"I miss you."

"I miss you too."

"Call me soon?"

"Sure. Love you."

"Love you too."

Eric said goodbye and ended the call. Ahead of him, the country road stretched on and on, ever deeper into the open farmlands. Cornfields turned to soybean fields and then back to cornfields again. Cattle herds occasionally shared the fields with horses and sheep and goats. Little patches of forestland cropped up from time to time, along with neatly planted apple orchards and even a Christmas tree farm, all punctuated with various farmhouses and barns and silos.

As the PT Cruiser's driver's seat began to grow uncomfortable beneath him and he realized just how far he'd strayed from home, he began to dread the long drive back.

And yet, he continued to pass driveways instead of turning around.

Finally, as he drove over a bridge, he spotted a perfect place to pull over. It was a little graveled drive at the far side of the small river, where fishermen could park and unload their gear.

Eric pulled off the road, but instead of turning around and starting home, he nosed the vehicle into the shade, put it in park and killed the engine.

He opened the door and stepped out into the morning sunshine, stretching his back and legs. The fresh air felt good and he realized that he needed this break.

He closed the door, then quickly opened it again and retrieved the phone that he'd deposited in the cup holder after his conversation with Karen. (He had barely won the battle with the seatbelt to get it *out* of his pocket; he wasn't about to try to wrestle with it to put the stupid thing back.)

When she first started making him carry the phone, he had a bad habit of forgetting it. And Karen had a bad habit of getting mad at him when that happened. It wasn't an ideal situation. It led to more than a few trivial fights. Over time, one of them had to give.

It wasn't her.

Cell phone properly deposited in his front pocket again, he locked the PT Cruiser's doors and strolled down to the river's edge to enjoy a few minutes out from behind the wheel.

Suddenly, and for the first time since waking from the dream that first night, he had no pressing desire to drive. He thought for a moment that he had beaten it, that he had finally driven far enough or long enough to have his fill of traveling.

But now he found himself being drawn along the riverbank and under the bridge.

Within minutes, he was around the bend and the rational part of his mind screamed at him to turn around.

This was far worse than his compulsion to drive. Now he was out in the middle of nowhere, utterly exposed and unprotected from the elements and in danger of becoming hopelessly lost. And yet still he walked.

At least he still had the phone. But how useful would it really be if something happened to him out here? As far as he knew, there was nothing for miles and miles but farmland and forests. How far could he go into this wilderness before he wandered out of the service area altogether?

A path appeared in the trees along the river bank and he found himself drawn there as surely as he'd been drawn to the river from his car. Leaving the water behind him, he made his way up a hill, through some thick brush and onto the neatly mown lawn of a modest, Victorian-style house.

His first thought should have been that this was private property and he had no business being here, that he'd be lucky if the owner didn't mistake him for a burglar and shoot him dead where he stood. Instead, he was compelled to walk to the back yard. Specifically, he felt drawn for some reason to a large, metal gate in the fence.

He walked up to this gate and rested his hands on the topmost bar. Beyond it, a narrow dirt path, little more than two dry wheel ruts in the tall grass, led away a short distance and then turned and disappeared into a field of tall and healthy corn.

"Ah. You finally showed up."

Startled, Eric turned to find an elderly woman hanging laundry up to dry just a few yards away. Even with his attention fixed on the gate and the path beyond, he was surprised that he didn't see her before

24

now. "I'm sorry," he said.

"No reason to be sorry," the woman told him. "At least you showed up. Better late than never, right?"

He wasn't sure how to respond to this. He'd meant that he was sorry to be trespassing on her property, yet this woman acted as if she'd been expecting him. But that wasn't possible. Even *he* didn't know how he came to be here.

"But we *did* think you'd show up two days ago."

Two days ago? That would've been right after his first dream. "I'm sorry, but show up for what, exactly?"

The old woman turned and looked at him. She was very skinny, with long, silver hair that was neatly tied back, deep creases around her mouth and an ugly blotch beneath her right eye. "You're going out there, aren't you?" She gestured at the corn behind the gate.

Eric turned and gazed out into the field for a moment. Somehow, he didn't like the idea of going out there, but she was right. The same strange compulsion that had lured him into this woman's back yard was definitely pulling him toward that field. Looking back at the old woman again, he said, "I honestly don't know what I'm doing here."

She stood looking back at him for a moment, considering him. Then she went back to her laundry. "Ethan always knew you'd come. Ethan's my husband, by the way. He always believed."

"That's impressive. *I* didn't even know I was coming until I got here."

If the woman heard him, she made no attempt to acknowledge it. "I can't say for sure that I ever believed it. Not until yesterday. Not until I saw *him*."

"Him?"

She didn't look at him as she hung a man's work shirt on the line. "The other one," she replied as if this made any more sense than "him." "I saw him with my own eyes, walking into the corn there. Scariest damn thing I ever saw. It was like he was only half there...all faded...like somebody standing in a thick fog...except there wasn't any fog. He just faded into the sunshine. Damn scariest thing..."

This conversation was only getting stranger. Eric turned and looked out at the little road again, wondering what was waiting out there.

When he looked back, the old woman was staring at the work shirt she'd just hung on the line. "Ethan fell the other day. Hurt his back. His hip, too. Doctor thinks he might not be able to walk so good anymore. Probably need a cane. I hate to see that. Once you get as old as us, you have to keep moving. When you stop moving, that's when you die. That's what my daddy used to say. He lived to ninety-eight. Made sure he walked at least a mile every day while doing his chores. Went out of his way if he had to. Then he hurt his hip and he couldn't walk anymore. Pretty soon, just like he always said, he never walked again."

Cheerful. He'd wager she was a laugh a minute at bingo night.

"You said you were expecting me?" asked Eric, hoping she would give him some sort of answer as to why he was here...or at the very least not tell him how she lost her mother.

"Oh yes. Definitely." Then she fell silent again as she withdrew a flowered housedress from her basket and hung it on the line.

"Okay." Apparently that was all he was going to get. Again, he turned and stared off past the gate. It was hard to look at the woman. There was something terribly sad about her.

"I gave him a red ribbon before he went in. That's good luck. Did you know that?"

"No. I didn't."

The old woman finished hanging her clothes and then picked up her empty basket and began walking toward the back door of the Victorian house. Without looking back at him, she said, "You should get going. I haven't been to the cathedral in a lot of years, but I remember perfectly well that it was a real long walk."

"Cathedral?"

But the woman was apparently done with their conversation. She entered the house and left him standing alone in her back yard.

Eric stared out into the cornfield for a moment. This was beginning to get spooky. He'd assumed that these urges to get in his car and drive were all in his head. He thought this even as he found himself getting out of his car and walking along the riverbank. But this woman had just told him that he was expected, as if he had been drawn here intentionally.

She also told him about "the other one." The one who looked like he was shrouded in fog, but without the fog. As if that made any kind of sense at all.

And she told him he was supposed to be looking for a cathedral.

It was beyond crazy. Either he just imagined this whole conversation, or she confirmed that he was here for a reason and not just because his brain was short-circuiting.

Or maybe they were both completely crazy.

He could still feel that strange pull, as if the cornfield were calling out to him. He did not want to go out there. Something was terribly wrong about all this. But he was fairly certain that he would find no peace by turning around and going home. And he certainly didn't want to converse any further with Mrs. Sunny Disposition.

Preparing himself for whatever weirdness awaited him on the other side, Eric lifted the latch on the gate and stepped through it to the other side.

Chapter Three

Eric walked through the tall grass between the sunken wheel ruts of the dirt road. He didn't like the feel of the tall corn on either side of him, the way it refused to let him see more than a few yards in either direction. Having already turned the bend, he could not even see the old woman's Victorian home anymore. Even the tallest peaks of its roof were quickly lost behind the endless stalks.

It was silly, but he found himself unwilling to stray past the ruts, as if something might reach out and snatch him away if he dared get too close. It was that woman's fault. Her insane rambling about the "other one" and how he was somehow shrouded in an invisible fog. It was a creepy thought, especially now that he was all alone out here, with nothing to be seen in every direction but corn.

She had obviously been delusional.

Yet, she had managed to make a strange sort of sense, too. Or at least more sense than his irrational compulsion to drive here in the first place.

He pulled out his cell phone and checked his screen. He was

surprised to find that he still had good service out here. There must be a tower somewhere nearby. He wondered how far he was from the nearest sizable town.

The road curved again and he turned with it, still keeping between the wheel ruts.

According to the old woman, he was looking for a cathedral. His immediate assumption was that he was looking for a large, ornately built church, but a cornfield didn't seem to be a very likely place for such a structure and he certainly didn't see any towering steeples rising over the corn. But then again, the woman also said it was a long walk. He wondered if this road would take him all the way there and if he would have to stare at the corn the whole way.

He knew that he should probably call Karen and update her on his whereabouts. But he also knew that she would just as likely be calling *him* any time to check up on him. And since she was the one who loved to talk on the stupid phone, he tended to let her do the calling.

He was trying to determine how he was going to explain to her why he left the PT Cruiser when he abruptly realized that something had changed.

He stopped and looked around, but he couldn't quite decide what was different. It was as if the light had changed, but when he squinted up into the sky, he saw that no clouds were passing before the sun. Yet everything suddenly *felt* colder and darker.

He turned around and surveyed the corn. The shadows seemed deeper somehow, the shade beneath the broad leaves darker, colder, more sinister.

That was ridiculous. Corn could not look more sinister. Broccoli, maybe. But corn was just corn. It was tasty.

Gazing forward, he saw that the plants were getting shorter as he went. He found himself passing through a strange swath of sickly stalks. It cut into the healthier, taller corn for about thirty yards to his right and curved out of sight to the left. It was as if the soil in just this one, narrow strip lacked the proper nutrients to fully sustain the crop.

As he passed through this odd area of the field, he checked his phone and saw that his signal had nearly vanished. A single bar kept flickering in and out, the words "NO SIGNAL" flashed at him as the little phone struggled to maintain its suddenly tenuous connection to the rest of the world.

He'd *always* hated cell phones. He hated the way people were always attached to them like a bad addiction. He'd met far too many people who were practically incapable of putting them down. They were constantly tinkering with them, as if they couldn't bear to be left unentertained for even a few minutes, constantly taking calls, sometimes in the middle of a conversation! People even *drove* with the stupid things, as if the roads weren't already dangerous enough. And it especially pissed him off when he caught his students playing with them in his class. He was notorious for his intolerance of cell phones in his classroom and still he had to confiscate the damn things at least once a week. He despised them and had proclaimed on occasions far too numerous to count that if every device on the planet abruptly quit working and they never made another one for as long as he lived, he'd continue his life quite happily.

But now that he was standing out here in this odd field, his signal cutting in and out, he felt a slow dread creep into him.

A soft rustling noise made him snap his head up. He scanned the

31

area around him, but there was nothing to see but cornstalks.

The hairs on the back of his neck were suddenly standing at full attention.

He told himself it was probably nothing more than a crow. Or perhaps a deer. But that eerie chill persisted. He began to walk faster, his eyes darting back and forth from the corn on his left to the corn on his right and back again, half expecting something to spring out at him, determined to drag him out into the sickly stalks.

Past the middle of the stunted patch, the corn grew taller again, and soon his vision was reduced to only a few shadowy yards.

Then, abruptly, everything felt different again.

Eric paused and looked around. The sky was still the same blue. The corn was still the same green. But everything suddenly appeared brighter somehow. That odd chill was gone.

He glanced back at the path behind him. It looked perfectly normal, except for the stunted stalks. Yet that feeling of uneasiness remained. He continued walking and glanced down at his phone again. The signal was strong and clear.

He stuffed the phone back into his pocket as he tried to see through the corn, but he had barely withdrawn his hand when the phone buzzed to life against his leg.

"Where are you?" Karen asked as soon as he answered.

Shaking off that strange feeling of irrational dread that had been creeping into his gut, Eric dismissed the weirdness of the corn and forced himself to relax. "I'm in a cornfield," he replied. "Where are you? What are you wearing? Are you naked? I like it when you're naked."

"Yes. I'm naked. I lounge around in my birthday suit all day when you're gone. Did you say cornfield?"

"I *did* say cornfield. You're never naked when I get home."

"Why would I still be naked when you get home? It wouldn't be relaxing with you around. What are you doing driving around in a cornfield?"

"I didn't say I was driving."

"Okay. What are you doing *walking* around in a cornfield?"

"Checking things out. Considering buying a farm. What do you think?"

"I think I wouldn't make a very good farm girl."

"Why not? Fresh air. Sunshine. Outdoors. The chores. 'Green Acres is the place for me.' The good life."

"I get allergic smelling hay."

"Well there go all my barn fetish fantasies. Thanks for leaving me empty inside."

"You'll get over it."

"I know I will." He scanned the field around him. Now and then he thought he saw something moving, but could not be sure it wasn't just the breeze churning through the leaves.

"So really, can we talk about you walking around in a cornfield? Because that's a little troubling."

"I've got to admit, I can see where you might think so."

"Yeah. Where's our car?"

"Parked it next to a bridge."

"Oh."

"Don't worry. I locked it."

"That's good. That makes everything all right."

"I'm glad. I was worried this was going to be an awkward

conversation."

"Why would you think that? You just abandoned our car and decided to take a walk in a cornfield. There's no reason at all to doubt the soundness of your mind."

"I have the most patient wife on the planet."

"Yes you do. Now please explain the cornfield to her."

"That's going to be tricky."

"I was worried it would be. What are you doing?"

"I don't know. Really. I have no idea what's going on. All I know is the farther I drove, the more sure I was that I was doing what I needed to do. And when I finally pulled off the road, I felt just as sure that I needed to get out and walk. I followed the river to a little path in the woods and I found my way to this house…"

In as much detail as he could recall, he described his encounter with the old woman and the enigmatic things she'd said to him.

"That's so weird," Karen said when he'd finished.

"I know."

The road curved to the right, winding ever deeper into the field, and again he was struck by that strange sensation of something changing. It happened only briefly this time, for merely a second or two, but the cell phone crackled in his ear as if he'd passed quickly through a tunnel.

"Do you think she really knew you were coming?"

"She couldn't have. I didn't even know I was coming."

Karen was quiet as she contemplated the idea.

"I don't think she was entirely there. She probably thought I was somebody else."

"Maybe… That stuff about the half-there man… That's creepy."

"I know. Kind of gave me a chill."

"I can believe she might've just been crazy, but it's really weird that she said she expected you two days ago."

"I know. That was a spooky coincidence."

"It was."

Again, something changed. At the same moment, the phone crackled. He stopped and began to walk backwards. After a few steps, everything suddenly seemed normal again.

This was interesting.

He began to walk forward once more. It seemed that he needed to walk almost twice as far as the first time, but that queer, shifting feeling came back as reliably as he could have hoped. There was a definite chill to the air here. And although the sky and the corn and the weeds and the earth remained unchanged, something about the underlying quality of it all seemed altered. It wasn't as if it had grown darker, exactly. It was, as crazy as it sounded, as if everything had grown *deeper*.

He couldn't wrap his head around it.

"Listen," he said as he glanced ahead and saw that the corn was becoming shorter again. "My phone's been cutting out a little in this field. I lost the signal completely just before you called. So if you lose me, don't freak out, okay?"

"I don't 'freak out.'"

Yes, she did. She simply managed to do it with considerably more grace than most. But he decided not to tell her this.

"You just worry about yourself. Don't get rattlesnake bit or anything."

"I'll watch where I step," he promised.

Karen's next words were gnarled into a sputtering of disjointed sounds.

"Karen?"

Another quick burst of noise crackled in his ears and then there was nothing.

"Karen…? Hello…?"

He ended the call and glanced around. Again, he had that uneasy feeling. On either side of him the corn became shorter and shorter until it was little more than sickly sprigs jutting out of the cracked earth, most of them half wilted, some completely dead. He found himself in an odd valley of pathetic stalks barely clinging to life and was unnerved by how silent it was here.

What was killing the corn? Was there something in the soil? Pollution, maybe? Or Radiation?

A hard shiver raced through his body as he imagined himself being slowly irradiated by something buried in the ground beneath him. Was he being exposed to something? Would it kill him if he remained here long enough?

Countless old movies began to surface from his memory, gleefully filling his head with thoughts of crashed alien spacecrafts that oozed terrible chemicals into the ground and filled the air with strange fumes, transforming harmless wildlife into gruesome and violent freaks of nature.

Why did it have to be a *cornfield?* Aliens loved cornfields. They were drawn to them like toddlers to coloring books.

He stepped up his pace to a near jog and soon the corn began to grow taller again, but the queer *deepness* remained.

Something rustled in the corn again. Something big. Something definitely not restrained to his imagination. He turned to face it, ready to defend himself, but he could see nothing. He was standing in an open strip of stunted stalks, completely exposed, searching the taller corn farther out.

"Hello? Is someone out there?"

Of course there wasn't. If there was, it would be someone with a chainsaw and a shirt made out of human faces. Why would such a person reply to a stupid question like that? It would spoil all the fun.

Eric began to run.

The corn grew taller and his visibility dwindled. He thought he could hear things moving all around him. An odd chittering noise rose from somewhere nearby.

Then everything abruptly became normal again. That strange depth was gone from his surroundings, the chill vanished and everything seemed once more to be perfectly fine.

He turned and looked behind him, but there was nothing there. It was just an ordinary dirt road winding through an ordinary cornfield. Again, the only thing out of the ordinary was the sickly-looking corn.

The cell phone buzzed to life in his hand, startling him so badly that he almost dropped it.

He took a moment to curse at the stupid thing before answering it.

"What happened?" asked Karen.

"Nothing. I just lost the signal for a minute there. Like I told you would happen."

"That was kind of scary."

"Just a lost signal," he repeated. He had no intention of telling her about hearing something in the corn. He didn't want to worry her.

Besides, he still had no idea what it was or how much of it had only been his imagination. It was probably nothing more than a deer hiding in the field.

He turned and began walking again. Ahead of him, the road was curving to the right and beginning to slope a little downhill.

Despite the chill he felt when he was in the strange area with the sickly corn, he now found himself sweating a little. It was going to be a very warm day.

"How goes the cake?" he asked.

"Still cooling. I'm getting ready to whip up the frosting. Strawberry pies are done. I have three caramel apple pies just about ready to come out of the oven and two blackberries ready to go in."

"See, it's probably good I'm not there. I can't behave myself around your blackberry pie."

"It does have an effect on you."

He followed the road around the curve, his eyes still searching the corn for signs of movement. Why didn't he hear it anymore? Where had it gone?

"I kind of wish I'd come with you."

"You have pies and cakes to make. And you hate long car rides. They make you sick."

"I know."

"I don't think you'd like cornfields, either, actually."

"I guess I probably wouldn't."

"Besides, I'm on an adventure, remember. You can't expect me to take a *girl* on an adventure."

"Oh, right. What was I thinking?"

Eric emerged from the corn into a wide, weedy clearing and

stopped, his eyes fixed on the structure that stood before him. All at once, the mysteries of the field were forgotten.

"Karen…"

"Huh?"

"I just remembered something from my dream."

"You did? What?"

"A barn. A big, red, wooden barn with peeling paint and a sagging roof. …And I'm looking at it right now."

Chapter Four

He recognized the monstrous red structure as soon as he saw it. It was not merely a vague recollection, but was instead perfectly vivid in every detail. It was exactly as he had seen it each of these past three nights, right down to the gaps between the boards and the rusted-through tin roof.

The memory of the barn from his dream—*this* barn—came rushing back to him in an instant, and with it came that awful feeling of gut-wrenching fear and foreboding with which he'd awakened each night. Though he could still remember no other details about the dream, not even the reason why this barn filled him with irrational dread, he was certain that he had seen this very same barn in his sleep.

But how? He'd never been here in his life. How would he even know that such a place existed?

"What do you mean you're looking at it right now?" asked Karen. "You mean it's real? It's *there*?"

"I'm looking right at it. It's here. I'm standing right in front of it."

"Are you serious?"

"Uh huh."

"How do you know it's the same barn?"

"I just do."

"But you didn't remember *anything* from your dream until just now."

"I know. But this was in my dream. This exact barn. I know it was. As soon as I saw it, I remembered it."

"Send me a picture of it."

"What?"

"Send me a picture. I want to see it."

"How do you expect me to—?"

"The camera on your phone, goofball."

"I have a camera on my phone?"

"Yes. You know that."

"No I don't." But he realized even as he argued with her that he *did* recall her telling him about the camera when she first gave the annoying little device to him. At the time, he thought the phone was an utter waste of money even without a camera in it. It was just one of dozens of extra features he'd never had any intention of using.

"Send it to me."

"How do I do that, exactly?"

Karen talked him through the process. He had to hang up to do it, but soon enough she was looking at the very same barn on her phone, seeing precisely what he was seeing.

He refused to admit that that really was kind of cool.

"That's a really creepy barn," agreed Karen after calling him back.

"Yes it is."

"You're sure this was in your dream?"

"Positive."

"That's really weird, Eric."

"Well, yeah."

"*Scary* weird."

"I know."

"What if…"

"What if what?"

For a moment she was silent. Then she surprised him by saying, "What if it's all real? You're…*feelings*. The things that old woman said. All of it. What if it's real?"

"You don't really believe any of that stuff, do you?"

"Do *you*?"

There was the real question. After all, if he didn't believe any of it, why would he be out here? Some part of him must have expected to find *something*. Otherwise he would have turned around long before he reached the county line. And he certainly never would have left his car.

"I don't know," he confessed. "I really don't."

"I can't decide if it's really scary or really kind of cool."

Eric found himself leaning toward "really scary" but perhaps that was just him. "Listen, I'm going to have to hang up for a little while."

"Don't hang up. I want to know what you find."

He was surprised to realize that he was already walking toward the door. "Even if I don't, I have a feeling I'm going to lose the signal again in a minute."

"Okay. Just… Please be careful."

"I will."

He hung up the phone and approached the barn. He thought he might find the huge, double doors locked or otherwise blocked off in some way. Given the condition of the barn, he wouldn't have been surprised to find the hinges sagging or broken, leaving the heavy doors weighted hopelessly into the dirt. If he were to tell the honest truth, he *hoped* that he would find his way blocked. But one of the two doors stood ajar, almost as if it were waiting for him.

Just above the doors, someone had mounted a bronze eagle with its wings spread in flight. The instant he looked up at this decoration, he recognized it. He'd looked upon it in the dream, just as he did now.

An eagle…

The only thing he'd been able to remember of his dream until a moment ago was that there was something about a bird. And here was a bird now, blatantly emblazoned right above the entrance of the rundown barn. Even if he could somehow convince himself that this barn wasn't really the same one from his dream, that it was just his mind playing tricks on him, he couldn't possibly deny the image of a bird so obviously placed above the entrance.

Eric tucked his cell phone into his front pocket, looked back one last time at the cornfield and the little dirt road that brought him here and then stepped through the door and into the shadowy interior of the barn.

Even the inside was familiar. The way the sunlight filtered through the gaps in the boards and the holes in the tin roof was exactly as he had seen it in his dream, down to the last detail. Even the weeds that were reaching through the many sunlit openings near the floor were the same. Every place his eyes fell, he found details he remembered. It was as if he'd been here a million times before, as if he'd spent his whole life here.

Except there was nothing as warm and comforting as a memory

of home. A deep and churning dread was rising in his gut. Something was very, very wrong here.

He began walking through the barn, toward the door on the far side, his eyes searching every crack and crevice for the slightest sign of danger. But the building was deserted. The stalls on either side were empty, with no evidence remaining of whatever animals they may have once housed. There weren't even any birds roosting in the high rafters above his head.

He wished he could remember more of his dream. What happened to him in the barn? What did he see? What did he find? Every surface, every beam of sunlight, every creak and groan of the aging lumber was familiar to him, yet he could not seem to remember anything beyond what he was looking at. It came back to him only as he saw it with his own eyes.

But some part of him, buried deep down in some far corner of his brain, must have still remembered it, because that awful, gut-churning fright remained. Whatever it was he'd found here in his dream, it wasn't pleasant.

An odd noise startled him and he stopped to listen, his skin prickling with gooseflesh. It came from somewhere on the other side of the far door, a sickly bleating sound, like nothing he'd ever heard before. He was no expert on farm animals, but to his ears, it was like the utterances of a wretched, starving animal.

That nauseous feeling in his belly grew.

Slowly, he crept toward the back of the barn, his eyes fixed on the second set of large, double doors that stood partially opened, just like the first. But while there was brilliant sunlight cutting through the shadows where he had entered the barn, the space beyond those far doors was dark and shadowy.

He felt a chill creep through him and realized he was holding his breath. He had to force himself to breathe normally.

Why was he so worried? What had he seen within these walls while he was dreaming?

When he reached the doors, he felt a cool draft flowing across his sweat-dampened skin and was reminded of the strange moments back in the cornfield, where the corn had withered. This was like those areas, he realized. It was connected somehow.

His eyes swept across the ground as he again wondered if some invisible poison might be soaked into the soil, undetectable fumes rising around him, invading his body, poisoning and twisting his mind.

He forced the unpleasant thought away and peered through the open doors.

For a moment, he was confused. He turned and looked back toward the sunlit front doors. The barn was big. Each set of double doors was more than large enough to allow entry for a sizable tractor, but it could not have been much bigger than this room when he stood staring at it from outside. Yet through this door waited a second room easily twice as long as the first. Empty stalls lined the walls on either side of a wide walkway that reached far past where the barn should have ended given its exterior dimensions.

It was impossible. It was like stepping inside an M. C. Escher work.

It had to be an optical illusion of some sort. There was no other logical explanation.

But then again, why would anything here be logical? Nothing he had done today was logical.

And even as he tried to make himself accept what was happening to him, he realized that he recalled discovering these same impossible dimensions in his dream.

Movement drew his attention to the far end of the second room. Something that appeared to be some kind of chicken was making its way across the floor near the next set of double doors.

Another bird…

As he watched it, he quickly realized that there was something wrong with the creature. Though small and plump, like a chicken, it wasn't moving like any barnyard fowl he had ever seen. It didn't hold its head up as it walked, surveying the room in lively jerks. Instead, it looked as if it were hanging its head in a curiously forlorn manner. Also, it didn't strut like a chicken. Instead, it moved in slow, lurching motions, as if on the verge of death. It was either the most depressed little chicken he had ever laid eyes on or there was something very not right about it.

Again, that awful bleating noise came. It seemed to come from beyond the far doorway. It reminded him a little of a lamb or a calf, but it was gruff and choked, like something slowly strangling to death in the jaws of a steel snare.

The chicken-thing continued its labored lurching, unfazed by the terrible sound.

Still standing in the doorway, Eric checked his cell phone. He wasn't remotely surprised to see that he had no signal. He returned it to his pocket and looked around again. The sunlight drilled through the holes in the rusted roof and the gaps between the boards in the walls, just like in the last room of the impossible barn, but it did not seem nearly as warm and bright as it should have been. The air felt cold against his skin. Even the sound of the gentle wind outside was muted. Only that awful bleating noise disturbed the stillness.

And yet, even the weirdness was familiar. His dream unfolded before him, promising to reveal to him in vivid detail why he had awakened breathless and afraid these past three nights, but only if he continued to walk in the footprints of the nightmare.

Glancing over his shoulder at the bright strip of sunlight once more, he braced himself for whatever horrors his nightmare still had in store for him and continued toward the far doors and the mysteries that waited beyond them.

Chapter Five

It *felt* wrong in here. The wrongness weighed down the air, seeming to ooze into his very pores.

And there was a stench, too. He hadn't noticed it when he was standing in the doorway, but as he moved deeper into the long, gloomy interior of the barn, it enveloped him. It was far worse than the odor of ordinary farm animals. It was a death-like stench, the sickly reek of decay.

He peered into each open stall as he passed it, finding one after another empty, just like in the previous room, until, about a third of the distance between the two sets of doors, he found a second chicken (or whatever the hell the thing was) sitting slumped in a corner.

He turned and approached the creature, but stopped short of the stall door. He wanted to see it. He wanted to understand what was so strange about it, but he dared not get any closer than absolutely necessary.

The wretched creature looked diseased. It was mostly bald, with black and gray mottled skin exposed except for a few small, blotchy patches of black and yellow feathers. It sat with its neck bent like a limp hose, the shriveled crest atop its head resting on the floor beside it. Its black, beady eyes stared blankly back at him.

He thought the poor creature had died, but then it flexed its useless, naked wings and uttered a loud noise that was far less a cluck than a swine-like squeal.

He doubted there was a force anywhere on the planet that could have prevented his feet from leaving the floor at that moment. His heart thumping hard against his ribs, his nerves electrified, Eric promptly left the freaky chicken to its roost and moved on.

What the hell was this place?

Three stalls down, he spied another of the strange fowl and he took a wide path around it, half-expecting it to dart out and attack him.

Another long and mournful bleating sound rose from the other side of the door and when he looked toward it he saw that there were now two of the ugly chicken things at the far end of the room. A second had just emerged from the last stall. Even from this distance, he could tell something was wrong with its feet, likely the cause for its odd, lurching gait. The ones in the stalls had been sitting with their legs tucked beneath them, hidden from view and he sure as hell wasn't going to pick one up for a closer look.

He continued to peer into the open stalls as he passed them, but he kept well between them and constantly ready to spring out of the way in case something small and barely feathered emerged with the intention of pecking out his eyes.

But as he approached the door, the two birds remained unconcerned with doing him harm. In fact, the nearest one loped away with greater urgency, as if it were *he* who was a monstrous mockery of nature.

Empowered by the birds' apparent wariness, he dared to take a moment and consider the nearest of the two. He could now see what was wrong with its feet. They were swollen and gnarled and clenched like bony fists. They walked not with their toes spread, like other birds, but upon the knuckles of their feet instead. But the true cause of their odd lurching appeared to be that their skinny legs didn't quite hold their weight. With every step they simply rose and then collapsed.

Earlier that summer, like he did every year, he'd visited the county fair and strolled through the various animal barns. He was well aware that there were many breeds of farm fowl, some of them remarkably ugly. Hell, your ordinary Thanksgiving turkey was no looker when you saw a live one close up. Even breeds with very few feathers weren't uncommon. But he'd never seen anything quite like these things. They weren't just ugly. They didn't even look *healthy*.

Again, he thought about the stunted corn and shivered.

More and more, he wondered if something otherworldly was at work here.

As he pushed open the door, he saw that the barn had a third chamber. That awful stench struck him with renewed force, knotting his stomach into an ever tighter ball.

At least a dozen of the ugly, loping chickens were stumbling around in here.

Again, he heard the sickly bleating noise and realized that it was originating from somewhere in this room.

He also could now hear the sound of buzzing flies.

His heart still pounding, he pushed on. It was strange how it seemed to grow darker without the light growing any dimmer. The shadows seemed to be taking on life and substance all their own, wholly separate from the shapes that cast them.

He paused as a realization came to him. Like the other two rooms, this part of the barn was familiar to him. He remembered it from his dreams. And he even remembered the strange chickens, now that he had seen them. In his dream he'd had the same reaction to them: disgust and distrust mixed with a certain morbid curiosity. But he realized now that he didn't recall seeing them in the previous room in his dream. And he didn't recall seeing as many in this room, either.

But of course, it had only been a dream. Not every detail would be perfect, he supposed. Not even in an apparently prophetic dream.

He started moving again and almost immediately his eyes fell on a shape far stranger than the creepy chickens. Inside one of the stalls to his right lay an animal as big as a cow, but with short, stubby legs and a long, limp tail.

He found that he remembered the creature as soon as he saw it, just as it looked now, and he felt as strongly drawn to the beast as he was repulsed by it.

Covered in short, charcoal gray hair, it lay facing away from him, its head pressed into the corner of the stall as if it were ashamed to exist. All he could make out were long, floppy ears and a short, blunt snout. A great, meaty sack, far larger than any cow udders he'd ever seen at any state fair, bulged from between its splayed and useless legs, at least a dozen teats bulging from it, some of them oozing a thick, sour-yellow substance that fell in thick ropes to the filthy floor beneath it.

The stench was strongest here. This stall had not been cleaned in a very long time. A foul stench filled the air and a swarm of flies shared the enclosure with the poor creature.

It was neither bovine nor swine, but something else entirely, and it looked at least as miserable as the half-dead-looking chickens.

He could almost believe that the fowl were merely some sort of new and exceptionally unbecoming exotic breed, but he was quite sure that these things should not exist.

Staring at it now, he realized that no one was ever going to believe that he actually saw these things. Even Karen, who trusted him as completely as any wife ever could, would never be convinced that he had actually seen such things. Telling her would only help convince her that her husband had utterly lost his mind.

Then he remembered his cell phone. The camera.

He pulled it from his pocket and saw that it remained out of service. For a moment he thought that his plan to prove his sanity had been foiled, but then he realized that he didn't need cell service to use the phone's camera. He snapped a single picture of the thing and then turned and snapped a picture of the nearest bird as well.

That would prove he wasn't crazy.

Or maybe it would prove that he *was* crazy. If all Karen saw when she received these pictures was a dozing cow and an ordinary chicken, he'd know it was time to pack up this silly adventure and check himself into the nearest psychiatric ward.

As he backed away from the sorry-looking creature and resumed walking toward the barn's back door, he heard the pathetic bleating noise again. Whatever creature was making that awful sound was in one of the stalls on the right-hand side of the room, near the end. He had only just begun to wonder if it was the same sort of creature that he had just seen when something to his left let out a long and irritable-sounding moan.

Jumping at the noise, he turned to see another creature staring at him through the wooden slats of the gate. It had huge, black eyes and a long, drooping tongue that hung from its gaping mouth and lay like a slab of raw meat on the filthy floor. Flies were crawling over the flaccid organ. Like the one in the other stall, it was lying on its side, its stubby legs spread around its bulging sack, seemingly incapable of standing.

Once more, his thoughts strayed to the stunted corn and those old movies about UFOs and horrific alien experiments.

Again the creature moaned at him. It was a disturbingly despondent sound.

He snapped another picture.

Feeling as if he might soon retch at the sight of these beasts, he turned his attention forward and continued on.

At least nothing here seemed especially dangerous. The birds fled as he approached, keeping their distance from him, no different from hundreds of other farm birds he'd seen. And the much larger creatures locked in the stalls didn't look remotely vicious. They didn't even look like they could move.

He approached the source of the sickly bleating sound. Even this didn't sound like anything dangerous. It was not an angry sound, but rather pitiful. It sounded miserable, not bloodthirsty. Yet he still felt reluctant to see it. If it was half as disturbing as the other livestock, he was not sure he could stand the sight.

But the stall from where the noise came was not gated like the others. Instead, the gate had been replaced with a ten-foot-tall, plywood and lumber door and chained shut so that it was impossible to see in.

He was relieved to be spared the sight of whatever was inside, yet the trouble someone had taken to shut the creature away enflamed his curiosity. Why? What would he find if he climbed to the top of the gate and peered over?

From inside, another long, pitiful call rang out.

In his dream, he had turned away without looking. He did the same now. He didn't want to see it. Whatever was inside, he was certain it would be far more disturbing than the other livestock. He didn't think it would be something he'd want to remember.

Ready to be out of this nightmare barn, he turned his attention forward again, just in time to see a tall, bearded man emerge from the farthest stall.

Startled, Eric stopped.

The man walked straight to the door and pushed it open. Bright sunlight spilled in, but somehow the barn's interior remained just as shadowy. As soon as he was gone, the door swung shut behind him.

Eric bolted for the door.

He ran past every stall, startling the limp-necked chickens into squealing fits as they stumbled over their own twisted feet and rubbery legs to get out of his way.

He reached the door without being attacked by mutant farm animals and shoved it open. Finally, he found himself back under the August sun.

Yet the chill in the air remained.

At first, he didn't know where the man went. Then he spotted him crossing the porch of an old farmhouse and entering the front door.

He wasn't sure how it was that he didn't notice the little house before he entered the barn. He assumed he'd been too preoccupied with the startling realization that the barn was actually a part of the dream that started all this craziness.

Hopeful for some answers, he hurried across the overgrown lawn and climbed the porch steps.

The house was in fairly poor shape. It needed a fresh coat of paint years ago and several of the windows had been boarded up. But he had no interest in discussing good housekeeping.

He knocked on the door.

"Hello?"

Nothing.

"Excuse me, sir? I need some help."

Still nothing.

"Hello?" He pressed his forehead to the screen door and peered inside. The living room was sparsely furnished and lacked any kind of decoration. It looked as if it hadn't been used in years. He pulled the door open and leaned over the threshold. A musty smell met his nose. *"Hello?"*

He stepped off the porch and stood in the doorway, listening. The house was eerily silent. As his eyes adjusted to the darkness, he saw that there was a thick layer of dust over everything. No one seemed to have lived here for quite some time.

But where did that man go? He couldn't have simply disappeared.

Or maybe he could have. Stranger things had happened already today.

"Hello? Can anybody help me?"

There was not a single sound to be heard.

"Where the hell did you go?" he breathed.

He walked through the living room and into the kitchen. There were no appliances except for a very old refrigerator. The shelves that he could see were bare. An old, rusty bread pan had been left on the counter next to the empty sink. The dust here was undisturbed.

At the far end of the kitchen was a door, but he couldn't make it open. If the man left through here, he must have locked it behind him somehow.

He returned to the living room and peered down the hallway. He could see a bathroom and a single bedroom. This house certainly didn't offer much in the way of space. It wasn't much bigger than his and Karen's first apartment.

He walked to the bathroom and flipped the light switch. In case the empty kitchen and accumulated dust hadn't been enough for him, the lack of power confirmed that this was no one's permanent residence.

He stood in the hallway for a moment, trying to piece together what had happened so far. Even ignoring the dreams and the weird compulsion to drive out to this freaky backwoods, there was plenty to think about. Was someone screwing with his head?

That old woman… Ethan's wife. She'd mentioned another man. "*Him.*" Could the vanishing figure he followed from the barn to this house have been the very same man who had frightened her yesterday? He hadn't seen anything like the invisible fog that she had described, but he'd only caught the two brief glimpses.

He stepped into the bedroom and looked around. The bed was stripped down to a stained mattress with broken down springs. There was an old wardrobe against one wall. The only other thing in the room was an old, tarnished mirror hanging on the wall opposite the doorway.

He walked over to the mirror and gazed at himself.

It was now that a thought occurred to him. The whole time he was in the barn, everything he saw also emerged from the buried memory of his dream. But here, inside this house, he had no such recollections. In fact, he didn't remember the tall, bearded man. He recalled exiting the barn and walking out into the tall grass and bright sunshine and that was all. The rest of the dream remained clouded in his memory.

What did that mean?

A horrible feeling began to creep into his gut again. But this was different than what he felt as he entered the barn. This was much worse, much more *urgent*.

A thought occurred to him: If this place wasn't in his dream, then maybe he wasn't supposed to be here.

He turned away from the mirror and began to walk toward the door, eager to leave these empty rooms, even if it meant returning to that nightmare barn. But as he passed in front of the wardrobe, the doors burst open and something shot out at him. An awful, convulsing shape exploded outward, snarling viciously.

Eric cried out and stumbled away from it, backing himself into the corner behind the bed.

Impossibly, the gnarled shape unfolded itself from the cramped confines of the wardrobe. It was difficult to make out. The thing was almost entirely black, seemingly enfolded in its own shadows, with bright red, glistening streaks undulating across its oily flesh. Every time he thought he could almost discern its shape, it changed, warping and flexing and coiling itself.

Something that looked like a hand with dozens of taloned fingers blossomed from the black and crimson mass and reached across the room for him.

Fairly certain that Narnia was not where it intended to take him, Eric leapt onto the stained mattress and threw himself across the bed and onto the floor on the other side. A blood-chilling roar shook the room as he scrambled back to his feet and bolted for the door.

He saw something from the corner of his eye and barely managed to duck out of the way as a heavy mass passed over his head.

Behind him, he heard the bed crash against the wall.

Somehow making it to the door, he ran down the short hallway, past the bathroom and into the living room before daring to look back over his shoulder.

Immediately, he wished he hadn't. A horrid mass of snaking black and blood-red flesh was boiling from the bedroom door, wicked claws tearing open the wallpaper and the carpet, decimating the plaster ceiling tiles. In the very center of the mass, a horrid face snarled at him, its gaping mouth revealing countless gnashing teeth.

Terrified out of his mind, Eric ran screaming through the screen door and onto the porch, where he found himself directly in the path of a charging bulldozer.

Chapter Six

Coherent thought failing him, Eric reacted less on calculated strategy than on pure instinct and adrenaline. Uttering a startled and, to his credit, a rather creative curse, he turned and leapt over the porch railing with the kind of grace he hadn't demonstrated in at least ten years. And then he sprawled face-first into the grass with *exactly* the kind of grace befitting him these days.

Behind him, the wooden porch burst into splinters against the onslaught of the dozer's blade.

Even over the roar of the engine and the resounding crash of cold steel against breaking wood, Eric could hear the thing that came out of the wardrobe. A terrible, rage-filled howl cut through the air and seemed to carve its way into his very soul.

Then there was only the thrumming roar of the machine.

Then even that sputtered into silence.

"You okay?"

Eric sat up and turned around to see what the hell had just happened. The first thing he saw was that it was not a bulldozer that had nearly flattened him as he fled the farmhouse after all, but rather an ordinary tractor with an impressive hydraulic blade mounted on its front. The blade was now firmly pressed against the front door of the house, preventing the wardrobe monster from following him.

He had no idea what was keeping it from lunging through one of the house's windows instead. It had been fully capable of throwing the bed across the room and tearing apart the hallway. But the house seemed to have fallen utterly silent in the wake of the tractor's unexpected assault.

The next thing his racing mind took in was the old man climbing down from the tractor's seat, the man who had likely just saved his life, but just as easily could have squashed him into jelly. All the easier for the monster to chew.

He was a tall, slender man, with hard, sun-beaten skin wearing dark, oversized glasses and a blue and white cap. "When I saw you go in there, I thought you were done for."

"Guess I almost was." He recalled looking back down the hallway and seeing that awful face clawing after him. He also recalled, now that the gripping panic had subsided and he was thinking back on it without the mortal fear of his imminent and violent death, that the screams he was spouting at that moment weren't exactly the manliest of cries.

Well, at least he hadn't wet himself. That would have to do, he supposed.

"Didn't Annette warn you about leaving the path?"

"Annette?"

The old man cocked his head, lifted his hat and ran a hand through his thick, gray hair. "No. I suppose she didn't."

Eric's eyes drifted back to the ruined porch. What was keeping that thing inside? He couldn't think of a single reason why a thing like that wouldn't still be tearing after him, yet the old man didn't seem remotely concerned about standing this close to the house.

"I guess she's still going on about Ethan."

Ethan? Ethan was the old woman's husband, he recalled. Now he understood. *She* was Annette.

"She never accepted it. He's been gone a while now."

At this, Eric turned and met the old man's eyes. Ethan was dead? Suddenly, he remembered the way she kept staring at the shirts as she hung them up, that profoundly sad look in her eyes. She talked about her father, and made it sound like she was worried that she might lose Ethan the same way. She even said something about giving him a red ribbon for good luck. But Ethan was already dead and gone. That was perhaps the saddest thing he had heard in a long time.

"Let's see if we can keep you on the path from now on, okay?"

Eric took a step back, surprised. "What? Oh. No. No way. I'm done with this nonsense. I mean…what the *hell*? I was just attacked by a goddamn…" He thrust his finger toward the farmhouse several times, his mouth moving with words he couldn't find. Then he pressed his hand to his face and rubbed at his eyes. "What…? What was that thing? Exactly?"

"Not sure what you call it," said the old man. "Just something *he* left behind when he came through here."

"'He?'"

"The other guy. Scary as all kinds of hell."

"Looks like he's half-hidden in fog, but there isn't any fog?"

"That's him. At least Annette gave you *something*. He passed through here yesterday afternoon. Left you that little surprise." He gestured toward the barn and added, "Left *that*, too."

Eric turned and saw a man walking toward them from the barn. It was the same man he saw before, the one he followed into the house. Tall, broad-shouldered, young, with a full beard. Before he could even begin to wonder how he had made his way back from the house to the barn, the man faded away before his eyes and was gone.

He blinked hard, as if that might correct the strangeness of what he had seen.

"Over there," said the old man, gesturing toward the house now.

When he turned, he saw the man again, this time walking through the dozer blade as if it wasn't there and the porch were still under his feet rather than folded into a gnarled pile of splinters in the tall grass.

"Can't hurt you. Not directly, anyway. It's residual. Repeats itself over and over again, several times every hour, ever since *he* came through here. You'll have to watch out for those."

"Clearly." Again, Eric's eyes drifted to the farm house.

"It can't get out," the old man assured him. "It's lost you. Unless you go back inside and stir it up again, it's done with you. By the way, name's Grant. Grant Stolyen."

"Eric Fortrell."

"Eric. Good to meet you. Sorry it's not the best of circumstances."

"Yeah. About that…"

"You want to know what the hell is going on?"

"I do, actually. I mean… Everything was fine until three nights ago. Then I wake up from a dream I can't even remember and every waking thought is 'I have to go! Now!'"

Grant nodded. "Three nights ago. So you ignored it?"

"*Tried* to."

"That's why you're so late then."

"Late?"

"You should've been here two days ago."

Eric recalled that Annette told him basically the same thing. "Late for what? What is all this?"

"Sorry, but I can't explain all of it. Don't actually understand all of it myself, to be honest. But I can try my best. You've probably noticed the cold spots by now."

He nodded. "And the stunted corn in the field. Light seems funny there, too. What is that? Some kind of pollution?"

"Nothing so simple."

"And all those mutant animals in your barn. I'll be honest, I was starting to imagine I'd find a crashed UFO or something."

"Again, nothing so simple, I'm afraid."

"Right. Why would it be that simple?"

"And it's not actually my barn. I'm the neighbor. I just keep an eye on things, but I don't go in the barn no more. Creepy bunch of bastards in there, ain't they? Give me the creeps. I kind of figured they'd die if I didn't take care of them, but apparently they don't need cared for."

"Nobody feeds them?"

"Not that I know of. Weird, huh?"

"Very."

"Anyway, I was talking about the cold spots. Those're the places where you're inside the fissure."

"Fissure?"

"Yeah. Like a *crack* between worlds."

"Worlds? What, like a wormhole?" Again, he thought of aliens and extra-terrestrial spacecraft.

"No. You're thinking of planets. I said *worlds*. *Dimensions*, if you prefer."

"Like parallel realities?"

"Sort of. Yeah. There's our world, the one we know, and then there's this other one. Scary-ass place, apparently. I think it's where those things in the barn came from."

Eric stared at him, trying to wrap his head around the very idea of this simple-talking old man explaining rents between alternate realities to him.

"Don't think I don't know how it sounds."

"Sounds crazy."

"Yeah. But you've already seen it for yourself, haven't you?"

"I guess I have."

"When you cross into the cold spots, into the fissure, you're actually in some kind of gray zone between the two worlds. It's like a border realm. Things can move back and forth there. You'll see some scary things there, let me warn you. And if you go too far into those areas, you could find yourself all the way out in the other world. And that's not somewhere you ever want to be."

Eric nodded. It sounded like good advice.

"You'll want to stick to the path or you'll never get where you're going."

"And where exactly is it I'm supposed to be going?"

"To the cathedral."

The cathedral. That's what Annette said, too.

"That's where the singularity is."

"The singularity?"

"The exact point where the two worlds meet. The rest of this stuff is just what bleeds through the crack that runs out from that point."

"And if I find this cathedral? Then what? What am I supposed to do there?"

"Hell if I know. I'm just here to keep the path open for you."

"And if I refuse to do it? If I just turn around and walk back home?"

Grant looked surprised, as if he'd never once considered the possibility that anyone wouldn't want to do these things. "Then *he'd* win."

"The foggy guy."

"Yeah. Him. Course, he might win anyway, with you running so late."

"And what happens if he wins?"

"I couldn't tell you. But I'm sure it'd be bad." And the look on his face suggested that he did, indeed believe it would be quite bad.

"Right." Eric took his cell phone from his pocket and checked to see if he had a signal yet. He didn't.

"That'll come back a little farther up the path."

"I haven't decided to do this. I don't know how much of this nonsense I even believe."

Grant shrugged. "You believed enough to come here in the first place."

"I *believed* I was having a stupid recurring nightmare that was making me feel crazy."

"But it wasn't just a nightmare, was it? You've already found that much out without my help."

That was true, but he still had no intention of taking on another wardrobe monster.

"Besides, the barn doesn't always work so good going the other way. It might not spit you back out in Annette's field."

"I had no intention of going back in there with those things." But as Eric turned, he realized that the cornfield was gone. The area behind the barn was now densely wooded. In fact, now that he was looking, he realized that the barn from which he'd emerged was not the same one he'd entered. This barn was much smaller and not nearly as old and rundown. "Wait…"

Grant laughed. "*Weird*, right?"

"Where's the other barn?"

"Annette's place is about fifty miles southeast of here."

"*Fifty miles?*"

"Give or take."

"But… My car…"

"It'll be fine."

Eric stared at the barn, trying to wrap his head around the idea of having traveled fifty miles by merely walking through a barn.

Two barns?

"But I meant what I said. I really wouldn't recommend trying to go back through the way you came. I'm not sure where people end up, but sometimes they never come back. They might even end up in that other world. If so, I don't envy them."

"So you're saying I can't actually go back?"

Grant stuffed his hands deep into his pockets and glanced away. "Well, you *can*. Technically speaking. I mean… You could call for a ride. I could show you the way to the highway. You just can't walk back the way you came."

"And if that's what I chose to do, you'd let me?"

Grant sighed. "I can't make you go. Only you can make that decision. But you need to understand that this is important. Without you... *he* wins."

Again with the "he wins" stuff.

"And what?" Eric pressed. "The world ends? We're plunged into eternal darkness? The Packers start a hundred-year losing streak? What? I mean, who *is* this guy? You guys are talking about him like he's the devil or something."

"I don't know who he is. I don't know what he wants. But he's *bad*. And he's trying to get to the cathedral *right now*."

"But even if I get to the cathedral first, you can't even tell me what I'm supposed to do."

"No, I can't. Only you know that."

"No, I don't. Remember? I'm the one who doesn't know anything about what's going on here? I'm the one who just walked into that house and almost got eaten by Anti-Narnia?"

"You saw it in the dream that brought you here."

"Oh. Well *that's* convenient, since I *can't remember that dream*!"

"Don't you?"

"No! Or..." Eric looked back toward the barn. "No. I *did* remember some of it..."

"It'll unravel itself as you go," Grant explained. "By the time you reach the cathedral, you'll remember it all. That's how you'll know what to do when you get there."

Eric stared silently toward the barn, considering. Now that he thought about it, he realized that he could recall seeing this second barn in his dream as well. In fact, he even remembered meeting Grant...except there had been no tractor involved in their meeting...because he'd never gone inside the house... They met in the yard, instead.

"And if you turn back," Grant added. "I can't promise you the dream will ever stop recurring. Even long after it's too late."

Eric met the old man's eyes and saw the depth of his emotions. He was truly sorry to have to say these things.

"This might be your only chance to be free of it."

Eric sighed. Continue this insanity or never sleep through the night again. He'd had better options given to him. But the choice seemed pretty clear. The whole reason he came here in the first place was to try to rid himself of his recurring dream.

"Okay," he said. "Show me where to go next."

'

Chapter Seven

Grant led Eric across the overgrown yard.

Along the way, Eric noticed that there were at least a dozen various bird houses displayed around the lawn. Some were mounted to tree trunks, others to freestanding posts, some dangling by chains from potted plant hangers. There was also a heavy-looking, concrete bird bath standing in the yard.

Whoever the former owners of this house might have been, they were obviously bird lovers.

Birds seemed to be the theme of the day. He even noticed that there was a lone hawk soaring high overhead, as if to punctuate the point.

He followed Grant through the tall grass, past the driveway and behind a little tool shed. There, he found another narrow dirt path, not unlike the one he'd followed through the cornfield.

"This will take you about a quarter of a mile into the woods before it becomes completely overgrown. At that point, there's another road out there. It's not easy to see, but you can make it out if you're looking for it. Does it look familiar, yet?"

It did. Peering down this path, he was sure that, like the barn, he had seen it in his dream.

"That'll be a clue. I'm betting that dream of yours was showing you what you were going to do *if* you got up that first night and came straight here. But it's two days later now and it looks like that other guy's trying to slow you down. Things are different. And where they're different, things are going to get dangerous."

"Like in the house." Eric remembered realizing at the last moment that he didn't recall seeing the house in his dream. The realization gave him pause and he decided to leave. He wondered now if making this decision *before* the wardrobe flew open might have bought him an extra second or two, perhaps making all the difference in his escape.

"That's right. And just like in the house, watch out for those residual ghosts. They'll probably be trying to lead you into trouble."

"Right."

"And you'll have your cell phone signal back, too."

Eric checked his phone and saw that he did, in fact have a couple of bars. He also had nine missed calls and a text message.

"That'll be useful too. You don't want to stray too far off the path. If you lose your way, use your phone. When you go too far into that border world, it'll cut out. As long as you have a signal, you're still home."

"Good to know."

"I can't come with you. But you'll meet Taylor up ahead. He'll take care of you."

Eric nodded. "Taylor. Cool. Listen, though. Can I really catch up to this guy if he has almost a whole day's lead on me?"

It was impossible to miss the deep look of concern on Grant's face. "I don't know," he confessed. "I sure hope so."

"Well then…" Unable to think of anything more to say, Eric gave Grant a wave goodbye and then started down the path.

With each step, the signal on his cell phone grew stronger. According to Grant, this meant he was still on earth.

And to think he came here with the intention of proving he *wasn't* crazy.

He checked the text message. It was from Karen, of course, and simply read: CALL ME.

He didn't like using the cell phone. He didn't even want to carry the stupid thing. He just wanted to throw it away. He rarely called her and almost always let her call him. He didn't want to call her now, either. And if the nine missed calls were any indication, he wouldn't have to.

And he was right. He had walked less than twenty paces when it began to vibrate in his hand.

"Eric!"

"Hi."

"I've been trying to call you!"

"Yeah. I just got your text. Didn't have a signal for a while there. But I'm okay."

"What's going on?"

"It's…um…" He glanced back the way he'd come. He expected Grant to be gone, but he was still standing there, staring after him. He waved. Eric waved back. "It's complicated."

"What do you mean?"

71

"Well… It's a little crazy, so… I really need you to open your mind for this, okay?"

Karen was quiet for a moment. He knew he had her attention now. Finally, she said, "Okay."

Eric told her everything that happened after he disconnected their last call and approached the barn, beginning with finding the eagle mounted over the doors. He told her about the impossible interior of the barn and the freaky chickens. He described the pitiful monstrosities he'd seen in the stalls. And he told her about the farmhouse and the monster that came out of the wardrobe. Finally, he told her about his conversation with Grant.

He couldn't say how he expected her to react to these absurd things he was telling her, but she only listened patiently. And when he was done, she only said, "So you've really got to find this cathedral, then."

"Yeah. I do. So you believe me, then? You don't think I've gone nuts?"

"You're no liar, Eric."

"I didn't ask if you thought I was lying. I asked if you thought I'd gone crazy."

She didn't answer.

"Of course you think I've gone crazy," Eric answered for her. "I'd think *you'd* gone crazy if you didn't."

"Well, that sounds sensible enough, I guess."

"Let me hang up and I'll send you the pictures I took."

"You have pictures?"

"I had to prove I wasn't nuts, didn't I?"

"Let me see them."

Eric disconnected the call and sent the pictures to her, exactly the way he'd sent her the picture of the barn last time. He didn't have any pictures of the wardrobe monster, but he wasn't remotely sorry he didn't stop to ask it to say cheese. However, he was beginning to wish he'd snapped pictures all the way through the barn so he could show her how much bigger it was on the inside than the outside, and a picture of the farmhouse both with and without the addition of Grant's tractor would have been helpful in validating his story also. But he was simply going to have to make do with what he had.

After only a moment, Karen called him back. "Remind me not to have you bring home milk and eggs."

"Freaky, right?"

"That is *definitely* some ugly livestock."

"So I'm not crazy?"

"Apparently not. These things are disgusting. What *are* they? They look *dead*. This is…"

"Crazy?"

"Well…yeah."

"I know it is."

"Do you really think you've gone fifty miles?"

"I don't know. I only have Grant's word on that. But the first barn was gone when I came out the other end and so was the cornfield. I can't say it's actually fifty miles, but I definitely went farther than I should have."

"That's so weird."

"Believe me, I know."

"But why you? I mean, if all this stuff is real, then why *you* of all people?"

"I can't even begin to tell you that."

The trees began to crowd the path around him. The road was less defined here, just as Grant had described. Soon he'd have to start looking for the other path, the one that was difficult to see.

"This is all really crazy."

"I know. But I think Grant was right. I feel like if I don't do this now, I may never stop getting up in the middle of the night and rushing out the door. And that's a pretty lousy way to live a life."

"I guess it would be."

He reached the end of the visible road and stopped. "Hey, I'm going to get off of here again so I can find this path. I'll talk to you in a little bit."

"Okay. Be careful."

"I will."

Eric pocketed the phone and turned slowly around, searching the forest. At first, he saw nothing but trees and brush. There was no sign of another path. But then he spotted it. It was to the right, almost completely overgrown, virtually invisible. From where he stood, however, he could see the way the trees lined up on either side of it, like a seam in a quilt.

He pushed through the brush and made his way along this secret path.

This was all familiar. He remembered this place from his dream. According to Grant, this meant he was on the right path. In the dream, it was two days ago. That explained the discrepancies in the barn, why the chickens weren't in the same places. They were wherever they would have been two days ago. On the other hand, the other creatures hadn't moved, justifying his hunch that the bloated things were incapable of moving around even within their own stalls.

He could hardly believe he was accepting this nonsense.

He pushed on, shoving through the dense foliage, thinking about his dream. He'd been drawn all the way to Annette's field by his peculiar urge to get in the car and drive (and then later get out of the car and walk) until he arrived at the gate in her back yard. But the dream didn't begin until he stood at the edge of the cornfield, looking up at the barn. He wondered how it was that he knew the way to the barn when it didn't seem to be a part of the dream. Was it simply a part of the dream that remained forgotten? Or had there been other forces at work in guiding him here?

He would probably never know for sure.

When the brush had thinned enough that he no longer needed both hands to push through it, Eric withdrew his phone again and fumbled through the address book Karen programmed into it for him until he found his brother's number.

"What's up?" answered Paul.

"Hey. I need a huge favor."

"How huge?"

"Pretty damn inconvenient."

"What do you need?"

"I need you to go pick up my PT Cruiser for me."

"Okay. Where is it?"

Eric gave him directions on how to find it as he followed the faint trail up the side of a hill.

"What the hell's your car doing way out there?"

"It's a real long story."

"If you say so. Where are *you*?"

"About fifty miles northwest of where I parked. I think."

"What are you driving?"

"Didn't say I was driving."

"Wait…what?"

"I'm out in the woods right now. Don't worry about it. I just need you to pick up the Cruiser. I think I'm going to have to find another ride when I'm done here."

"What the hell are you doing in the woods?"

"Like I said, it's a really long story. Will you do it?"

"Sure. Yeah. I can do it."

"Thanks. I owe you."

"Yes you do. Does Karen know where you are?"

"Yes, Karen knows where I am."

"You're seriously acting weird today."

"You don't know the half of it."

"What?"

"Nothing."

The phone crackled as he approached the top of the hill and he took it away from his ear long enough to look at the display and see that he was again losing the signal. When he put it back to his ear, Paul was saying something. His voice stuttered through the static.

"What was that?"

"I said it'll be a couple of hours before I can drive out there."

"That's okay." He hadn't expected him to leave immediately. Paul owned his own construction business. He had the freedom to leave work to run errands, which was why Eric called him instead of having Karen take care of it, but he didn't expect him to drop everything and go. "There's no huge rush. Listen, my phone's cutting out so…I'm…"

He trailed off as he crested the top of the hill and looked down off the other side. "Whoa."

"What?"

Before him lay a landscape vastly different from the cornfields and forests he'd seen so far. The path continued down the other side of the hill, widening as it went. The trees thinned. Rocks jutted up from the ground. About two hundred yards in front of him, the earth was split by a wide gorge.

"Eric? What's going on? Are you still there?"

"Yeah. But I've got to let you go. I'm losing my signal."

"Okay. Call me later, though, okay? Let me know what's going on."

"Yeah. Sure."

Eric disconnected the call and stood staring at the gorge that blocked his path. The road led right up to the ledge, where a dangerous-looking rope bridge waited to carry him to the other side.

Chapter Eight

Eric made his way down the hill and stood at the end of the bridge. It was a simple suspension bridge, with old, wooden slats that he wasn't sure would hold his weight. But at least the bridge was supported with thick cables and not flimsy ropes, as he'd first thought. Still, it inspired very little confidence as a means of safe crossing.

Was he really expected to use this thing? Grant never said anything about risking his life on a terrifying deathtrap. That seemed like something that should come up.

Several fat crows were perched along the cables of the bridge, a murder of bad omens.

He looked down into the gorge. There was water at the bottom, but if it was a hundred feet deep or only a few inches, he couldn't tell. Either way, he had no desire to test his high diving abilities.

The terrain here was strikingly different from the farmland he'd become familiar with. Was this the gray area Grant was talking about? Or was he looking at some of Wisconsin's natural glacial features? The cell phone remained dead, and that odd chill was in the air again, suggesting that he was no longer in the Wisconsin he knew. At least not entirely. But the sun still shined brightly in the sky and nothing more sinister than the architectural deathtrap waited to claim him.

Eighty feet above the surface of the water, the bridge was clearly the product of an evil and deranged mind.

Gingerly stepping out onto the planks, he felt it immediately begin to sway beneath his weight. The crows took flight, apparently smart enough to know the makings of a disaster when they saw it.

It was frightening as hell. Yet even as he eased his weight out onto it, he realized he had done this all before.

In his dream.

At least he knew he was going the right way. Now he only hoped that he wouldn't get out over the middle of this gorge and suddenly recall that his dream ended with him plummeting to his death.

Although heights generally didn't bother him much, it was already clear that he was going to make an exception in this case.

Not feeling any giddy urges to run out and jump up and down, he stalled a moment by studying the transformed landscape around him. But this turned out to be a poor decision as he had barely surveyed the trees behind him when he caught sight of a creature watching him from the cover of the brush.

"You've got to be kidding me…" Eric breathed.

The thing was still too far away to see clearly, but it resembled a cross between a coyote and a deer. It had short, powerful-looking legs, a long neck and a blunt tail. Its head looked too large for the rest of its body and it appeared to be covered in blotchy, gray fur. It was clearly far more agile than the nightmare livestock he'd observed while passing through the barn. Even as he watched, it stalked closer to him, one paw after the other, oversized head low to the ground.

The thing was not even remotely familiar. For some reason, it had not been there in his dream. He'd set out across the bridge without seeing anything more frightening than the bridge itself.

He didn't like that the creature was new. New was bad. New was unpredictable. New meant that he couldn't rely solely on his dream to get him through this ordeal.

Obviously, he was done procrastinating. He turned back to the unpleasant task at hand, gripped the thick cables and began making his way across.

Almost immediately, he was impressed by how utterly terrifying the experience was. The whole structure swayed beneath him, tilting him left and right with each step, threatening to tip him over the edge and send him speeding toward the water below with far less poise and grace than an Olympic high diver and at least as much noise as a terrified teenage girl in a Halloween haunted house.

About a third of the way across, he risked a look back.

The creature had advanced, but it wasn't stalking him across the bridge. Instead, it was busily sniffing the path where he'd walked, studying his scent.

Maybe it wasn't interested in a snack. Maybe it was only curious about him.

Or maybe it just liked to smell its food before every meal.

He sensed that this was neither the time nor the place for reckless optimism. He turned his eyes back to the planks in front of him and continued across the bridge. The closer he crept toward the middle, the more the bridge moved beneath him. He could feel every faint breeze that blew past.

Glancing back again, he saw that the creature was sitting at the end of the bridge, watching him.

It was probably waiting for him to fall. That would save it the trouble of catching him. And the impact would likely tenderize his flesh nicely. Yummy.

Or perhaps it was just waiting for his clumsy ass to reach the other side so it could cross without him shaking the bridge to pieces from under them both.

Carefully and far too slowly, Eric made his way past the middle of the bridge. He could hear the planks creaking, threatening to snap.

He didn't like this at all. His heart was racing. His hands ached from gripping the cables with all his strength. His body was tense, his teeth clenched. Afraid that the mere sight of the chasm beneath him would freeze him with fright, he kept his eyes fixed on the path at the far side of the bridge.

He could feel himself trembling. It wouldn't have surprised him if his very heart gave out before he could reach the safety of the far side of the gorge. But with one step after another, he made his way steadily across.

When he was nearly at the end, he realized that he was muttering curses and couldn't quite remember when he started doing that.

Finally, he stepped onto solid ground again and turned to face the creature, convinced that it would be charging toward him.

But it remained where it was, watching him, apparently uninterested in eating him, but perfectly content to watch his amusing antics as he fled.

Wondering if it would eventually come after him or if it would simply wander off again, but not waiting to find out for sure, he hurried along the path, up the next hill and into the next valley, where the trees grew thinner still and the jagged rocks jutted even more prominently from the ground.

The forest that had mysteriously appeared from cornfields was itself quickly giving way to what looked like the foothills of a mountain range. The hills grew taller and steeper and rocky bluffs broke the earth like great, yawning grins.

Behind him, the creature had not yet followed him over the hill and he could see no other signs of life to give cause for concern, but he kept his optimism reigned well in.

The path wound to the bottom of the valley, followed it down for about a hundred yards and then jutted up and over the next rise. Eric followed it step-by-step. Grant had warned him not to leave the path, and he intended to obey him to the letter. He did not even dare to cut the corners for fear that he might find himself rapidly and unexpectedly plunged into an even stranger and more hostile landscape.

His phone remained dead.

Nearing the top of the next rise, he turned back and saw that the creature was making its way down the previous hill, its snout to the ground, sniffing at his trail.

Picking up his pace, he climbed the next hill and started down the other side. The trees were denser here, the jagged rocks less pronounced. The path wound around several mossy boulders and then cut through the dense underbrush at the bottom of the hill.

As he reached the cover of the brush, he looked back again in time to see the creature crest the hill behind him. It lifted is snout from the ground and stared back at him, its oversized head cocked curiously.

Movement caught his eye and he spotted a second creature

making its way along the top of the ridge toward the first. A hot, twisting feeling grew in his gut as he wondered if the beasts would grow bolder in packs.

Paranoid that they might chase him if he bolted, he forced himself to maintain only a fast walk as he moved into the cover of the brush.

Ahead of him, the trees on the left of the path gave way to another cornfield. The path wound around behind the field, toward a number of small buildings about half a mile away. If he could reach those buildings before the creatures worked up the courage to run him down, he'd be fine.

Looking back over his shoulder, he saw neither of them chasing after him.

Then something growled at his left hip.

Chapter Nine

Having scratched the high dive off his bucket list already, Eric discovered that he might have had a promising future in either Olympic high jumping or on *Dancing with the Stars*. Although neither venue was particularly appropriate for the sailor-worthy curses that escaped him even as he realized the sound was nothing more than his cell phone vibrating.

Clearly, he had returned to Wisconsin's calling area.

Hoping that, if nothing else, the creatures were now concerned about catching a freakish hopping strain of Tourrette's and wouldn't want to eat him anymore, he answered the damn phone.

"How goes the quest?" Karen asked.

"Peachy," he replied, his heart still pounding from the fright.

"You okay?"

"For now."

"What's wrong?"

"Nothing. Just jumpy."

"Where are you?"

"Not sure yet. Another cornfield. I see some buildings up ahead. I'm going to check them out."

"Be careful."

"Obviously."

"Don't go near any more wardrobes."

"You don't have to worry about that. I'm over Narnia for good."

"I prefer Hogwarts anyway."

"Me too."

"Paul called. He said you asked him to pick up the PT Cruiser."

"I did."

"He said he'll be over in a little bit to pick up my key."

"That was fast."

"He was concerned."

"I'll bet. He probably thinks I've lost my mind."

"Well you *are* wandering around in a cornfield. Again."

"True."

Karen fell silent.

"Do *you* think I've lost my mind?"

"No."

"Really?"

Again, she fell silent. Eric waited it out. Behind him, the creatures still hadn't emerged from the woods and he grew paranoid that they might try to circle around through the corn instead.

"I really don't think so," she decided at last. "I mean, you sent me the pictures. Unless you're playing a really elaborate prank on me—which I really doubt you'd be dumb enough to do—"

"That *does* sound like a stupid thing for me to do."

"Yes. It does. But if you're not…then I don't know how else to

85

explain it. Either this is all real…or…you've gone completely nuts."

"And that's the simplest explanation," Eric concluded.

"You said you were seeing creatures that don't exist. Monsters. You said you jumped fifty miles by walking through a barn."

"Well…I was *told* fifty miles. I don't actually *know* it was fifty. Could have been just one."

Again, Karen fell silent.

"So did you tell Paul I was going crazy?"

"I told him about your dream. Not about…all the other stuff."

Nothing rustled in the corn but a faint breeze and the half-coyote-half-deer things had not emerged from the forest. He was still not halfway to the safety of the buildings and he did not even know for sure that those structures actually equated civilization and therefore safety. For all he knew, the buildings had been abandoned years ago and since claimed as dens for the very creatures he sought to escape. In that case, Karen might not be the only one getting her lunch delivered to her home.

On the other hand, he didn't know for sure that these things wouldn't hesitate to follow him right up to someone's door and disembowel him right on the welcome mat.

"He was worried."

"I know."

Something rustled in the corn. Was it just the wind? A rabbit?

"I think you should send him those pictures. Let him know what's going on."

"You think so?"

"Just consider it. Maybe he can help."

He searched the corn, but could see nothing.

"Maybe. We'll see. But listen, I need to hang up again for a little while."

"Okay. Call me back."

"I will." Although he knew perfectly well that *she'd* call *him* long before he'd get around to it.

Eric hung up and looked back the way he came. The absence of the creatures was worse than knowing they were following him. It was far too easy to imagine an entire pack of them gathering under the cover of the corn, stalking him, preparing to pounce.

But nothing showed itself as he made his way to the far end of the field and around the curve.

Ahead of him, the buildings loomed silently. Six small structures and one much larger structure were clustered around a center courtyard. Even before he reached them, he could tell they were no longer in use and his heart sank at the realization that this might not be the safe haven he was hoping to find.

Now and then something would flit around in the field, and once a pair of crows shot up and took flight, startling him into another fit of cursing, but nothing more showed itself. The creatures were either uninterested or they were biding their time for some reason.

In the dream, he recalled feeling nervous about the corn, about all the things that might be hiding in there, just out of sight, watching him. He remembered hearing a lot of noises in the field, but hadn't seen anything to justify his fears. The strange hybrid of coyote and deer had still not shown themselves.

Apparently, Dream Eric had arrived on time like a good boy and therefore didn't have to deal with all this extra crap.

Noises taunted him, the corn rustled threateningly, yet he

somehow made his way along the road to the cluster of buildings without being set upon by ravenous beasts.

As he walked out into the overgrown yard, he realized he was standing in some sort of abandoned campground. The six smaller buildings were cabins, the larger likely contained a meeting room and cafeteria, probably an office or two. He could see the posts where a volleyball net used to be, an old basketball court, a half-dozen picnic tables and several concrete fire pits.

There was also an old, cheesy-looking totem pole displayed at the center of the yard. Most of the paint had faded or flaked away, leaving much of it unrecognizable without a close inspection, but the one on top was clearly a bird of prey with boxy, outstretched wings.

As he looked around, everything he saw came back to him. Just like with the barn and the bridge, he had been here in his dream, which meant that this was precisely where he was supposed to be. But where, exactly, was he supposed to go from here? Grant had only told him to follow the path, which he did. He even crossed that stupid bridge.

So where to now?

Looking around, he caught sight of a hefty bald man in a pair of baggy shorts and a dirty tee shirt. He was walking out from behind one of the cabins and was now crossing the tall grass toward the front door of the main building.

Taylor.

Eric broke into a jog. "Excuse me! Hey!"

But the man walked into the building without acknowledging him.

Assuming he hadn't been heard, Eric hurried after him. He had almost reached the building's front steps when he suddenly realized that something was wrong.

He stopped running and stared into the open doorway. This was remarkably similar to the man he'd seen leaving the barn and then entering the house. The *residual* man.

He had followed that one into a place he wasn't supposed to go. And here he was, chasing this person, merely *assuming* that it was the man Grant told him to expect.

His eyes fixed on the darkened doorway, he began to back away.

"Wise choice."

Twirling around, uttering an incoherent cry, he found himself face-to-face with an elderly black man with kind eyes and a gentle smile.

"Sorry to startle you."

"No, it's fine. You'd think I'd be getting used to it by now." He glanced around the empty courtyard. "Where the hell did you come from?"

"I was in cabin four when I saw you run by." He gestured at one of the smaller buildings.

"Oh."

The old man was dressed in worn jeans and a light work shirt, not that different from Grant, he realized. There was a tool belt around his waist that appeared to contain very few tools, a stark contrast to the similar belt he'd so often seen Paul wearing while at work. His always looked so laden with heavy tools that he should barely be capable of walking.

"I was hoping to catch you before you did something stupid, but it looks like you're already onto that trick."

"Yeah. Fell for the residual thing back at the barn. Lucky for me, Grant saved my ass. I take it you're Taylor?"

"Taylor Parlorn."

"Eric Fortrell."

"Pleasure to meet you, Eric."

"You the groundskeeper here or something?"

"Not officially. But I do keep my eye on things."

"Because of the fissure," Eric guessed.

"Because of the fissure." Still smiling, Taylor turned and walked toward the nearest cabin and Eric, having not been given any instructions on what he should do next, followed.

"So you guys are what? The honor guard or something?"

Taylor stepped into the open doorway and surveyed the interior of the cabin for a few seconds before pulling the door closed. Turning around, he replied, "Something like that."

Eric followed him to the next cabin. "What is this place? Or *was*, I guess."

Taylor stopped and turned to face him, his smile broadening. "About forty years ago, it was a naturist resort."

"Naturists?"

"Naturists, nudists, whatever you want to call them. This was Gold Sunshine Resort." He turned and continued to the next cabin. *"Clothing optional.* Naked people everywhere. Naked swimming. Naked sunbathing. Naked volleyball. Naked basketball. Naked campfire singing."

Eric laughed. He couldn't help it. It just seemed so completely absurd that he should find himself in an abandoned nudist resort of all places. And then there was the way Taylor kept pronouncing the word "nekkid."

"I didn't know there were nudist resorts in Wisconsin."

"Well, I can't imagine it was all that popular a hobby in the wintertime, to tell the truth."

"I wouldn't imagine so, either."

Taylor stepped into the second cabin and Eric followed. A piece of plywood that had been mounted over a broken window had fallen and was lying on the floor. Taylor picked it up, produced a hammer and some nails from his belt and fixed it back over the window. That done, the two of them exited the building and Taylor closed the door firmly behind them.

"Something happened here," Taylor said as he walked back out into the sun. "Something bad. I don't recall which story was true and which were just rumors, but the place closed down. It's been sitting here empty ever since."

The idea that something bad had happened here was unsettling.

Eric turned and caught sight of the two creatures that had been following him. They were standing between the farthest two cabins with their backs to the cornfield. Apparently they *were* hiding out there. They had probably been watching his every move. As he eyed them, a third crept out into sight.

Taylor followed his gaze. "I see you've got some admirers."

"Looks like it."

"They're real curious creatures, but pretty well harmless."

"Are they?"

"Oh yeah. Like most animals, really. I've never heard of them attacking a person. Not even in large packs."

"Huh."

"Ugly suckers, though, ain't they?"

Looking at their too-large heads and mangy hides, he couldn't argue. But there was also something almost endearing about them, too, now that he knew they weren't determined to tear out his throat. They had a characteristically puppy-like quality.

Remembering the cell phone's camera, he pulled it out and snapped a picture of the three animals. "I still have reception," he noticed.

"Yep. We're in Wisconsin."

Eric sent the picture to Karen, thankful again for the opportunity to prove that he wasn't completely out of his mind. Obviously, he was only *partially* nuts at best. "Speaking of Wisconsin," he said. "How far have I gone this time?"

Taylor gave him another endearing smile. "You're about eighty-five miles north of where you left Grant."

"Sonofabitch."

"Pretty cool, huh?"

It wasn't entirely *un*-cool, he had to admit.

Eric glanced around the resort. "So where do I go now?"

Taylor scratched the gray stubble on his chin. "Well... That's the problem, isn't it?"

"There's a problem?"

"There is."

"Of course there is."

"You see, you're supposed to follow *that* guy."

Eric turned in time to see the bald man making another trip into the largest of the seven buildings.

"But I'm not supposed to trust them."

"I know. But he's standing between you and the path to the cathedral."

Eric's heart sank. "So this...*him*...whatever he is...set another

92

trap for me. Except this time I can't avoid it."

"Looks that way."

"Another wardrobe monster?"

"Wardrobe monster?"

"The thing back in the farmhouse…" He shook his head. "Forget it."

Taylor shrugged. "I don't know what you saw back at the farmhouse and I don't know what you're going to find in here. But I'm sure it's going to be nasty."

"Great."

"If one of these things starts after you, it'll keep coming until it catches you or loses its focus. If you can find a way to distract it, it'll forget about you and go back to sleep."

Eric nodded. He recalled Grant telling him that the wardrobe monster wouldn't harm him as long as he didn't go back in to stir it back up.

"It'll have to be something big, though. You won't be able to just throw a stick. It's got to be something it won't see coming. Something sufficient to tear its attention away from you utterly and completely."

"Like a tractor coming through the front door?"

Taylor laughed heartily at this. His voice carried over the open fields around them and startled one of the curious, coyote-deer creatures into retreating a few steps toward the safety of the cornfield. "Oh damn…" he gasped, nodding. "Good old Grant. Yep. That'd definitely do it."

Eric recalled how close that stunt had been for him. If Grant's timing had been just a little off, things could have turned very bad for him. At the time he hadn't known why he would take such a risk, but now he understood. Anything less than that and the thing would've simply kept coming. It would've chased him down and killed him.

Now he stared at the main building, wondering if he might not be running dangerously low on luck. He didn't like the idea of going in there. He had no clue what might be waiting for him. And he didn't have a tractor.

Looking back the other way, he saw that all three of the creatures were still watching them. One was lying down, its oversized head resting on the ground in front of it, its big eyes staring back at him.

"I'm not going to have any help for this one, am I?"

Taylor was wiping at his eyes. The smile quickly faded from his kind face. "I'm afraid not."

"Do you at least know what I'm looking for? Where I'm supposed to go?"

"The stairs at the back of the kitchen shouldn't be there."

"I'm sorry?"

"They shouldn't lead anywhere. But they do."

"Oh. I get it. Thanks."

"Sure thing. And as for what *he* left for you… Just trust in yourself. You'll find a way. Use the advantages you have."

"I don't have any advantages."

"That's not true."

"Not unless blind ignorance and dumb luck count for anything."

"They *do*, actually. But you have more than that. For starters, you have the *dream*."

"The dream," Eric repeated. He recalled Grant telling him that the dream would help guide him. It would show him things that were different between now and when he should have come. But he already knew something was different. The difference was precisely what concerned him.

"Trust in yourself," Taylor said again.

"I'll try."

"Good luck."

"Thanks."

Eric glanced back one more time at the creatures that were watching him and saw that they now numbered four. Another had joined the first three while he was looking the other way.

He was willing to take Taylor's word that they weren't dangerous, but he still didn't care for the idea of them gathering in large numbers.

He walked across the courtyard toward the main building. It was still difficult to imagine people running around here naked.

As he climbed the steps, he looked back one last time at Taylor, who smiled broadly back at him and waved.

Eric waved back, then turned and walked inside.

A large, open room that probably served as a cafeteria and a meeting room as well as a dozen other purposes waited just inside the front door of the main building. A very large fireplace stood in the center of the wall opposite him. Six aged ceiling fans hung from the high ceiling. Eric tried to imagine people in this room, eating, dancing, playing games, all of them stark naked. It seemed strange to him, utterly alien, in fact, but he was sure a great many people would also find his fascination with Shakespeare equally boggling. To each his own, he supposed.

Off to the right was an open door leading into a small room, likely a management office. Next to that was a storage room. Farther down along that wall were restrooms. He could see the gender signs on the door, which struck him as a little bit funny in a nudist resort. What was the purpose in segregating public bathrooms if those using it were unconcerned with privacy?

Maybe it was because no self-respecting female would care to share a restroom with the gender responsible for the kinds of abominations Eric had discovered in far too many public restrooms to count.

His eyes drifted to the far left, where a hallway waited.

He was already familiar with the building. He was here in his dream. He explored all these rooms. He could describe them if he wanted to, without even entering them, though there wasn't much to describe. The building was mostly empty.

The kitchen was off the hallway. The stairs Taylor described to him were behind a door on the far side of the right-hand wall, in the corner beside the refrigerator. Except that there would be no refrigerator. The appliances had been removed long ago.

The stairs led down. But this building had no basement.

He had no recollection of whatever monstrous thing the foggy man left for him, of course. According to Grant, the dream only showed him what he would have seen if he'd come here immediately after waking from it the very first night. At that time, the foggy man hadn't been here yet. But last night, something in this building changed. Something was here now that wasn't here before. And it wasn't going to be gentle about revealing itself.

It was going to scare the living hell out of him.

Ignoring the rooms on the right, he turned left and walked to the hallway. Then he stood in the kitchen door, staring in. Ugly tile floors. Bland countertops. Stained ceiling tiles. Spider webs and dust. He could see the faded shadows on the walls where the refrigerator and stove once stood. Directly across from him was the back door with a grimy window that let in the sunshine.

He focused on the dream, tried to remember every detail he could, but he couldn't find anything that was changed. Everything seemed utterly untouched.

Cautiously, he stepped forward, his eyes watching the cabinet doors for any sign of movement, ready to bolt at the first sound of a creaking hinge.

But nothing attacked him.

Just to the right of the back door, directly between the corner and the refrigerator's lingering shadow on the wall, stood the door to the mystery stairs. He walked to this door and then looked back into the kitchen again, holding his breath with anticipation.

Still nothing jumped out at him.

He turned and opened the door.

Nothing awful waited behind it. There was only a narrow hallway leading to a dark set of stairs.

Again, he looked back at the kitchen, half-expecting something to be rushing toward him now, but still there was nothing.

He dared to hope that perhaps the foggy man had left the trap on the other side of the building and that he wouldn't have to deal with another wardrobe monster.

Then he glanced at the back door and saw a terrible face staring in at him.

Chapter Ten

Eric wasn't entirely sure whether the door exploded before or after he ran screaming down the hallway. He also couldn't recall which obscenities actually made it out of his mouth and which ones became knotted together into incoherent nonsense as he rushed precariously down the dark and narrow stairs.

He did not dare look back, but he could clearly hear the thing tearing after him and uttering horrible, unearthly noises that filled him with indescribable terror.

He did not notice when the concrete walls changed, but by the time he reached the bottom of the stairs he was no longer inside the resort's main building. He was now running along a narrow concrete path between a tall stone structure and a dense hedge.

Off the stairs now and at a full run, he finally risked a look over his shoulder. The thing was nine feet tall, pale green with sickly black blotches. Huge, grotesque legs, like deformed tree trunks, pounded the concrete almost at his heels. He saw massive arms reaching out for him, terrible claws slashing the air like the blades of some hellish machine.

And that awful face… Oozing, bloody eyes, pulsing gashes for a nose, countless gnarled and jagged teeth gnashing together. But it was worse than all of that. He couldn't quite grasp the entirety of everything he saw before he could no longer bear to look at it. Despite having a face, he didn't think it had a head. And though it had arms and legs, it lacked a discernable torso. It also had many other appendages, most of which he could not seem to even comprehend.

Eric ran. He reached the end of the stone wall and turned the corner. He found himself in some kind of overgrown garden. He dodged an ivy-covered statue and an ornate bird bath, ducked under a low limb and barely avoided falling into a weed-choked fish pond before launching himself over a stone bench and darting behind a small, brick structure.

Behind him, he heard a series of crashes punctuated by his pursuer's terrifying yowls.

Already, he was gasping for breath, his body aching. He couldn't go on like this much longer. He had to find a way to break the monster's focus. But how the hell was he supposed to do that? He could barely think clearly enough through his terror to keep running.

A set of steps ascended a small hill. At the top he would find a patio with enormous, fifty-gallon planter pots overflowing with gnarled weeds. He remembered these pots perfectly. They were in his dream. They were clay, with ornate designs. They looked very expensive.

Rushing up the steps, he realized that he had a marginal advantage here. He did not recall being attacked by a monster in his dream, so he must have had time to explore. That meant that he was already at least minimally familiar with this place.

The patio was located against one wall of the enormous structure that had somehow replaced the main building of the abandoned resort. Though he still didn't know what this place was, he suddenly recalled that there were signs of construction. It was obvious that no one had been here in a very long time, but the last time anyone was here, all of this was either still being built or undergoing repairs because just off the patio stood an aging set of scaffolding.

He had barely passed the first pair of giant planters when he heard the distinct sound of one of them shattering.

Uttering another stuttering barrage of curses, Eric forced himself somehow to run even faster, rounding the ledge and racing along the narrow, paved path that ran alongside the building and past the scaffolding.

Quickly, calculating his movements, he leapt onto the side of the scaffolding and began to scramble upward, desperately hoping the whole thing wouldn't collapse or tip beneath his weight.

He dared a quick look down in time to get his foot out of the way of a slashing claw and scurried upward with renewed energy, spouting a frenzied string of words that he was pretty sure were not words at all but merely half-assembled grunts and terrified blubbering.

Something crashed against the bottom of the shaky structure. He heard the clanking of metal rods striking the pavement and felt the platforms lurch beneath his feet, tilting perilously to one side, threatening to spill him into the reaching arms of the monster below.

He forced himself not to look.

Slipping between the support rods and onto the highest platform, he immediately began to crawl on his hands and knees back toward the far end of the structure as it wobbled beneath him, praying it would continue to support his weight.

Another crash. Another reverberating clang of metal against stone. Another sideways lurch.

His heart thundered in his ears. He swore loudly, his voice cracked and shrill. If he survived this, hopefully he'd recall this moment in a manlier light, but right now, he just couldn't make himself care about that sort of thing.

Rising to his feet, he surveyed his surroundings. He saw that he was standing just under the guttering, within reach of the roof. He also saw that the beast was climbing over the far side of the scaffolding.

Something beneath him finally gave way. The scaffolding jerked, tilted. A thunderous clattering rose up. The wooden platform snapped. The monster dropped with a shriek. Eric felt it move beneath his feet.

The very next instant he was clinging to the edge of the roof, his shoes scraping the brick surface of the wall, trying to find a footing as the entire structure beneath him collapsed into a pile of metal and wood with a clamor that might have carried for miles.

He could almost imagine hundreds of those coyote-deer things lifting their oversized heads and looking this way.

Desperately, he clawed his way upward, trying to pull himself to safety.

He glanced down to see what kind of mess waited beneath him, hoping there wouldn't be a half-dozen steel bars jutting upward at him, waiting eagerly to run him through. What he saw was the monster rising from the wreckage, its horrible face glaring up at him.

"Oh come on!"

Freshly fueled by the panic of realizing that he had failed to break the beast's focus and therefore remained in imminent mortal danger, Eric somehow managed to hook his leg over the edge and pull himself onto the roof.

Gasping for breath, he dragged himself away from the ledge as huge, yellow claws sank into the shingles and that grotesque face peered over the gutter at him. Its bloody eyes were filled with rage.

"Just go away already!"

He scrambled to his feet and ran up the slope of the roof to the peak, scanning these new surroundings. None of the rooftop looked remotely familiar. Apparently, if he'd come the first night, he would not have found any reason to climb up here and enjoy the view. He would have simply wandered through the grounds around this building, strolling leisurely.

This must be karmic payback for all those times he crabbed at his students for procrastinating on their papers.

Looking back, he saw that the monster had already climbed onto the roof and was now moving toward him, its teeth gnashing horribly. He still couldn't quite make out how the thing fit together. Its huge arms hung at its sides, its claws almost dragging at its feet. Those other limbs seemed to slither strangely around it. They weren't quite tentacles, but they weren't quite arms, either. He couldn't seem to comprehend them. Its green and black skin reminded him of tree bark, as if the thing were nothing more than a particularly ugly old tree come to life.

There was nowhere to go. He was now stranded on the rooftop with no way down. He might as well have locked himself in a room with the thing.

Out of ideas, Eric simply ran. He made his way across the rooftop, toward the far side of the building, where the taller portion of the structure met the two shorter wings, hoping desperately that he would find a window he could escape into or a ledge from which he could climb safely down.

The monstrosity followed him, snatching at him with its claws. Its strange, unearthly cries filled the air at his back, drowning out all other sounds, even the thunderous pounding of his heart.

Something caught his foot and he fell. Kicking and thrashing, he tore free of his shoe and rolled down the slope of the roof. The rough surface of the shingles ground against his exposed skin, but he barely noticed the pain. His only conscious thought was that he had to keep moving. He had to put distance between himself and this monster.

Coming to a stop, Eric tried to lift himself onto his hands and knees, but the thing was already upon him again, its terrible cries right on top of him.

He threw himself out of the way.

It seized his arm.

He kicked at it, yanked his arm free and rolled again.

The shingles bit his elbows, his forehead, his nose. They burned his belly and back where his tee shirt rode up.

His left hand slipped over the edge of the roof and he found himself looking down at a four-story drop. Hard concrete waited patiently to break his bones.

Built on a slope, the building was much taller on this side than it was on the side he'd climbed. There was no way down and nowhere he could go that this thing couldn't follow him.

Out of places to run, he rolled onto his back and looked up as the monster leapt atop him, its huge foot crushing down on his thigh. He cried out, his voice tinged with sharp pain and numbing terror.

The world around him swirled into a chaotic blur.

This seemed to be it. He was out of places to run. He was going to die.

A huge mass of yellow claws passed over him. His ears were filled with the howling and yowling and shrieking of the beast. A hot flash of pain painted itself across his face, his shoulder, another across his leg.

He felt himself sliding closer to the ledge. He clutched for something to hold onto, but his arm flailed uselessly at the air high above the ground. His shoulder inched out over the drop.

If the creature didn't tear him apart, he would fall to his death.

The creature's weight shifted. Its foot rolled across his thigh, threatening to break his leg.

Claws dug into the shingles beside his head. The gutter tore away beneath his shoulder with a great screech of shredding metal.

Teeth snapped before his face and he jerked his head away, closed his eyes, braced himself for the agony to come.

Then the creature's foot was no longer on his thigh. Its unearthly yowling suddenly and rapidly receded.

A heavy thump, a clanking of aluminum as the gutter followed the beast down.

Eric lay there, gasping with fear.

He could hardly believe it. In all the commotion, the monster's foot had slipped over the edge.

It fell.

And by some miracle, he didn't.

Carefully, he pulled himself away from the edge of the roof and then rolled onto his stomach. He was trembling badly. He did not dare try to stand for fear that he might yet manage to fall to his doom.

Seconds passed. Then minutes. Everything remained quiet.

The monster was silent.

Finally, he crept back to the edge and peered over.

He could see the shredded guttering lying on the pavement, precisely where it had landed, but the monster was gone.

Apparently, a four-story fall was as effective at breaking a monster's focus as a charging tractor.

Yet he hesitated to believe that he was really so lucky. It couldn't actually be over. That he should survive by nothing more than a simple misstep on the part of the monster was utterly absurd. Surely the thing must simply be circling around, looking for another way up here.

He stood up, retrieved his lost shoe and made his way back up to the peak of the roof, where he sat down. He was still trembling, his heart still thumping. He couldn't seem to quite catch his breath. He didn't feel like he'd ever be normal again.

He looked down at his leg and found that his khakis were torn. There was a long cut visible through the rip. He was bleeding, but not profusely.

His shoulder, he found, was worse. Blood trickled down his arm, soaking the sleeve of his tee shirt and dripping from his hand. And his face was bleeding, too. A shallow, but freely flowing cut ran from beneath his left eye to just under his left ear.

How he managed to not get his entire face peeled off was beyond him.

He'd received other, smaller injuries as well, including a gash in his ankle, which he received when he lost his shoe, and two bloodied elbows from rolling around on the rough shingles. He had friction burns all over his stomach and lower back. His face was scraped up, his nose and forehead raw.

There was a first aid kit in the glove box of the PT Cruiser, he recalled. As if that would do him any good.

He pulled his cell phone out, confirmed that he still had no signal and then pocketed it again.

He was on his own up here.

The cuts on his shoulder were the ones he needed to worry about. He rolled up his sleeve so that the fabric covered the entire injury and then pressed his hand against it and stood up.

The first thing to do was find a way down from here. He couldn't go back the way he came, obviously, but perhaps there was another way down. Preferably one that didn't involve breaking both his legs.

Chapter Eleven

Circling around the taller, middle section of the building's roof, Eric finally located a window he was able to break.

Slipping inside, he found himself in a small, unfurnished bedroom. It was dark in here, gloomy, despite the white walls and the bright sunshine outside.

No one came to investigate the sound of breaking glass, but he hadn't expected to be confronted. The overgrown yard had suggested that no one had been here for a very long time. And if all the noise of the monster's horrible cries, his own screaming and cursing and the stomping around on the roof hadn't alerted anyone to his presence, much less the deafening cacophony of the collapsing scaffolding, then it was fairly safe to assume that no adequately concerned homeowner was currently present.

In his defense, however, he *was* courteous enough to at least knock at the window before kicking in the glass.

Besides, anyone who could afford to build a place like this certainly wouldn't miss the cost of replacing one window. Insurance would probably cover it anyway.

Still, he couldn't help feeling a little guilty.

Quickly, not caring to linger any longer here than was absolutely necessary, he made his way through the door and into the hallway.

Like with the roof, nothing here was remotely familiar. Perfect, reliable, two-days-ago Eric, who didn't put off getting in his car and driving to Weirdness, Wisconsin just because that was an insane thing to do, never had to break into this building to get down off a roof. Two-days-ago Eric never got into situations like this. He was on time, he did everything right the first time and he was always Mom's favorite.

And he didn't get his ass handed to him by nine-foot-tall towers of yowling teeth and claws, either, apparently.

He tried to recall the things he'd remembered about the yards outside. Everything he'd seen had suggested that this building was empty, deserted. But it wasn't completely rundown. It was relatively clean in here. Just a heavy layer of dust and a few small cracks in the plaster.

For the most part, the house still looked new. But as he peered into one room after another, he found them all completely empty, as if no one had ever actually moved in.

But why spend this kind of money and never even use the place? What happened here?

Still keeping pressure on his bleeding shoulder, Eric made his way along the silent hallway, peering into bedrooms as he went, searching for a stocked bathroom. But although most rooms had private baths, none of them had any towels or running water.

At the end of the long hallway, he found a stairwell that took him down to an elegant but eerily empty foyer. Ignoring the exterior doors for now, he made his way deeper into the house again, peeking into room after room, until he at last found a guest bathroom with a towel.

With no water, he was unable to clean his wounds, but he was at least able to tear the towel into strips and use it to wrap his bleeding shoulder.

He probably needed stitches, but he doubted very much that this strange journey through the fissure would include a rest stop in a hospital emergency room. Unless of course said hospital was long deserted and haunted by demonic brain surgeons.

That wouldn't surprise him.

Finished with his shoulder, he examined his leg and decided it was fine. The creature had only grazed him with its claw. He was more upset about the pants, which were still fairly new.

He stood up and examined his reflection in the mirror. The cut on his cheek wasn't bad either. It, too, had already quit bleeding, but not before a large portion of the left side of his face had become covered in gore.

He looked awful. He didn't exude any of the manliness of a bloodied action hero fresh from a hard-won victory. He just looked like an out-of-shape extra in a bad horror movie.

He took the last of the towel, spit into it and began wiping at the blood. It was now, as he leaned close to the mirror, trying to see through the gloom, that he glimpsed someone standing in the doorway, watching him.

Simultaneously jumping, shouting, cursing and flailing, he reeled around to see who was there.

But he was alone.

He ran from the bathroom and looked around, but there was no one there.

"Hello?"

The house remained silent. *Perfectly* silent, now that he was listening to it. Not a sound reached his ears but the thumping of his own heart.

A shiver raced through him.

Had he only imagined the figure in the doorway? He hadn't seen it very clearly. There were no lights. The bathroom was dark. And it was only there for a split second.

Standing there, wondering if it was even possible to imagine something so startlingly realistic, he remembered what Grant told him about using the memories from his dream as a guide. If he couldn't remember it, it wasn't somewhere he visited in the dream. If he didn't go there in his dream, then it was presumably not somewhere he would have gone on the first day. In other words, it was not somewhere he should be.

Having somehow managed to escape the foggy man's second trap, he had assumed it was safe to linger. But he'd already determined that he never entered this house in his dream. Therefore, he was off the map.

Here there be monsters, he thought, and another violent shiver raced through him.

He was still holding the last strip from the torn towel in his hand. He glanced down at it, considering what to do with it, and decided to stuff it into his back pocket. It was no substitution for a fully stocked first-aid kit, but it was better than nothing.

Now he returned to the foyer and quickly made his way past the staircase to the front door, only to find it locked tight.

Heart sinking, he turned and pressed his back to the door, his eyes wide open.

The house was no longer silent. A low, rumbling groan now swelled through the room, as if rising from the very floor beneath his feet.

Monsters, he thought. *Here there be monsters…*

Chapter Twelve

This sucked.

It wasn't even fair. He survived the foggy man's trap. He beat the monster. All he'd wanted was to patch up his wounds and move on.

The whole room reverberated with that strange groaning. It seemed to pass right through him, shaking him all the way to his core. Suddenly, he was convinced that something very bad was going to happen if he remained here.

Where the hell was he? What was this place?

The door at his back was sealed shut. He was unable to escape that way. With no other choice left to him, he bolted back across the foyer from where he'd come, down the hallway and through the dining room into the kitchen.

Behind him, the groan swelled into an angry roar.

Spotting another door in the kitchen, Eric ran for it, jerked at the handle, but like the doors in the foyer, it wouldn't open.

He turned and scanned the kitchen. Like the rest of the house, it was bare. There wasn't even a carving knife he could pretend was an adequate weapon.

Now he realized that the groaning noise had changed. It no longer seemed to be rising from the floor. Now it seemed to be specifically coming from the foyer, as if the source of the noise was collecting itself into a singular location. In his mind, he could almost see something forming there, a vague shape slowly drawing itself together, materializing from thin air.

But this was merely his imagination. He'd always had a good imagination. Until now, he'd always considered it an asset. Now, he could do without the horror movie that was stubbornly playing in his mind, adding to his overwhelming fear.

He didn't need his imagination to realize that it was getting closer. He could hear it moving toward him. He could almost *feel* it.

Another hallway led away from the kitchen, toward the back of the house. He took it.

Behind him, the groaning tightened into something like a voice. It became a moaning, and then a wailing. The sound chilled his blood.

Another set of stairs waited at the end of the hallway. Remembering the window by which he'd entered the house, he climbed three flights of steps two at a time, hoping he'd find himself back in the same part of the house.

By the time he remembered that there was no way down from the roof (the whole purpose of actually entering the house in the first place), he'd already found himself in another hallway, making his way past numerous spacious bedrooms.

He paused at an intersection between two corridors and considered his choices.

Something about the layout of the house confounded him. It was

113

less like a house than a hotel, but not nearly as convenient.

Behind him, the wailing began to fade into something more like a murmur. Somehow this struck him as even more unsettling.

He turned left and ran to the end of the hallway. There he found yet another staircase, which he took down one flight to a large, spacious room that might have been either a banquet room or a ballroom.

This didn't feel right. He had the strangest sensation that he wasn't traveling through this house in any logical way. As odd as it sounded, it seemed like he was jumping from one side of the house to the other.

He stood in the middle of this room and turned slowly in a circle, listening.

Suddenly he wasn't sure where the murmuring was coming from. It seemed to be moving, originating from one door, then another on the other side of the room, then back again, then to the far corner.

What the hell was going on?

He considered breaking a window and fleeing the house the way he entered, but there was nothing to break the glass with. There was nothing in the house that wasn't built in. And the windows in this room were too high to kick out with his foot.

He chose a door at random and fled, hoping desperately that he didn't run headlong into something horrible. He found himself in yet another hallway.

Now the murmuring was behind him. And it was transforming again, growing, swelling into something even more disturbing, something he could almost comprehend.

Somehow, he felt certain that he never wanted to know what this horrible voice was saying.

Desperate, terrified out of his mind, he ran to the end of the hall, descended another set of steps as quickly as he could, and rushed down yet another hallway.

He stopped. The murmuring was now a muttering. And it was coming from in front of him.

Again, he had that weird sensation of traveling through the house in weird ways. Though he'd just descended a flight of stairs, he had the strangest feeling that he had actually ended up on a *higher* floor.

Another hallway intersected this one at its midpoint. He hurried there and listened, but the muttering seemed to come from every direction at once.

All these choices seemed wrong.

He turned back the way he'd come and was surprised to see a young girl standing in the middle of the hallway, staring back at him.

She was perhaps thirteen, older than the little girls in *The Shining*, but still he managed to appreciate the similarities. She was dressed for summer in a pair of yellow shorts and a pink halter top, with long, brown hair and a pretty face. She was barefoot.

Seconds passed between them as the muttering rose, words that he desperately did not want to hear beginning to take form. His heart was racing. He couldn't move. He didn't know what to do.

Then the girl held a hand out to him. "Hurry," she said. "Come with me."

Going with the creepy little girl in the haunted house seemed like a very bad idea. But the alternative was *definitely* a very bad idea, so he took a leap of faith and ran to the girl.

She took his hand and led him into one of the rooms.

It appeared to be a bedroom, though there were still no

furnishings. A single door stood on one wall, leading into a bathroom. She led him through this bathroom, through another door and into another bedroom, revealing both rooms to be part of one suite. Then she led him through the door of this second bedroom and out into the hall, right back where they started. Except that it was *not* exactly where they started. This wasn't the same hallway.

Before he could grasp what just happened, she led him into another room, through what looked like it should be a closet but turned out to be a staircase, and then emerged into a living room of some sort, past what he was pretty sure was not the same kitchen he'd visited before, to another hallway that led them to yet another bedroom.

Every time they passed through a room, the mutterings grew fainter, until they were little more than a distant humming.

One last door carried them from a bedroom into some kind of electrical room with several massive fuse boxes mounted to concrete walls. There, the girl let go of his hand and sat down on the floor with her back against the wall and her knees drawn up in front of her.

This room was utterly silent.

"We'll be safe here for a little while."

"Okay," said Eric, looking around. The walls and floor were concrete. Water lines passed from left to right overhead and thick bundles of cables ran across the ceiling and walls in every direction.

"What's your name?"

"What? Oh. Eric."

"Eric," she repeated. "I like that name. I'm Isabelle."

"That's a pretty name," Eric replied.

"Thanks." She smiled sweetly and stared up at him without saying another word.

Eric stared back at her for a moment. He had no idea what he should say, where to even begin. This was already, without a doubt, the strangest day of his life. It had decisively won that title pretty well as soon as he'd finished that first enigmatic conversation with Annette, but he was repeatedly finding himself facing ever-weirder oddities as the day went on. And this mind-boggling house-hotel hybrid seemed to possess a weirdness of such profoundness that it classified as an oddity *among* the other things he'd seen.

"So…" he began at last, "you want to tell me what all that…*stuff* back there…"

"What the hell's going on?"

"Yeah. That covers it, I think."

Isabelle smiled. "I can't really explain all of it. I don't actually *get* most of it, honestly. Like, I don't know why this particular room is safe. There's no electricity, so it's not that. But I think maybe it's all the metal and wiring. Whatever it is, he doesn't like to come down here."

"Who's 'he?'"

"Altrusk."

"Altrusk?"

"Used to be Isaac Altrusk. Though, I'm pretty sure that was a fake name. He was a petty con artist turned cult-leader turned creepy recluse turned…well…whatever he is now."

Eric was surprised by the maturity of the girl's vocabulary. Most of his high school students wouldn't be able to come up with such a description.

"He started Gold Sunshine Resort."

"The nudists?"

"Yeah. It was all a load of crap, though. He was a perv. It was just an excuse for him to look at little girls naked."

"Yuck."

"I know. But it was actually pretty smart, too, because most people didn't care to look too hard at what went on in a nudist resort. And what he was *really* interested in was the fissure."

"The fissure?" He almost asked her how she knew about the fissure, but common sense kicked in at the last moment. She was obviously pretty familiar with it, since she was currently *in* it.

"Yeah. I don't know how he found it, but he did. And he built the resort on top of it to hide it while he built *this* place on the other side. I think he envisioned it as some kind of palace."

"Where did he get the money for something like this?"

"Conned people out of it, mostly. But he didn't build the whole thing. He only started it. Then, at some point, it just kind of…finished itself."

"Wait…how does that work?"

"Like I said, I can't explain all of it. The place has a mind of its own. You saw how it is. It takes you places you aren't going. Doors that should go one place spit you out somewhere else. It'll make you crazy if you're not careful."

"Did it make Altrusk crazy?"

"Oh yeah. Totally bugshit."

Eric chuckled.

"The house is built right *into* the fissure somehow. It takes on some of its properties. That's why it warps space and stuff. But it's a lot more than that. Something about the world on the other side of the fissure… It's a bad place. It distorts things. And it distorted the *hell* out of Altrusk. Like, at some point, he just decided he wasn't going to furnish the house. He lived here for years without any furniture. He slept on the floor. He ate at the kitchen counters."

"At least he kept towels in his bathroom," Eric recalled.

"*Some* of the bathrooms."

"What happened to him?"

"Eventually, the house just swallowed him. He stopped being Isaac Altrusk—or whoever he *really* was—at all. Now he's just Altrusk."

"And that was him making all that noise out there?"

"Uh huh."

"And what would happen to me if he caught me?"

There was no humor in her expression when she replied, "You'd be swallowed too."

"Good to know. Let's put that on the list of things we don't want to happen. So is there a way out?"

Isabelle smiled up at him. "I think I can open the door for you. But it'll be dangerous. Altrusk won't want you to leave. And he knows you're here, so he'll be looking for you."

"I see."

"You might as well sit down. He's going to need a little while to calm down. He's got the house all coiled up right now. If we're going to get to the door, we'll need it to not be so jumpy."

Add that to his growing list of things he never thought anyone would ever say to him.

He did as she said and sat down on the floor, his back against the wall, facing her.

Isabelle smiled at him.

Eric removed the cell phone from his pocket and saw without any surprise whatsoever that he still had no signal. Even if he wasn't way off the path and deep inside a freaky alternate reality house with an attitude, he was sure he wouldn't have a decent signal inside these concrete walls.

He glanced up at his young companion, suddenly concerned. "You said Altrusk was a pedophile?"

"He was a little too into little girls, yeah."

"He didn't... I mean you weren't one of his...?"

"Oh. No. *So* yuck. He never touched me. Not sure if he ever actually touched any of them really, he was never that brave. He just...leered, mostly." She shuddered at the memory. "And then after he changed...well, I don't think he cared much about sex at all after that."

"That's good. But how did you get here, then?"

"My parents were members of his club. We vacationed at Gold Sunshine. A lot."

"So you were one of the...?"

"Nudies. Yeah."

"Oh. Sorry. I just didn't know."

"Yeah. It's weird. When we wear clothes, nobody can tell the difference."

Eric laughed, but he couldn't help feeling embarrassed. "I guess so. I just never knew a naturist before."

"We did *own* clothes. It was kind of an optional thing."

"Sorry. I didn't mean to offend."

"You didn't. I totally understand. I mean it was my parents' choice, not mine. I didn't even know it wasn't something everybody did until I was about seven or eight."

Now another thought occurred to Eric. "Wait... I thought the resort's been closed the past forty years."

"Thirty-six years, actually."

Eric stared at her, astounded by what she was suggesting.

Isabelle lifted her hands in a mock expression of shock and said, "Surprise!"

"You've been here for thirty-six years?"

"Yep."

"So you're... What? A ghost?"

"Not exactly. I don't think I'm actually dead. I'm just...different now."

Eric sat there. It was difficult to imagine. "How did it happen?"

"I went nosing around where I shouldn't've. Found my way into the kitchen stairway. Altrusk always said it was his personal wine cellar. Off limits. But there wasn't any wine down there. I wandered out into the yard here, same way you did. It was all a big, incredible adventure until I found a way inside. Then I got real scared real fast. It was crazy terrifying. I don't even remember most of it. I just remember screaming."

Eric felt a shiver creep through him.

"Then I was just here."

"And you're aware of how much time has passed?"

"Yeah, that's weird too. I'm *aware* of time. But I don't actually *feel* time. It doesn't have any effect on me anymore."

"Weird."

"I know, right? I think I'm only *aware* of time because I still have a connection to my family. I can constantly feel my parents. I can get into their thoughts from here. I can see how time passes through them." She paused for a moment and stared down at the floor, her pretty smile gone. "I was with them when I first disappeared, when they went

121

through all that hell, but they don't know it. They're still alive today. They still think about me every day."

"I'm so sorry."

She made herself smile again and gave him a little shrug.

Suddenly, Eric recalled his conversation with Taylor. He said something bad happened at the resort, something that closed it down. He said he didn't recall what really happened, suggesting that there were multiple stories, but apparently it was that a thirteen-year-old girl went missing.

He looked down at his phone, considered it. Then he lifted it and snapped the girl's picture. He wasn't entirely sure why he wanted the picture. Maybe there was something he could do for her. Assuming he actually survived this house of horrors.

"Are there others like you trapped here?"

"Yeah. But they won't come out. They're too afraid of Altrusk. Some of them are afraid of you, too."

"Me?"

"People just don't come here. Ever. This place doesn't even exist to people. So you must be a bad thing."

"I see. But what makes you different from them?"

"I'm not sure. I think it's just that I refuse to give up. Like I said, I can still feel my parents out there. I have to keep thinking there's got to be a way back to them. Over the years I learned some things about the house."

"But you never found a way out?"

She hesitated. "I might have found one way. But I'm too afraid to try it. There's a room hidden somewhere in the house. *You* couldn't get to it. You have to be...like me. There's a doorway there. It doesn't go anywhere else in the house. I'm sure of that. But I don't know where it goes. Every time I've tried it... It hurts. It's like an electric current. It cuts into me, makes me pull back. I can't stand to go in. And I don't have the courage to force myself to go through because I'm not even sure it's really a way out. It might actually kill me, instead. And I just can't do that to my parents."

"I don't blame you."

She gave him a sweet smile. "So what about you? What are you doing here anyway?"

Eric laughed. If only it was as simple as nosing around where he wasn't supposed to be. He told her his story, beginning with the dream and ending with him stranded inside this house.

"That must've been Altrusk you saw in the mirror. Sometimes he appears like that, just standing there for a second. I don't know if it's something left of who he used to be or what. He doesn't last long. He kind of flickers through the house like that and then disappears back into it."

"That's weird."

"Totally."

The two of them fell silent. Eric reflected on all that Isabelle had told him and was surprised to realize just how easily he'd begun to accept these things. He began this day by rationalizing every odd thing he experienced and cramming it into whatever form of rational logic he could make himself believe. The recurring dream that filled him with terror and woke him with a driving conviction that he must get out of bed right now and leave, that there was somewhere he desperately needed to be, could only have been some form of repressed emotions, perhaps nothing more sinister than a subconscious desire to get out and see the world before he grew too old. The woman hanging her laundry, Annette, was only an old and addle-minded widow whose nonsensical ramblings were not prophetic, but merely coincidental. Even the barn was a fabrication, an optical illusion, a game of special effects. Even when he knew that his explanations no longer made sense, he clung stubbornly to them because these things simply *could not exist*. And then he met the wardrobe monster. Grant. The coyote-deer with their amusingly oversized heads. And all that had transpired to lead him here, to this queer little room. He was not forced to accept every word as God-given truth, but he *was* forced to accept that he did not have a rational explanation. Whether Grant and Taylor and now Isabelle were telling him the truth or not, it was the only explanation he had.

If he survived this, he was going to have an entirely new respect for all things paranormal and strange.

"He's gone up to the library."

"Altrusk?"

She nodded. Standing up, she said, "That's at the far end of the house. Top floor. He's still looking for you, but he's calmer now. So is the house."

Eric was now on his feet, too. He was pleased to hear that the house was calmer. That was good. Apparently.

"We may not have another chance. He doesn't like coming down here, but when he doesn't find us anywhere else, he eventually will."

"Okay then. What do we do?"

"I've been able to open some of the doors here a few times, even though I can't leave. Some have been easier than others. We're going to head for the parlor. I'm not sure why, but that door's always been the easiest for me. If I can get it open, I think I can get you out. But we'll have to hurry. He'll feel us before we can get there, but I know the house well enough to make it a fair chase."

"Are you sure I'll be able to leave?"

"No. I'm not. But I know Altrusk used to come and go before he was completely changed. I'm hoping you can, too. Besides, it's the only chance you've got."

There was no arguing with that logic. "So if I don't make it, I could end up stuck here like you, right?"

"You could," she admitted. Then, hesitantly, she added, "Or you could die."

Eric nodded. "Okay then."

Isabelle opened the door and peered out into the hallway. Finding it clear, she took his hand again. Her skin was warm, solid. Nothing about the feel of her revealed that she no longer existed in this world the same way he did.

"Hold on to me," she told him. "If we get separated, you won't stand a chance."

"Got it."

She looked up at him now, her eyes soft. "By the way, if you do end up stuck here, I'll keep you company. Even if you're crazy."

Eric smiled down at her. "That's…*lovely*," he told her. "Thank you."

She smiled brightly up at him and then led him out into the bedroom through which they'd entered the electrical room.

Chapter Thirteen

Isabelle led him by the hand through the empty bedroom, across a hallway, into another bedroom and through the bathroom door into what proved to be not a bathroom but a very large garage.

"He's noticed us," she warned.

"Already?"

"He's a part of the house now. It's kind of hard to keep things from him."

"How long do we have?"

"Not long. But he's restricted by the house just like we are. Weird as this place is, you still can't walk through walls."

They ran through the empty garage as a low, strumming reverberation began to rise in the walls around them. Upon reaching the far door, they passed through it and emerged from what should have been the linen closet of a small bathroom.

Trippy.

Out of the bathroom, through another bedroom and into another hallway, where they raced to the far end, opened a bedroom door and immediately ascended a wide set of stairs as the whole house began to tremble with a warbling, muffled tone that Eric once again realized contained words that he desperately did not want to hear.

A door at the top of the stairs deposited them in a large dining room.

"We're almost there."

"Thank God."

They ran through the dining room and directly into another bedroom, into a closet and up another flight of stairs as the unnerving thrumming rose into a terrifying roar of voices.

"We have to hurry!" screamed Isabelle as they burst through one last door and into what must have been the parlor that she described.

There were large windows spaced all along the outer wall and a pair of matching French doors directly in the middle. Isabelle led him to this door and then let go of his hand as she seized the handle. The door did not budge.

"Don't listen to it!" she cried.

Eric realized that the muttering had become a sort of chant. Words he didn't yet recognize flowed over him, filling him with deep and inexplicable dread. He clamped his hands over his ears and tried not to listen.

Isabelle pulled at the door, her bright eyes fiercely fixed on the handle, her jaw clenched, her muscles taut. She looked intense, as if she were giving it everything she had, both physically and emotionally.

He began humming loudly to himself to cover the disturbing sound of the chanting, desperate to avoid hearing it. There seemed to be something profoundly evil about the voice.

Looking back, he saw something enter the room.

It had a vaguely man-like shape, but was little more than a smoky haze rippling through the air. Dark shadows etched themselves across the wall and carpet, snaking out from the shape at its center. Somewhere in the middle of the mass, an evil pair of eyes glared at him, as if not from a man's head, but from his belly.

Altrusk.

There was a sound like fabric tearing apart and Eric looked back to see Isabelle slowly inching the door open, the small cords in her neck standing out with the exertion.

"Go!" she screamed at him. *"Go now!"*

The chanting suddenly gave way to an insane shriek.

Altrusk darted forward.

Eric wasted no time. He bolted through the door and out of the house.

Free now, he turned quickly and seized Isabelle's wrist. "Come with me!" he cried.

Dark, twisted arms wrapped around her, clutching her, pulling her backward. A terrible voice howled with fury.

Eric held fast.

"Just go!" Isabelle screamed. *"Leave me!"*

"No! I'm taking you with me!"

"I can't!"

"Try!"

"No! I *physically* can't!"

Eric's eyes dropped to her hand and he saw that her fingers were sinking into the door, binding her to the house. He knew she was right. Whatever happened to her, whatever Altrusk did to her, it had somehow fused her into the house. But he couldn't bear to leave her.

She didn't belong there.

"Just go!" Isabelle screamed again. "I'll be fine! He can't hurt me anymore!"

The dark, snaking fingers crept up her arm and reached for his hand. In another moment, those foul tethers would coil around his wrist and he would be dragged back inside to suffer fates worse than madness and death.

"Go! Before it's too late!"

His heart breaking, Eric let go.

The door snapped shut like a steel trap and left him standing there, staring at his own reflection in the window. Instantly, all was silent. Nothing stirred. There was no movement behind the glass. All that remained were shadows and dust. Both Altrusk and Isabelle were gone.

Feeling profoundly numb, Eric turned and gazed around. He was on the patio. He ran by here while fleeing the monster. To his left was the planter it shattered as it raced after him. Rich, dark soil and fragments of clay were spilled across the pavement. To his right was the pile of broken scaffolding.

Again, he was struck by the forgotten memories of his dream. Everything came back to him. He walked past here, calmly, curiously, wondering about the purpose of this building that looked so elegant but appeared abandoned. Nothing pursued him. Nothing shattered the planter. With no need to flee for his very life, he never climbed the scaffolding. It never collapsed. He was never stranded on the roof and therefore never needed to break into the house to get down.

He never met Isabelle.

That version of him simply walked on by, around the corner of the building, utterly and blissfully unaware.

His heart still pounding in his chest, a deep aching inside him, Eric began to walk in that direction.

The house loomed over him, monstrous in size and eerie in its silence, but otherwise perfectly unremarkable. There was absolutely no way to know that the rooms and hallways did not lead where they were supposed to, that a man who had become a monster stalked unwary trespassers…that a young girl was hopelessly trapped inside.

It was difficult to breathe.

In the dream, he'd wandered these grounds for a while before discovering the little path that weaved through the garden and into a dense thicket of trees. But because of the dream, he already knew it was there. He followed the path and left the house of Altrusk behind him forever.

Once he reached the other side of these trees, once the house was completely out of view, Eric succumbed to the weakness in his legs and sat down in the middle of the path, where he stared despairingly up at the bright sky.

The trees swayed gently in a soft breeze. A hawk was circling lazily overhead. Inexplicably, the world carried on.

His phone rang.

Apparently, he was home again.

He fished it from his pocket. It was Karen.

"Thank God, Eric. I've been trying to reach you for like two hours now."

"I'm sorry."

Apparently, something about his voice revealed his distress because she immediately asked, "Are you okay?"

"Yeah." But his voice was unconvincing.

"What's wrong?"

"She's gone."

"What?"

"Isabelle. She's gone. I couldn't save her."

"Baby, what are you talking about?"

"She's just a little girl. Just a girl… And I couldn't save her…"

"God Eric, what happened? Talk to me."

"I never should've gone inside. I didn't know. Never could've known. But she saved me. She saved me and *I* couldn't save *her.*"

Karen fell quiet.

"I'm sorry."

"No. It's fine."

"It's just hard right now."

"I can tell."

"I just need a minute."

"You want me to call back later?"

"No. It's okay." And it was. He didn't have time to sit down and cry. He had to keep moving. The cathedral waited. The foggy man might already be there. He couldn't stay here, couldn't fail again.

He stood up and continued walking. "I'm okay."

"Are you sure?"

"Yeah. Just… Just talk to me for a little bit, okay?"

"Okay. Well… You want to tell me what these things are that you sent me a picture of?"

"Picture? What things? Oh!" Now he remembered. Before entering the resort's main building, back in the world before Altrusk, while he was still speaking with Taylor, he'd snapped a picture of the

131

three creatures that were watching them. He'd completely forgotten that he sent it. "Just some things I saw following me. Taylor says they're harmless. Basically some freaky breed of wild dogs or something."

"Taylor?"

"Guy I met. Friend of Grant and Annette, I guess."

"Oh. Well I didn't know what was going on. I got this picture and then you stopped answering your phone.

"Sorry. Didn't mean to worry you."

"You were just gone for so long."

"Didn't feel like so long. What time is it?" He looked at his watch.

"Almost noon."

That wasn't right. "My watch says it's not even eleven yet."

"Well it's almost noon here in the real world."

Eric compared his watch to the time on the phone. They matched.

"I wasn't gone that long..." he said. He'd lost over an hour while stuck in Altrusk's insane house.

"What?"

"I don't know." He closed his eyes. His head hurt.

"Well I was worried. I was starting to think these things attacked you after you took the picture."

"Like I said, I was told they're pretty well harmless. Other things out here...not so much."

"What other things?"

Eric told her about the abandoned nudist resort and the monster that was waiting for him behind the kitchen door. He described his terrifying flight through the garden and up onto the roof. He told her of his lucky escape. Somehow, he even managed to tell her the rest of the story as well, including his encounter with Altrusk and losing Isabelle. It all poured out of him. He couldn't seem to help himself.

"That's horrible," Karen said when he'd finished. "I'm so sorry you had to go through that."

"Me too." He remembered Isabelle promising him that if he became a permanent addition to the house, like her, she would keep him company, and he found himself struggling just to hold back a tear. It wasn't fair. None of it was fair.

"Are you all right? How's your shoulder?"

"It's okay. I've stopped the bleeding." *For now*, he thought but didn't dare say. He didn't keep the injury from her, but he might have sugarcoated it a bit. She didn't have to know that he probably needed stitches. That would only worry her needlessly. She already had more than enough reasons to worry about him, most of them far better than a few nasty cuts.

"Where are you going now?"

Eric gazed ahead. "I have no idea."

"Anything coming back to you from your dream?"

"What I'm looking at now. The path. Actually, I guess it's more like a road. It's all familiar, like I've been here before. But only as I see it. I won't know what's around the bend until I get to it."

"Not the most useful of abilities then, is it?"

"No. But it does come in handy. I can immediately tell if anything's changed, if there's something that shouldn't be there."

"At least you have that, then."

"Didn't help me much in that kitchen, though," he recalled. *And it didn't help me save Isabelle*, he thought.

"But it's *something* at least."

The path wound around a thick grove of trees and then emerged into a small clearing at the edge of a large lake. An old boat dock stretched out over the water. As soon as he saw it, he knew something had changed.

"Speaking of which…"

"What?"

"I just came across a boat dock."

"And…?"

"The boat's missing."

"The foggy man?"

"As far as I know, he's the only other one who's been here."

"That's not good. Are you sure you took the boat in the dream?"

Eric looked around the clearing. There was a path that led left along the bank, but he didn't recall going that way. Though the details leading up to it were still piecing themselves together, he was sure he could remember climbing into the boat. He wondered why he would do that. He wasn't very familiar with boats. The idea of rowing out into the middle of a lake—especially an *unfamiliar* lake—was a little unnerving.

He moved closer to the path, intending to examine it more closely, and heard the phone crackle. Now it all came back to him. In the dream, he'd tried to go around the lake, but he found that he couldn't go left or right without losing his cell phone signal and therefore straying off the path. The only option was to use the boat.

"Yeah, I definitely took the boat."

"So now what are you going to do?"

That was a damn good question. He returned to the dock and peered off into the water. A pair of ducks swam lazily near the shore to the right. Farther away, he spied a second pair. But there was not another dock within sight. No more boats. No way forward. He was confident he couldn't swim across. "No way forward but by sea and nary a dinghy to me name."

"Yar. Seems ye be screwed."

"Yar indeed."

Eric sighed. He really wished he could catch a break. His heart really wasn't into this right now.

"You okay?"

"No."

"Come on. You can figure this out. Isn't there anything in the dream that can help you?"

"I don't think so."

"You said Grant, Taylor and Annette all acted like they expected you, like they *knew* you were going to be there. If they aren't entirely crazy—and you've sent me *pictures* that prove there's *something* to what they say—then there must be some kind of force out there behind everything you're doing. I mean, maybe it's God. For all we know. That force, *whatever* it is, must have known that you might run late and that the foggy man would beat you there. Doesn't that make sense?"

"Sort of…"

"Then I can't imagine a force that wise and powerful wouldn't see this happening. There's got to be another way."

"Wow."

"What?"

"You."

"Well, I do hate it when you're down on yourself."

Eric smiled. "Thank you."

"You're welcome."

"I'm going to hang up and see if I can work this thing out."

"That's my guy."

Eric disconnected the call and stared off the end of the dock for a moment, trying to recall every detail of the dream.

Karen was right. Something was out there, some greater force watching over everything. There had to be. These things were not merely random, after all. They had obviously been set in motion long ago. And this was not the kind of problem that should have gone overlooked by such a power.

And yet, that meant that this greater force had also foreseen that he would meet and then lose Isabelle.

He closed his eyes and forced her from his mind. He couldn't let himself dwell on that now. Later. He would think about her like she deserved *later*. Right now, he had a problem to solve.

Opening his eyes again and gazing down at the water where the boat should have been, he could remember every detail of it. It was an ordinary johnboat, green where the paint was still visible. It had only a small trolling motor that was a pain in the ass to start, but it worked.

He remembered pulling away from the shore, using his cell phone for a compass. It let him stay in this world and not drift into the other one.

He recalled looking back toward the dock, half-expecting the boat's owner to come running out of the woods, shouting at him. But no one was there. It had been silent. The entire shore had been peaceful that night.

The entire shore…

Now he remembered.

He'd scanned the lakeshore up and down as he moved away from the dock. It was about a hundred and fifty yards to the right, which would be his left as he stood on the dock looking out at where he would have been in the dream, looking back. It had been dragged up onto the shore, half-hidden in the brush. Another boat. Smaller than the one that had been tied at the dock, and much older, with no motor.

Any other time, he would have assumed that such a boat would be useless, its bottom likely rusted out, incapable of holding his weight. But if he was right... If *Karen* was right (and how often was she wrong, really?), then that boat was for *him*.

Just in case.

Maybe it's God, Karen had said...

Eric felt a chill creep through his body.

Shaking it off, he turned away from the lake and frowned. Retrieving that other boat was going to be tricky. For one thing, he'd already determined that the path leading over there was sunk into that gray zone between here and the other world. That meant leaving the path, which Grant specifically told him not to do.

He crossed the small clearing and followed the path into the trees. He watched the signal on his cell phone sputter and die in the space of just two steps and then tucked it back into his pocket as he searched the trees around him.

Though the sun still shone brightly overhead, the shade here was deep and cool. The air had a completely different quality. There was a subtle reek that might have been nothing more than a dead fish somewhere along the bank or it might have been a small taste of whatever foul atmosphere blanketed that other world.

How easy would it be to step off the edge and be lost forever?

The very idea was dreadful.

Less than fifty yards from the clearing, the normal sounds of the woods were lost and an eerie silence overcame the area. The hairs on the back of his neck prickled and he became acutely certain that he was not alone out here.

Somewhere in the trees, something rustled. He thought he heard a branch snap, a whisper of a footstep in the leaves.

He tried to tell himself it was only his imagination, but his experiences so far today had all been powerful examples of why he should never dismiss anything as only a fabrication of his mind.

Yet he somehow managed to make it all the way to the boat without being mauled or disemboweled or viciously leg-humped by something from another world.

The path did not pass directly by the boat. A thicket of brush stood between him and it, effectively hiding it from view except from the perspective of another watercraft, making him wonder once more if it might have been left here specifically for him to find.

Pushing through this brush, he considered how he was going to proceed once he reached the boat. The easiest way would be to simply push it right into the water and climb inside. But sometimes the easy way was also the wrong way. He had no idea where the gray area ended and the other world took over. It was too easy to imagine pushing away from the shore and making his way back toward the dock, only to find himself hopelessly adrift in that dark and hostile world, never to return.

But then again, dragging the boat through this dense brush and then back along the path to the dock did not seem like a reasonable solution, either.

Arriving at the boat, he peered inside. The bottom was badly rusted. Given a choice, he would not have risked it. But he wasn't left with a lot of options.

At least it actually *had* a bottom.

Something rustled loudly in the branches of a nearby tree and Eric looked up in time to see a large, ape-like shape settle there.

Chapter Fourteen

Covered in shaggy red fur, it looked a little like an orangutan except for its enormous hands and ghastly face. The moment he met its crazed, yellow eyes, it exposed a ghastly mouthful of massive teeth and uttered the most terrifying shriek he had ever heard in his life (which, given the events of only the past few hours, was actually saying something).

The question of whether it would be better to backtrack with the boat and launch it from the dock or simply cast off from where it sat became utterly moot. So did any concern he had about the seaworthiness of the craft. Taking hold of the port side, he shoved it backward into the water and threw himself into it as the Stephen King equivalent of Curious George dropped from its branch and came loping after him, shrieking insanely.

Managing somehow to position himself upright in the boat without capsizing it, he immediately realized that there were no oars with which to row to safety. Swearing loudly, Eric turned and plunged his right arm into the water, splashing wildly in an effort to make the boat move.

Meanwhile, Furious George continued his noisy tantrum. Long arms flailing wildly, massive teeth exposed, the angry creature charged out into the water, splashing and shrieking.

Eric didn't seem to be going anywhere. The boat began to turn lazily, slowly spinning in a circle as if utterly unconcerned about the angry monkey that apparently wanted to eat its passenger.

But even as Eric began to realize the futility of his crazed paddling, he also noticed that the creature refused to follow him any farther than a few feet from the shore. Peering back over the side of the boat, Eric realized that the thing did not seem able—or at least particularly willing—to swim, which was a stroke of amazing luck since it turned out that he made a lousy propulsion system for a boat.

Somehow managing to point the bow toward the dock while keeping one eye on his angry, hairy friend, he allowed himself a moment to ponder the best route forward. He considered removing his shoe and using it as an oar. They were *already* soaked from his awkward boarding of the boat as he scrambled to escape the creature. But he decided that they wouldn't offer much more surface area for pushing the water than did the palms of his hands.

He also evaluated the boat, noting that it *did* seem to be taking on water, but not catastrophically. He could probably keep it afloat indefinitely as long as he took a moment now and then to bail the vessel.

Furious George, still shrieking, turned and splashed back up onto the shore again, apparently having determined that he had made his point.

Relieved to see the beast leave, Eric bent over and paddled on one side of the boat and then the other, gradually pushing himself toward the dock. He was concentrating on this task when something heavy clanged against the side of the boat. Looking up again, Eric watched as George picked up a second rock and hurled it at him, this time striking the surface of the water three feet in front of him.

A third sailed over his head.

"Hey!" he shouted.

George didn't seem terribly fazed by this exclamation. He picked up a larger stone this time and bounced it off the side of the boat.

Eric swore loudly and paddled faster.

Another rock landed loudly inside the boat in front of him.

"Knock it off!" he yelled. The words were barely out of his mouth before he felt the next rock sting his right knee and he fired off a particularly insulting insinuation about the ape's parentage.

The creature threw its hands in the air and shrieked at him again, showing him all of its awful teeth. They were huge. He couldn't quite fathom how they all fit in the damn thing's mouth. It didn't seem possible.

Swallowing those enormous teeth back into its mouth, the hateful thing snatched up another stone and sent it hurdling straight at Eric's face.

He threw his arms up to shield himself and felt it bounce off his right elbow with a sharp sting.

"Don't make me come over there and kick your ass!"

George was so terrified that he chucked an even larger rock. Luckily, it fell short.

Apparently, he wasn't going to talk his way out of this mess. Keeping one eye on the creature to watch for incoming headshots, Eric continued paddling, now trying to aim the boat farther from the shoreline. Twice he had to duck incoming stones, but for the most part George turned out to be a terrible pitcher.

He did not fail to appreciate how lucky he was.

When he'd moved far enough out into the lake that none of the thrown rocks reached the boat, the beast threw its huge hands up and shrieked at him again.

Eric replied by showing him both his middle fingers and suggesting that it should copulate with itself.

It was important to occasionally vent one's frustrations. It was healthy.

Remembering his phone, he quickly pulled it out, checked that it was still dry and snapped a picture of the beast. A pissed-off monkey was going to go great in his scrapbook with the mutant livestock and big-headed coyote-deer.

He returned the phone to his pocket and resumed paddling. Slowly, he made his way back to the dock, ignoring the primal shrieks from the shoreline.

He would have liked to have tied the boat off at the dock and gone in search of something to use as an oar, but he didn't dare return to the shore for fear that Furious George might still be sore about his impolite language. He suspected that it might not be able to come all the way into this world. Otherwise, what kept it from attacking him before he went searching for the boat? What kept it from wandering into the nearest town and terrifying the locals? Or climbing the nearest water tower and swatting at passing airplanes? But he didn't dare make any assumptions.

Deciding it was better to not take any chances, Eric resigned himself to making do with only his hands to paddle the boat.

Using his dream as a guide and frequently checking the phone to make sure he hadn't drifted into that other place, he slowly crept across the surface of the lake.

When his arms had grown sufficiently tired and while he was still much closer to the dock than the far side of the lake, he decided to take a break. He sent his picture of George to Karen and waited for her to call him, which only took a couple minutes.

He let her know that she was right, that once he accepted that there must be a solution to the problem, he was able to find one.

Karen was happy to have helped (and even happier, he suspected, to be right). She was also disturbed by the nasty monkey. "That is one ugly primate," she declared.

"It had an even uglier disposition."

"So where are you now?"

"Out on the lake."

"Still?"

"It's slow going with no oars."

"I'll bet."

"And I have to stop occasionally to bail water."

"That's not good."

"No. But it's a slow leak. I think I can stay ahead of it."

"Any idea yet where you're headed?"

"I remember crossing the lake. I still can't recall where I ended up."

"Well at least you're on the right track."

"Hopefully my new monkey friend isn't waiting for me on the other side."

"That would suck."

"It would. And he'd probably have enough time to beat me there, too. In the dream, my boat had a motor."

"Dream You gets all the breaks."

"He really does. He was always much more popular than me in high school, too."

Eric wiped the sweat from his brow. It had been hot most of the day, but it was particularly hot out here in this boat, with the sun beating down on him. He bent over the side and began to paddle again as he talked. At least the water was cool on his skin.

"By the way, I did an internet search for 'Gold Sunshine Resort' while I was waiting for you to finish trading insults with your monkey."

"He *so* started it."

"I couldn't find any news reports or anything," she continued, "but I did find a missing persons report for an Isabelle Albin."

Isabelle…

"Says she went missing from Gold Sunshine Resort in nineteen-seventy-eight at the age of thirteen. That's really sad."

"Is there a picture?"

"There is."

"I have a picture, too."

"You do?"

"I snapped it while we were waiting for Altrusk and his devil house to calm down so we could make a run for it."

"There's something you don't hear every day."

"It's a day of firsts all around."

"It is. Send me the picture. I want to see."

Eric hung up and sent her the picture. In just a few seconds the phone rang again.

"That is just freaky!"

"Same girl?" As if he really needed to ask.

"It is. I can't believe it. This is totally nuts."

"That's just the kind of day I'm having."

"Crazy," she said again. "I can't believe she's been there this whole time."

"I know."

"Wow."

"Did you find anything about Isaac Altrusk?"

"I didn't. I should look for him."

"Isabelle said it was a fake name. He was a con artist before he became...whatever he is now." Eric recalled Isabelle telling him that he used to be Isaac Altrusk, but now he was just *Altrusk*. Her words were no less creepy now than they were then.

"I'll see if I can find anything. You keep that boat on top of the water."

"Aye-aye, Captain."

"Bye."

Eric pocketed the phone and resumed his paddling. A full minute had not passed before the phone rang and he had to stop again to answer it. This time it was Paul.

"Hey. I just turned off the Interstate down here, looking for your Cruiser."

"That was fast."

"I finished early. I brought Kevin to drive my truck back." Kevin was Paul's nineteen-year-old son.

"Thanks a lot. I appreciate it."

"Sure thing. What's going on, anyway, where are you?"

He considered lying, but he didn't see the point. "I'm in a leaky old boat, trying to make my way across a lake without any oars."

"Okay…" said Paul. "That's…um… *Okay*. So you're okay, then? Doing all right?"

"Yeah. Just tiring. Hard to row with your hands."

"Have you tried using your shoes?"

"Thought about it. But a shoe doesn't have much more surface area than your hand, when you think about it."

"Yeah, I guess so."

Eric smiled. It was always fun tripping up his brother. Thinking of Isabelle, he asked, "So you think I'm completely bugshit yet?"

"I wouldn't say *completely*. Yet."

"What did Karen tell you?"

"Just about the dream."

"It was more than a dream. It was all real."

"Real, huh?"

"Yeah. Everything's coming back to me. And then some. You wouldn't believe what I've seen today. I don't even know where to start. The mutant livestock. The wardrobe monster. The nudist resort. I was almost eaten by a goddamn *house*!"

"*Nudist* resort?"

"Really? All those things I just said and *that's* what you want to hear about?"

"I've never been to a nudist resort," Paul pouted.

In the background, Eric heard Kevin announce that *he* wanted to check out the nudist resort.

"You'd make an awful nudist," Paul affectionately informed his son.

Eric heard Kevin point out that nobody would want to see Paul's fat ass naked, either.

"It's been abandoned since the seventies," Eric said.

"Bummer."

"You don't believe a word I'm saying, do you?"

"I believe something's going on," Paul assured him.

"Right. Well then, hang up."

"What?"

"Hang up. I've got something I want to send you."

"Okay…"

Eric disconnected the call and located his picture of the ape creature. He sent it to Paul's phone and then resumed paddling while he waited for him to call back. It didn't take long.

"Hello?"

"What the hell is that thing?"

"I'm not entirely sure, but I just barely got into this boat before it tore my face off."

"That's the freakiest thing I've ever seen!"

In the background, he heard Kevin exclaim something about the thing's wicked-looking teeth using more expletives than strictly necessary.

"I wish I could tell you it's the freakiest thing *I've* ever seen, but this guy's not even close to the same level of freak as Altrusk."

"Are you really serious? I mean, *really*? This isn't some stupid practical joke?"

"Because everybody knows what a mean practical joker I am?"

"Well… No. I guess not. I just… I mean… This is *weird*, okay?"

"I *know* it's weird. *I'm* the one out in the damn leaky boat without any oars!"

"Eric, this is really messed up. Maybe we should come find you."

"No. You can't. I don't even know where I am right now. I could be hundreds of miles away. And it's way too dangerous to come the way I did. There's way worse things than that pissed-off monkey blocking the path." Specifically, he was thinking of the resort monster waiting to devour anyone who passed through the kitchen to use the stairs to Altrusk's yard. "Just get my car back home for me, okay? I'm going to have to go. I have to bail the water out of my boat again."

"You're really in a damn boat? *Really*?"

Eric held the phone out over the water as he splashed with his free hand. "This is the sound of me paddling a goddamn boat with my hands," he said loudly enough for his voice to carry to the receiver. Putting the phone back to his ear, he said, "Good enough?"

"I believe you."

"Good. Now really, I've got to hang up before I sink."

"You're going to call me back, right? Tell me what's going on?"

"Call Karen. She'll catch you up. She can send you some more pictures, too."

"No shit?"

"None at all. Now I've got to go."

"Okay…"

Eric hung up the phone, considered it for a moment, and then snapped a quick picture of himself giving a thumbs-up against the backdrop of the lake. He sent the picture to Paul and then pocketed the phone and began splashing water out of the bottom of the boat.

When he'd rid himself of as much lake water as he could, he sat up and looked around.

He was still a long way from the far shore. And he had no idea what might await him when he finally reached it.

As he dipped his hand into the water again, his eyes drifted back to the dock and the path that led into the forest behind it. Over the tops of the trees, he could just see one of the highest peaks of Altrusk's house.

It still felt wrong that he was leaving Isabelle.

But he had no idea how to help her. All he could do was hope that someday he could find a way to come back for her.

It was the only thing that made it bearable.

Chapter Fifteen

Eric eventually found that by stretching out over the bow of the boat and dipping both hands into the water on either side, he was actually able to propel the craft at a more respectable speed.

The downside was, of course, that the bow of the boat was hardly designed for comfort. It was especially uncomfortable on his left shoulder, where the resort monster slashed him as it tumbled off the roof of the Altrusk house.

He wasn't sure how long he'd been on the water now. At least an hour, he was sure, maybe much closer to two. His exposed arms and the back of his neck were beginning to get sunburned. With no warning that he was about to embark on such an adventure, he'd had no more opportunity to apply sunscreen than he'd had to retrieve the first aid kit from the PT Cruiser's glove box.

He was about to take a break, perhaps bail some more water, when suddenly the bottom of the boat ground against the bottom of the lake.

Surprised by this abrupt end to his forward momentum, he sat up and looked around. The lake was no longer a lake at all. It had suddenly transformed itself into a marsh. Huge trees loomed ahead of him, creating a dense canopy that plunged the surface of the water into eerie shadow. Looking back the way he'd come, he saw that there were more trees behind him that he did not remember passing. He could not see the dock at all.

Checking his phone, he saw that he no longer had reception. He'd drifted back into the gray zone.

Yet these trees were familiar. He'd seen them in his dream. He searched the water around him and then saw it there, the other boat, drifting lazily between two trees, abandoned by the foggy man as he continued forward through the marsh on foot, just as he now recalled having done in his dream.

He peered over the side of the boat, down into the water. It was obviously only a few inches deep if the boat had run aground, but the mud and silt made it impossible to see anything down there. The stagnant stench of rotting vegetable matter rose up around him.

This was going to suck.

A lot.

Consigning himself to the unpleasant task at hand, Eric clumsily stepped out of the boat and stood up in several inches of mud and soggy leaves.

To say that trudging forward was unpleasant was akin to saying that gas prices seemed a smidge high. The air here was heavy with humidity. Every step was a labored effort, and produced a foul odor that seemed to wrap him in an inescapable cloud of stench, making it nearly impossible to catch a fresh breath. His mind insisted on torturing him with thoughts of fat leeches and venomous serpents. It didn't matter that there were no dangerous water snakes in Wisconsin. In his stubborn mind, even alligators and crocodiles, vicious snapping turtles and anacondas as large as freight trains prowled these waters.

After all, he'd been fairly sure there were no nasty-tempered apes in Wisconsin, either, until a short while ago. His cell phone confirmed that he wasn't entirely still in the world he knew. Who could possibly say what kinds of things might call *these* strange waters home? With every step he expected something mean and ravenous to spring up from the mire and sink vicious teeth into his flesh, or simply drag him screaming down into the murky depths, never to be found.

In his dream, he'd waded through these very same waters and recalled seeing nothing stirring beneath the surface. But he also did not yet recall exiting the marsh, so there was still time to remember something terrifying. It would probably return to him only when it was too late. And even if the dream never revealed a monstrous danger lurking in the bog, it did not necessarily mean that it wasn't there. After all, the dream did not warn him of the toothy ape or the coyote-deer. And for all he knew, the foggy man may have left him another surprise hidden somewhere in the mud.

But step-after-step, he found nothing waiting to rend his flesh and crush his bones.

After another half-hour of sloshing through the reeking muck, a memory *did* return, however. In his dream, he saw a strange shape moving purposefully through the water, too large to be any known snake or turtle.

The memory now returned to him, Eric scanned the area for the same shape, but it was nowhere to be seen.

He pushed on, eyes wide open.

The trees drew closer together as he walked, the canopy above him denser, mottling the sunlight upon the surface of the foul water. More and more frequently, his feet struck the roots, threatening to trip him and send him sprawling into the muck, but somehow he managed to keep his footing.

His legs ached. Bugs swarmed around him. Mosquitoes threatened to bleed him dry. The humidity was stifling. And still he could see no end to this miserable marsh.

The creature in his dream wandered off and did not return.

How was it, he wondered, that a scary swamp would prove to be free of monsters determined to devour him (with the notable exception of the damned mosquitoes) while a farmhouse and a nudist resort nearly killed him?

Finally, he came to an area where the earth rose above the surface of the water in places, allowing him to walk on dry land for brief periods of time. It was on one of these small islets that he stopped and sat with his back against a tree, resting his weary legs.

He checked his cell phone, confirmed that there was still no signal, and then snapped a picture of his surroundings to add to his scrapbook of crazy things he saw and did on his twisted wonderland adventure.

It was odd, now, to think that he started this insanity in a cornfield.

Cursing, he slapped at another mosquito and then glanced up in time to see an enormous shadow pass overhead.

Leaping to his feet, he looked up to see what appeared to be a massive black bird soaring past above the trees and out toward the lake from which he'd come.

He could see very little detail through the branches, and might have mistaken it for a small and extremely low-flying plane if it wasn't utterly silent.

Not caring to be carried off like a field mouse, and not daring to assume that it would do no such thing should it see him, he stepped out into the water and continued on his way, his eyes drifting repeatedly to the sky as he went.

He didn't recall seeing a giant bird in his dream, which was weird, now that he was thinking about it, since the bird theme was the only part of the dream he could even remotely remember until he found the barn at the far end of Annette's field.

The trees grew denser still, crowding together until he had to struggle over their tangled roots and squeeze between their fat trunks.

Then, just as abruptly as he'd run the boat aground and found himself within the marsh, he stumbled out from between the trees and found himself once again in a cornfield.

"The hell?" he muttered, looking back at the crowded trees behind him. From here, he could see no sign that any marsh existed, only a dense thicket of trees, all of which were native Wisconsin pines and oaks and maples. He couldn't seem to remember when the swamp cypresses ended, but he must have been pushing his way through a genuine Wisconsin forest for at least the past few minutes.

Even the humidity had vanished. Although the air remained hot, it was a much dryer and more bearable heat.

In his dream, he'd had the exact same experience. Therefore, he was confident that he was still where he was supposed to be. And checking his phone, he found that he had his signal back.

He also had thirteen missed calls and a text message that read,

WHERE ARE YOU?

He should call Karen. She was clearly worried. But he was sure that if he just waited a few minutes, she would call him. And, as it turned out, he had barely started pushing his way through the corn when it began to vibrate impatiently in his pocket.

"What happened to you?"

"Sorry. I was off-world for a while there."

"You've been waiting your whole life to be able to say something like that, haven't you?"

"Actually, yes."

"I couldn't find anything about an Isaac Altrusk. But I didn't have time to search too hard."

Eric wasn't sure what good it would do anyway. The Altrusk house was well behind him now. He doubted he'd ever see it again. And poor Isabelle…

"How's the cake?" he asked, not caring to dwell on the poor girl he'd been forced to leave behind.

"Coming along."

"Get the pies done?"

"Yeah. I've got cookies in the oven now."

"I should leave you alone more often."

"No, you shouldn't. So where are you now?"

"Back in a cornfield."

"Oh. Beats a leaky boat."

"It does."

"So you got across the lake okay?"

"Lake turned into a swamp. Had to hoof it through the bog."

"Yuck. Better you than me."

"Yeah, you wouldn't have made it."

"Oh you think so?"

"I know so."

"Really?"

"Yeah. It ruined my shoes."

"Oh. Yeah, I wouldn't've made it."

"That's what I'm saying."

"Piss off any more monkeys?"

"Not yet. Saw a big bird though. Huge. Like a plane."

"Scary."

"It was."

"Well I'm glad you're okay."

"So am I."

"Paul called me, said you told him I could tell him what was up."

"I did."

"He was freaking out about your monkey picture."

Eric smiled. "*That* got his attention."

"Yes, it most certainly did."

"So you told him my story?"

"Uh huh. Sent him those other pictures, too."

"Good. He won't think I'm crazy anymore."

"No. I'm pretty sure he believes you now."

"Good. Did he find the PT Cruiser?"

"Yeah. Him and Kevin were parked by it when he called. They should be on their way back with it now."

"Excellent."

Eric stepped out of the corn and found himself standing on another dirt road, nearly identical to the one where this strange adventure first began. He almost expected he had come full circle, that soon he would find himself back at either the barn or Annette's backyard gate.

"So any idea where you're going now?" asked Karen.

"Nope. Stupid dream's still only coming back to me as things happen. But I found a road through the corn, so at least I'm not walking completely blind."

In his dream, he'd turned right, so he started walking in that direction. Hopefully, he wouldn't walk five miles only to recall that, in his dream, he'd found a dead end and had to turn back.

"I'm going to hang up and see where this road goes."

"Okay. Call me soon."

He didn't know why she continued to tell him that. She knew damn well it would be *her* who called *him*. It always was.

Eric stuffed the phone back into his pocket and continued walking. A few hundred yards ahead, the corn on his left gave way to pasture and a barbwire fence separated him from a few dozen cows.

He was studying the animals for any sign that they may turn around and bare huge sets of angry gorilla teeth at him or some other terrifying thing, but they appeared to be nothing more than ordinary cows.

His phone rang again.

Grumbling, he answered it. It was Paul.

"What's going on? You still stuck in that boat?"

"No, I ran out of lake, had to get out and wade through a swamp. Now I think I'm back in Wisconsin. I see cows."

"Sounds like Wisconsin."

"Have any trouble finding the Cruiser?"

"Nope. It was right where you said it was. Safe and sound."

"Good. Where are you now?"

"Kevin's on his way back to your house with the Cruiser. I stuck around to do a little snooping."

Eric stopped walking. "You're doing *what?*"

"I checked out that old lady's house. What did Karen say her name was? Annette?"

"What the hell are you doing at Annette's house? How did you even find it?"

"Karen said you followed the river and found a path. I went looking for it."

Karen apparently hadn't skimped on the details.

"Why would you do that?"

"Why not? She wasn't home. Nobody answered the door."

"You're not missing anything. She kept talking about her husband, how he was probably going to die soon. Then I found out he's been dead a while already. Not a cheerful chatter. You really don't want to have a conversation with her. I told you to pick up the car and take it home, not try to follow me. I *specifically* told you not to try to follow me."

"Relax. I'm just having a look."

"There's nothing to see! Things didn't start getting completely weird until I walked through the barn and by then it was too late to turn around! If you go there, you'll be stuck. And then we'll have to find someone to go get *your* car."

"You really think I can't go back through the barn?"

"I was told a lot of things I don't have any reason to doubt. One of them was that if you go back through the barn the other way, you might not come out at all. If you go through the barn like I did…" Eric closed his eyes. "Tell me you didn't already find the barn."

"It was kind of hard to miss once you made it through the corn."

"Damn it, Paul…"

"The things in there were way freakier in person than in your pictures. What the hell was in that boarded-up stall? I couldn't see in."

"Where are you now?"

"I'm at the end of the driveway in front of that old house. There's a paved road with no shoulders, no center line. I had to come all the way down here to find a signal so I could call you."

"Listen to me," Eric said. "Do not go back there. Just start walking. Try to figure out where you are. Don't go back into the barn and sure as *hell* don't go into the house."

"I wouldn't know how to get into the farmhouse. In case you forgot, there's a tractor parked in the door."

Well, it *was* good to know he hadn't imagined that. Although he found himself wondering why Grant hadn't moved the tractor. Maybe he busted something when he plowed through the porch.

"I'm serious. You saw what was in the barn. You know I was telling the truth."

"I do. I took some pictures of my own, even. God, those things in the stalls were nasty!"

"Then you have to believe me when I say you could die out there."

"Okay. I get it."

"Really? Because you said you got it last time I talked to you and now you're stranded fifty miles from your car."

"*Really*. Don't lecture me. I'm just trying to help."

"How is you getting yourself killed going to help me?"

"I'm not going to get myself killed. Did I really go fifty miles?"

"*I don't know*. You need to listen to me. *You're in danger*. Inside that farmhouse is an old wardrobe with a monster inside it. If not for Grant and that tractor, I'd be dead right now! That thing will hunt you relentlessly until it kills you unless you can find a distraction big enough to break its focus, which—believe *me*—is not easy to do when you're running for your life and scared out of your skull!"

"Okay. Fine. But what did you do next?"

"You don't need to know what I did next! You need to start walking and you need to *keep* walking! Just leave. And then you can start thinking about how you're going to get home."

"Karen said you made your way to the nudist resort from here."

"Seriously? The nudists? Still? There's no one there, Paul! Get over it!"

"I know there's no one there. But Karen said you made your way there from here and all you found along the way was those weird dog-things that you told her were harmless."

"Taylor told me they were harmless. I don't know for sure that he was telling me the truth. And I don't know that there isn't something else out there in those woods, something that *is* dangerous. A big, red, pissed off ape, maybe?"

"Just calm down and listen to me."

"I'm not going to calm down! Like I don't have enough to deal with out here without worrying that you're going to go poking around in all the places I was almost killed today because you won't believe me when I say it's not safe!"

"I *do* believe you! That's the whole fucking point! I'm not cool with just sitting around all day and waiting for my little brother to call and tell me he's still alive, okay?"

Eric ran a hand through his hair. He wasn't sure what to say, so he remained quiet.

"This is some really weird shit," Paul went on. "I needed to check it out for myself, okay? It's not about me not trusting you. I mean, think about it. All these things you're seeing... None of it should be possible. But not only is it real, *you're* out in the middle of it all. What would you do if you were me? If *I* was out there and you were just the guy who was picking up the car, what would you do?"

Eric remained silent. He couldn't deny that Paul was right. If their positions had been switched, he would have gone through the barn, even if he knew it meant ending up stranded.

"Well?"

"Fine. But if you were in *my* place—"

"I'd be pretty pissed about you following me. I know."

"Good."

"But I want to go to the resort."

"I'm telling you, you'd make a terrible nudist."

"I know, but besides that... I figure that resort... What was it called?"

"Gold Sunshine Resort."

"Gold Sunshine. Stupid name."

"I *have* heard better names."

"I don't have a clue where I am now, but I think Kevin could probably find Gold Sunshine Resort and pick me up."

"There's a monster inside the biggest building there. It almost killed me. Tore up my shoulder pretty bad. I only survived by dumb luck. It's blocking the only way forward. Even if you did survive, the next stop is the lake. I took the last boat. No going around it unless you want to run into the monkey with the huge teeth. And he doesn't get over things quickly. Also, I might've insulted his parentage."

"So the resort's as far as I could go. Got it. I'll call Kevin, see if he can find the address."

"The place closed in nineteen-seventy-eight. He might not be able to look up the address on the internet."

"He'll figure it out. If not, I'll find my way to the highway like I did here and find somewhere to ask for directions."

Eric didn't like the idea of Paul wandering around in the fissure. It simply didn't seem like a good idea, no matter how he rationalized it.

"So how do I get there from here?"

"You swear to me you won't go any farther than the resort, and you won't go into the biggest building."

"I won't. I promise."

"You better not. I swear to God if you go near that building I'll see to it you never taste Karen's chocolate truffle cheesecake again."

"You wouldn't!" Karen's chocolate truffle cheesecake was Paul's favorite desert. She made it every holiday. And she made him one every year for his birthday. He couldn't get enough of it.

"I would. In a heartbeat. Don't push me on this. She'll side with me when I tell her you're out here with me."

"Fine. I swear."

"Really?"

"*Really*. You already said the way is blocked. I believe you. I've been to the barn. Those things in there were scary as hell. Shit, the barn *itself* was scary as hell. I mean, it just kept going! I'm really not interested

163

in running into anything that's actually dangerous."

"I can't say for sure there's not something dangerous waiting for you anyway. Anything could be hiding out there. You'll have to be careful."

"I will."

Eric sighed. "I'd really rather you just walk home from there."

"Noted. Just tell me where to go next."

"There's a little tool shed backed up into the woods. The path is behind it. When it gets too overgrown, you'll have to look carefully to find the next path. It's hard to see. You'll have to take the bridge. Hope you like heights."

"What kind of heights are we talking about?"

"You'll just have to see for yourself, I guess."

"Nice. I'm going to get off of here and call Kevin."

"Be careful."

"I will. Bye."

"Bye."

Eric pocketed the phone again and continued walking. He didn't like that Paul was here in the fissure. It worried him. But on the other hand, at least he'd validated his experience in the barn. As crazy as all this was, he would not have been surprised to hear that no such barn existed and that everything he'd experienced today had all been inside his own head.

It was like Karen finding Isabelle on the missing persons list and connecting her to a real Gold Sunshine Resort. It didn't prove that someone wasn't messing with his mind, but at least it was some measure of evidence in favor of his sanity.

Add to these things the pictures he'd taken and he could at least remain confident about the soundness of his mind.

He squinted up at the hot sun, wiped the sweat from his face again and continued on toward whatever mysteries awaited him ahead.

He watched the cows as he walked. He'd never been particularly fond of cattle, or any farm animals for that matter. They smelled terrible. They were filthy. They drew flies. He preferred them fully prepared and placed neatly on his plate with a side of vegetables and a potato. But now he was simply happy that they weren't throwing stones at him.

In fact, given all that he'd been through, all that he'd seen, they looked almost majestic standing out there.

Then the one closest to him lifted its tail and took a crap right in front of him.

Of course.

Eric moved on, his eyes fixed on the road before him again.

He wondered how much farther he'd have to go. For that matter, how far had he actually gone? Grant told him that his trip through the mutant livestock barn had carried him some fifty miles northwest. Taylor later informed him that he'd traveled another eighty-five miles due north after crossing the gorge on that terrifying bridge. Since then, he'd passed through that shadowy otherworld twice, once past the Altrusk house and once through the marsh.

But as far as he knew, he didn't jump forward when he passed the stunted corn in Annette's field. So maybe he hadn't jumped those last two times, either.

Or maybe he was all the way in Canada by now.

Thinking back on it, he recalled Karen's assertion that it was almost noon when his watch and phone had only read a little later than half-past ten. At some point, it seemed that he'd lost more than an hour.

Could that be true? If the fissure could distort space in such a way that he was flung forward fifty and eighty-five miles at a stretch, why couldn't time scrunch down so that the minutes had passed considerably more quickly inside Altrusk's house?

He didn't have time to consider it further. Movement caught his eye to his left and he glanced over in time to see several of the cows running from the far corner of the field as if something had spooked them.

On an ordinary day, he would not have thought anything about it. On an ordinary day, there simply wouldn't have been any *reason* to think anything about it. But today had been no ordinary day by any stretch of the imagination. Today, he would be a fool not to be concerned about what might have spooked the cows.

Shielding his eyes from the sun with his hand, he scanned the far corner of the field, but he could see nothing more than corn beyond the fence.

Perhaps the cows were just restless. Or perhaps one of them had stirred up a hornet's nest or a rattlesnake.

Or perhaps there was something extremely unpleasant in the corn.

He remembered the first cornfield, between Annette's back yard and the mutant barn, the sickly, stunted corn that was his first glimpse of the strange effects of the fissure. He'd heard something moving in the corn, something he couldn't quite see, something that had filled him with dread that he assumed, stupidly, was senseless.

Now he wondered again what it was that had moved in the corn back in that field. And he wondered if it was here, too.

He turned and scanned the field behind him, listening.

Suddenly, it felt like something was watching him. Was that simple paranoia? His imagination running away from him just because he'd begun to think about these things?

He needed to get a hold of himself.

If there was something truly dangerous in this area, would a farmer be able to keep his cows here? It didn't seem likely. And a quick glance at his phone revealed that he still had a signal. He wasn't in that other world right now.

He stood in the middle of the road, as still as possible, forcing himself to breathe slowly and listen.

Seconds ticked away. Nothing moved in the nearby corn. The cows settled across the field and returned to their grazing.

It was okay.

He was fine.

He looked back out across the field and saw a dark shape standing by the fence, watching him.

Chapter Sixteen

His eyes fixed on the shape at the far side of the pasture, Eric began to move again.

It wasn't fair. He was still in Wisconsin. (Or at least on *Earth*.) The corn was tall and healthy, not at all stunted, the shadows beneath them still soft and shallow. Nothing should be here.

But of course, he knew no such thing. He was likely only a short distance from the fissure, as he'd been since he first arrived at Annette's house. And those curious coyote-deer creatures had followed him right up to the abandoned cabins of Gold Sunshine Resort, where a clear signal allowed him to send their picture to Karen.

The shadowy thing moved along the far fence, keeping pace with him.

It was difficult to make out. It was a solid shape against the corn, but was the same shades of green. It walked on two feet, upright like a man, but was at least seven feet tall. It dwarfed the fence posts in front of it and stood an entire head above the tops of the corn stalks behind it.

Eric swore under his breath. He was tired. He didn't want to keep running. He needed a break.

But he wasn't going to get one.

Something moved behind him. He turned, startled, and glimpsed a green head ducking back down into the corn.

Another one.

He swore again. Glancing forward quickly, he saw that the pasture came to an end a short distance ahead and he would soon have the blinding corn on both sides, his vision further reduced.

Across the field, the first figure was now moving faster toward the corner of the pasture.

He heard the one on his right moving through the corn, creeping closer.

He decided to run for it.

Immediately, the shape across the field broke into a run as well and the corn rustled violently as another rushed between the stalks somewhere behind it.

Scanning the fields around him, he saw several more green shapes rise up and peer over the corn at him, some of them already moving to track him.

From every direction, crows took frenzied flight as the corn came alive with predators. He was surrounded.

Stringing together a few of his favorite obscenities, Eric ran as fast as his legs would carry him, which, it seemed, was not all that fast in comparison to the things that would happily chase him down and devour him.

The creature on the other side of the pasture reached the end of the fence and passed into the corn. Its head and shoulders remained visible over the stalks for only a moment before it lowered itself out of sight, vanishing like a diving submarine.

A few seconds later the pasture was behind him. Tall corn obscured his view on both sides. He could hear large things moving among the leaves.

He recalled passing through here in his dream. He also recalled hearing things in the corn. He recalled being afraid. But he did not remember seeing the creature across the pasture. He did not remember being surrounded and chased.

He tried to recall what was different between then and now. The conversation with his brother… He'd raised his voice a little, angered and afraid to hear that Paul had wandered into this mess against his wishes. Had that extra noise drawn them?

Ahead of him, a tall shape streaked with shades of green to match the colors of the summer corn darted into his path and he came to an abrupt halt only a few paces away.

Feet apart, long, sinewy arms held tensely out at its sides, its body lean, but powerful, it was at least as terrifying as the resort monster. It had no neck, only a muscular bulge attaching the lower half of the head directly to the torso. An insect-like mass of glistening eyes took up most of its face and a huge, gaping maw extended almost to its swollen belly. He saw no teeth. Instead, it seemed to have row after row of fine, bony ridges, as if this thing did not tear and chew its food, but rather shaved meaty morsels from its victims, all the better to leave its prey alive and squirming while it feasted.

Eric didn't know for certain that this was true, but it came easily enough to his maddeningly vivid imagination in the split second before he cried out in a shrill and embarrassingly un-masculine voice and bolted into the field.

This seemed like a stupid move, even as he shoved blindly through the first of the leafy stalks. Clearly, the cornfield was their domain. They used its cover for stealth, careful to keep their heads down whenever they moved. It was a dangerous gamble, but he was sure he couldn't outrun these things on the road. His only chance was to hope that the corn would allow him the same cover it lent them, evening the playing field a little.

Of course, these creatures probably had a much better sense of direction than he did. After only a few seconds of pushing through the stiff cornstalks, he was already uncertain which way was which.

Leaves rustled all around him. He could hear heavy footfalls on the dry soil. Once, he even saw something green and black streak by in a nearby row. But for now, he seemed to have bought himself another moment of life, though he had absolutely no idea how he was going to make the most of it.

He came to a stop between two rows of corn and crouched there silently, listening.

They were all around him, moving through the corn, searching for him.

There must be a way out of this. He remembered the lake. That second boat. And before that, the scaffolding that bought him the extra few seconds to escape the resort monster. The universe had so far appeared to be stacked in his favor.

So what was he supposed to do now?

He tried to remember his dream. He was walking down the road between the corn, frightened by the strange movement in the field and a cold certainty that something was watching him. But he didn't recall seeing one. They remained out of sight.

One came too close. A darkling shape in the shifting stalks spooked him. He ran. Around him, things ran with him.

But he couldn't yet remember what happened next.

Far to his left, one of the creatures emerged from the corn and stood with its back to him, searching. Stretching its body to its full height, it peered out over the corn, likely searching for the telltale movement of cornstalks.

As quietly as possible, Eric slipped between the stalks and into the next row before it could turn and see him.

His gamble seemed to have paid off. The very same thing that gave them their stealth was now hiding him from them. If he hadn't still been utterly terrified, he might have smiled at the justice of it all.

But it was far too early to celebrate.

At that moment, his cell phone rang. Its eager buzzing sounded at least as loud as a chainsaw motor to his startled ears, and it was more than loud enough to draw the attention of the gruesome pack of creatures he was hoping to escape. He could see the one he'd just avoided turn and look right at him.

Shit.

Eric shot to his feet and ran.

A huge, groping hand snatched at him. He cried out and leaped out of the way, changing directions, only to catch sight of something tearing through the corn directly toward him.

He changed directions again, crying out as the heavy leaves battered his face.

Something uttered a gut-wrenching roar directly behind him.

The goddamn cell phone kept buzzing at him.

"This is *not* a good time!" he growled.

As he ran, the corn suddenly began to shrink around him, withering away, and a chill cut through the August heat.

The remains of a very old tractor appeared, covered in rust and half buried in the parched soil. He veered toward it, seized the wheel and vaulted over the metal seat, hoping to slow down his pursuers.

He risked a quick look back over his shoulder and saw three of the grotesque creatures converging on him, undeterred by the pitiful obstacle.

He turned forward again, running even harder, and barely avoided colliding with the broad trunk of a tree.

He didn't even have time to wonder what the hell a tree was doing in the middle of a cornfield before the ground abruptly dropped from under his feet and he went sprawling down the side of a steep hill, cursing all the way to the bottom.

He landed hard in a dry creek bed, the gravel digging into his palms and elbows as he skidded to a halt, his injured shoulder flaring with pain.

But he had no time for pain. He had to keep moving.

Sitting up, he found himself bathed in deep shadows. Huge trees towered over him, surrounding him.

There was not an ear of corn in sight. He now seemed to be in a dense forest.

Looking back up the hill he'd just maneuvered with even less grace than he might have handled an advanced ski slope, he saw a half-dozen tall shadows peering down at him, several of them already making their way down the hill after him.

Scrambling to his feet, Eric took off again, following the dry streambed along the ridge as fast as his feet would navigate the rough terrain.

He didn't recognize any of this. As with his ill-conceived venture into the Altrusk house, he was way off the map.

He tore through a thicket of brush, spooking a small flock of birds and catching a cluster of painful thorns in his right forearm.

For several minutes he ran, occasionally glancing back over his shoulder and always finding the yawning visage of one or more of the creatures close behind him.

He recalled now that he had continued to run along the road in his dream, past an area where the corn had grown stunted and small, to an old wooden bridge with planks that creaked underfoot as he raced across it.

By the time he reached the other side of the bridge, the things in the corn were gone and he never even saw what they looked like.

On-Time Dream Eric was a lucky son of a bitch.

A path crossed the streambed, offering surer footing, and Eric swerved to follow it even as the snarling and grunting behind him grew unnervingly close.

He crested a hill and raced down the other side. Around him the trees grew larger and taller. They were the biggest trees he'd ever seen in his life, at least as big as the giant California redwoods that he'd only seen in magazines and on television.

The blue sky seemed to pull away above him and the shadows deepened until the gloom began to envelop him. It seemed to be growing dark out, though it was still hours before sunset.

In his dream, the corn gave way to more pastures filled with cows. The sun shone brightly above. He'd begun to sweat. In one field, a young and playful palomino mare trotted up near the fence to investigate him.

The horror had ended as quickly as it had begun, leaving him shaken, but still unharmed.

Here in the waking world, Eric glanced behind him, but he could no longer tell the monsters from the shadows. Even their snarls had mingled together until he could no longer discern how close they were getting or from what angle they might pounce.

He rounded a curve in the path and glimpsed a light between the massive tree trunks ahead of him.

Hopeful for a miracle, he willed himself to run even faster, though he was rapidly losing strength.

The light turned out to be shining from the windows of a small church. But the sight that greeted him did not appear even remotely holy. The windows were glowing blood-red, casting a crimson light across the rocky ground, as if the entire area were bathed in gore. The building itself was badly in need of repair. The paint was almost entirely peeled away, the shingles warped and buckled. Even the steeple seemed to be askew, as if some great and unholy force had shaken the whole structure, nearly toppling it to the ground.

It was easily the last place on earth he would have chosen to stop for a quick Sunday school lesson, but the horde of flesh-crazed predators at his back made it difficult to be snobby.

He bounded up the steps onto the small, concrete landing in front of the door and yanked on the handle.

Naturally, it was tightly locked.

Glancing back, he saw the shadowy shapes stalking across the blood-tinted clearing, closing in on him.

He beat on the door. He shouted, pleaded for someone to open it. There had to be someone home. Why else would there be lights?

The creatures were right behind him.

He darted right, toward the corner of the building, intending to run around behind the church, but another creature appeared in his path, blocking his way and bringing him to a halt before he had even reached the end of the landing. They were everywhere.

He turned and pressed his back to the wall, his fists doubled, his jaw clenched, his eyes fixed on the nearest of the creatures, resigned to stand his ground as long as possible, though he was sure that wouldn't be long. They were so big. He certainly didn't stand a chance.

Maybe he should have answered the phone when it rang. It might have been his last chance to say goodbye to Karen.

As the first of the monsters reached out with its long, green hands, the church door slammed open. A thunderous boom assaulted Eric's ears and imploded the top half of the nearest monster's head.

A second and third boom likewise disfigured two more of the creatures before the first had fully collapsed into a heap on the church steps.

Then, as he stood there with his hands pressed over his ringing ears, someone seized the sleeve of his tee shirt, hauled him bodily into the church and threw him to the floor as the door slammed shut behind him.

Sitting up, Eric turned and found himself staring into the barrel of a large-caliber rifle.

Chapter Seventeen

This was definitely not the most welcoming congregation he'd ever attended.

"Why the fuck are you here?" boomed the man staring down at him over the weapon.

"Is 'I don't want to be eaten by those things outside' not an acceptable answer?" asked Eric as he gazed down the barrel. "Because I may not be able to think of a better one with that in my face."

The man glared at him and did not lower the rifle. His eyes were dark and piercing, determined. They were not the eyes of a man who appreciated his kind of humor.

"Okay… Just back it off a little." Eric had never had a gun pointed at his face before. He was surprised to find that he wasn't pants-wetting terrified. Instead, it was an impressively surreal feeling. He was too distracted by the absurdity that he should find himself at the business end of a firearm to be too afraid. As a result, he managed to meet this man's piercing gaze with a fair amount of dignity, if not exactly action-hero bravado. "Those things chased me here. That's all. I was looking for the cathedral."

This seemed to be the wrong thing to say, because the man pressed the barrel of the rifle against the side of his nose. "This ain't no fucking cathedral."

Now Eric felt a little more of that carnal fear. This guy clearly had a talent for this. "I didn't think it was." And this was perfectly true. He hadn't thought to make any connection between the cathedral and this church until now. The only thought that crossed his mind when he first laid eyes on the little structure was that it didn't look as warm and welcoming as he thought a church should look.

Sometimes first impressions were spot-on.

"That's just where I was going when those things came out of the corn," he continued.

"Corn creeps."

"Corn creeps? Really? That's what they're called?"

"It's what *I* call them."

"It's a good name for them," Eric decided.

The man's eyes narrowed. He regarded him for a moment longer, the rifle barrel still pressed to Eric's face. Then he abruptly turned away and placed the weapon gently on the seat of a chair that was standing next to the door. "So you're *that* sorry bastard."

Eric rose warily to his feet, still half-expecting to have his head blown off his shoulders. "I'm sorry, but exactly *what* sorry bastard am I?"

"The sorry bastard that's going to die screaming in the festering asshole of the almighty cathedral."

Poetic *and* frightening. Nice. "Maybe you're thinking of somebody else?" hoped Eric.

The man let out a snort of a laugh. "Sorry to break the news to you."

"Probably not as sorry as I am."

The man was tall and lanky, with lean, muscular arms and an impressive mane of unkempt blond hair. "Probably not. What's your name? Actually, forget I asked. I don't want to know. No reason to know a dead man's name."

"Eric."

"Or you could just fucking tell me anyway."

"I don't intend to be a dead man."

"Don't matter what your intentions are. We all die."

"Then I don't intend to die *today*."

"If you say so." He turned away and slid open a small window built into the door. The feature appeared to have been added somewhat recently, and without much care for aesthetics. It was little more than a short length of two-by-four held in place by several metal brackets. Eric noticed that it was mounted at the perfect height for the man to aim the barrel of his monster-busting rifle through. While peering out into the unnatural gloom, he said, "I'm Father Billy."

This caught Eric off guard. "You're a priest?"

Father Billy looked back over his shoulder at him. "No."

"Oh."

Looking back out through the homemade peephole, the man who called himself Father Billy but was not a priest did not explain why he called himself "Father" when he was not a priest, but instead said, "You sure stirred up a shit storm out there. I'm amazed you made it all the way here. They ain't the fastest-moving fuckers, but they've got damn long strides. Those long-ass legs of theirs."

He certainly had far more colorful language than any "father" he'd ever known. Even his *actual* father had never strung together the kind of imaginative description that Father Billy used next. Not even when he hit his thumb with a hammer. And that was always good for encouraging creativity in vulgarity.

Deciding not to discuss the ethics of using such language inside a church, even a church in an advanced state of disrepair and possessing eerie, blood-red windows, he said, "So they're still out there, I take it?"

"At least twenty of them, not including the three I put down."

Twenty... "What are they doing?"

"Eating their dead."

"Oh." He wasn't sure what was more disturbing, the fact that these things were cannibalizing their fallen pack-mates or that this man could speak such a reply without a hint of disgust in his voice.

"Yeah. Nasty bastards. They're extremely opportunistic. They won't expend any energy to hunt if there's something easier to eat. Even if it's one of their own. It's actually a good thing. Because if you can kill just one of them—or even just cripple it— the rest will forget about you and turn on it. Of course, if you're stupid enough to go wandering around the fields without a gun, you're pretty well fucked."

Ignoring the insult that was quite obviously aimed at him, Eric stood up and looked around. The interior of the church was a mess. All the pews had been shoved against the walls like a barricade and a rough campsite had been assembled in the middle of the room. A pile of blankets lay surrounded by glowing lanterns, coolers, an assortment of propane tanks and jugs of water. And lots of trash.

"Do you live here?"

"I do."

"With those things right outside?"

"They're not always here," Father Billy explained. "And they never come out at night. It's always been safe to go out after sunset. Well… *Mostly*."

Eric looked up at the windows. It wasn't the light that was blood red, but the window panes. He wondered whose decision it was to do that and what it was, precisely, that they were thinking. From this side they did not glow at all. There was not enough light reaching down through the dense trees. "How can you tell when the sun's set?"

"You can tell."

He'd have to take Father Billy's word on that, he supposed.

He felt an odd, crawling sensation on his arm and looked down at himself, expecting to find a bug on him. Instead, he saw several large thorns protruding from his skin. Fat drops of blood were slowly making their way down through the hair on his arm, toward his wrist. He'd forgotten about those. He picked them up running through some brush. At the time, he'd been far more concerned with escaping the things pursuing him than with a few insignificant thorns. One by one, he began to pluck them out, marveling a little at how big they were and how much blood they let out.

"I don't know why they don't come out at night," Father Billy went on. "It's strange. You'd think it'd suit them."

"Where do they go at night?"

"Don't know that, either."

"Why do you stay here? Why not just leave one night?"

Father Billy shrugged. "I like it here. It's private. *Usually*."

"If you say so."

"I do. Stumbled across this church a few years ago. Seemed

wrong to just leave it empty to rot. Didn't figure God would like that very much. So I decided to keep it company. It felt right. Even the corn creeps couldn't make me leave. After a while, I even took to calling myself *Father*. Just because I thought this church *deserved* a Father, even a shitty one."

Eric supposed he could find no real fault in that logic. There was, after all, something about the thought of a church abandoned and left to rot. That was powerfully symbolic. He could see how a certain kind of person might be compelled to stay.

"They're fascinating in a way," Father Billy said, still staring through his homemade peephole. "Come look."

He stepped out of the way and Eric took his place. Immediately, he saw the swarm of creatures that had fallen over their dead companions. Now that he was right next to the door, he could *hear* them, too. They snarled and grunted as they fought for every scrap. And even that did not entirely cover up the awful sounds of them slurping and tearing at their morbid meal.

"See the one that's different?"

Eric scanned the dozen or more creatures that were moving around the yard and quickly found the one he was talking about. Unlike the others, it was hunched over, its long arms dangling toward the ground. It was much fatter, with a huge, drooping belly and a much broader chest. It looked considerably clumsier than the others, and much slower.

"That's a male."

"No kidding?"

"Only the females hunt. The males are too slow and stupid. They don't care about much more than eating and fucking."

Even as Eric watched the creature, he noticed that it seemed to be following one of the females around, as if waiting for a chance to pounce.

"It may take him hours, but eventually he'll ambush one of them and have his way with her. Makes her mad as hell. You should hear the noise."

Eric didn't think he cared to hear the noise these "corn creeps" made when they mated. He was fairly certain that it was one of those sounds he could go his entire life without hearing and not be left feeling remotely unfulfilled. But that might be a rude thing to say aloud. Father Billy seemed genuinely proud of his knowledge of corn creep mating practices.

He turned away from the door, happy to be moving away from the nauseating sound of tearing, cannibalized flesh, and found a chair to sit in. "So am I stuck here until nightfall, then?"

"Maybe. Just depends how long they stay. Sometimes they can be stubborn. Linger right up until twilight. Other times, they'll get bored and head home early. But by the time the sun's fully set they'll be long gone and you can get back on your way."

"Wonderful." Eric didn't care for the idea of completing the rest of his journey after dark. It was already creepy enough out here without adding the ambiance of nightfall.

Father Billy peeked out one last time at the corn creeps and then slid the panel closed. "Look at the bright side," he said, turning to face him. "It'll give you time to consider what you're really doing." He turned and walked toward the corner, where several cardboard boxes were stacked. "There's still time to give up this suicide mission."

"And then what? Go back home and have the same damn dream

every night?"

"Right. The dream. Forgot about the dream… I hear it'll drive you mad if you don't do what it wants."

"Seems that way. Feels so desperate, like I *have* to go. I jump out of bed every night in a blind rush. I just want it over with."

Withdrawing a small, plastic container from the topmost box, Father Billy said, "It'll be over all right. I'm telling you, you won't live through the night."

"You seem awful sure of that."

"I am." He tossed the plastic container to Eric. "First aid kit. You should really patch up that arm."

"Thanks." Eric looked down at his shoulder and saw that the makeshift bandage he'd made from the scraps of Altrusk's bathroom towel had slipped off the wound at some point during his flight from the corn creeps. It probably happened when he went tumbling down that steep hill. Fresh blood had spilled down the entire length of his arm.

"That looks pretty bad."

"I know."

Father Billy sighed and sat down in another chair, facing him.

"You know," said Eric as he removed the useless towel and began to clean the cuts in his shoulder, "everyone I've met today seems to know a hell of a lot about what's happening to me."

"I'm sure they do."

"But nobody seems to want to tell me why I'm here or even what it is I'm supposed to be looking for. All anybody will tell me is that I have to go to the cathedral."

Father Billy ran a hand through his long hair as if uncomfortable.

Then he said, "The old folks aren't what they appear to be. That's the first *I'm* going to tell you and the first thing you really need to know."

The old folks. Those could only be Annette, Grant and Taylor. It had been pretty obvious that they were not simply random senior citizens he was happening across. They all had been expecting him. They all knew about his dreams. And they all had advice for the difficult road ahead. Though Annette had been considerably less helpful than the other two.

"The next thing you need to know is that there's nothing but death waiting for anyone who goes inside the cathedral. I don't know what you think makes you any different, but I promise you you'll die just as easily as everyone else."

Eric unrolled some gauze and laid it over the gouges left by the resort monster's wicked claws as he considered these words. He had no less reason to doubt this man than he did Grant Stolyen and Taylor Parlorn. The fact of the matter was that this was the first anyone had said about the cathedral other than telling him that it was his destination. He'd simply assumed that he would find an answer to all his troubles there. But if Father Billy was right, all he'd find waiting there were the cold, open arms of death.

In his pocket, Eric's phone jumped to life, buzzing against his hip. Surprised, he pulled it out. "Didn't know I had any reception here."

"You don't," said Father Billy, staring at the phone. "Or you *shouldn't*. We're pretty deep inside the fissure."

No number was displayed on the screen. Neither was there an "UNKNOWN NUMBER" or "TOLL FREE CALL" or any of those other messages that always really meant "WE'RE NOT TELLING YOU WHO WE ARE BECAUSE WE KNOW YOU WON'T

ANSWER IF WE DO." (Stupid survey takers and telemarketers.) The screen simply remained as it looked when no one was calling. Yet the phone continued to vibrate in his hand.

He pressed the call button and held it to his ear. "Hello?"

He thought he heard his name spoken to him, but it was too garbled with static to be certain. "...out...use...old you a...kay...elp..."

"Hello? Who is this?"

But the line was dead again.

Eric returned it to his pocket. "That was weird."

"Must've been some kind of freak interference or something."

He took a roll of tape from the first aid kit and began securing the bandages. This was a poor substitute for stitches, but it was the best he was going to get. It was much better than a torn hand towel, at least. "I guess so."

"Maybe that happens sometimes. I wouldn't know. I don't have a cell phone."

"I'd give you mine if I could," Eric grumbled. "I hate these things. Wife makes me carry it."

"Way I hear it, they can come in handy out here."

"Works like a compass. I know. If I lose the signal, it means I've wandered into the fissure." Not that it did him any good when he had to run for his life from a pack of voracious corn creeps.

"Well, I see the old pricks didn't send you in completely clueless."

"First one did, actually. The other two were a little better."

"But they didn't tell you what was waiting for you."

"No. They didn't tell me anything about the cathedral."

Father Billy nodded knowingly and leaned back in his chair.

Eric stared back at him. "And what about *you*? How do *you* know about all this stuff?"

Again, Father Billy ran a hand through his hair. His eyes wandered across the room. "You learn a few things out here. That's all."

"No. That's *not* all. You're sitting there, telling me what an *idiot* I am for even being here, reminding me that the only people I've had to trust this whole time won't even tell me the whole story…and *you're* keeping secrets from me right now."

Father Billy stared at him for a moment. It was hard to tell whether he was considering what he'd just heard or simply thinking about backhanding him. Then his brow furrowed as he seemed to realize something. "Does it seem quiet to you?"

Eric didn't notice anything. It had seemed pretty quiet to him all along.

"I don't hear the corn creeps anymore." He stood up, concerned, and walked to the door. Eric watched him slide the wooden panel over and peer out. Immediately, he jumped back, as if startled, and then pressed his face to the opening again for a better look. "Who the fuck is that?"

Eric jumped up from his seat, tossed aside the first aid kit and moved to join him at the door. When Father Billy stepped aside, he peered out and saw that all the corn creeps were gone. The three dead ones remained on the steps, half-devoured, but the rest had fled. And it was no mystery what spooked them. Standing there in the middle of the yard, looking back at him, was the black shape of a man who appeared to be half-concealed in a dense fog.

Except there was no fog.

Chapter Eighteen

"The foggy man..." Eric breathed.

There was nothing out there to obscure his vision, yet the mysterious figure was partially faded from view in the gloom, as if he were shrouded behind a heavy haze. It was exactly as Annette first described him, and every bit as terrifying as he'd imagined.

"Friend of yours?"

Eric turned and looked at Father Billy. "You don't know about the foggy man?"

"Should I?"

"He got here before me. He's supposed to be trying to get to the cathedral first."

"Then what's he doing *here*?"

Eric had no idea. "He's been leaving these...*things*...along the path. Monsters. Two of them have tried to kill me so far."

"Monsters?"

Eric peered outside again. The foggy man was no longer there, gone as quickly and mysteriously as he'd appeared. In the spot where he'd been standing, there was now a large box. "What the hell?"

Father Billy pushed him aside and looked out. "Where'd he go? What's with the box? You expecting a package?"

"Nothing I'd care to open."

Father Billy turned and looked at him, his eyes narrowed. "You said he was leaving *monsters* for you?"

"Yeah. One was in a wardrobe in an old farmhouse. The other came through a kitchen door in an abandoned resort."

"What did they look like?"

"Hard to explain. Huge, kind of—"

"Hard to explain? Or hard to *comprehend*? Like you just can't quite make parts of them out no matter how hard you looked?"

"Yeah. I guess. I was too busy running for my life to look very hard. All I know is I'm supposed to break their focus."

"Break their focus…? Aw *fuck*." He pressed his face to the peephole again and stared out at the box. "He's leaving you fucking *golems*? I can't believe this shit!"

"Sorry."

"It's a little fucking late for sorry! He's already dropped another one off. At *my church*! Son of a bitch even *gift-wrapped* it for you!"

"How considerate."

Father Billy cursed bitterly and slammed the peephole closed again. "I need to think."

"So what the hell's a golem? Isn't that some kind of fairy tale creature or something?"

"Jewish folklore, actually."

"You're Jewish?"

"No."

"Right. Didn't think so."

Father Billy sat down again and rubbed tiredly at his eyes. After a moment, he said, "So how the hell did you get away from the other two?"

"Guy named Grant drove a tractor through the front porch of the farmhouse to stop the first one."

"Not bad. And the second?"

"Fell off a four-story building."

"Impressive."

"Lucky, actually."

"Impressive luck, then."

"I'd rather not rely on luck to get through another one."

"Me neither."

Eric stood beside the door, staring at Father Billy. "So why is it you know about golems, but you don't know who the foggy man is?"

"I never claimed to know everything."

"No. You only *acted* like you did."

Father Billy glared up at him. "I've had some experience with the weird, okay. I used to be mixed up in some pretty heavy shit."

"Heavy like waking up from crazy dreams with irresistible compulsions to drive out into the country and then go strolling through a deadly crack in the universe? That kind of heavy shit?"

"Not *exactly*, no. More like I used to work for some people who made weird shit like this 'crack in the universe' their business."

Eric lifted an eyebrow. "Now *that* sounds interesting."

"It was. I've seen some weird-ass things, let me tell you."

"So you guys were…what? Like Men in Black or something?"

"What? No. Nothing so glamorous. It was… Well, to be honest, I couldn't tell you *what* it was. At first, I thought it had something to do with the mafia or something. I was hired by a guy named Saulkin. Never even knew his first name. This guy's job was to find—as he put it—'items of interest.' I never knew what these items were. I never even *saw* the items. I just ran errands for the guy. I gathered information. Me and two other guys. That was our job. We weren't supposed to ask questions."

Eric sat down across from him, interested.

"Wasn't always ethical work. I don't know who Saulkin worked for. Never met them, but I heard they were some scary-ass dudes. It didn't take long for me to realize that I was in real deep with something way more fucked-up than the mafia."

"And you came across these golems working for Saulkin?"

"No. I never actually saw one. But I heard about them. There was supposedly this guy who knew how to make them. Used to hear about a *lot* of things like that."

"So, what kinds of things *did* you see?"

"Mostly I just heard things. But I did have a run in with some kind of witch."

Eric raised an eyebrow. "A witch? Really?"

"She was *some* kind of crazy-powerful bitch. Turned two hard-trained men into raving lunatics and made a third vanish off the face of the earth, all between breakfast and lunch."

"Wow.'

"Yeah."

"How'd you get away?"

"Crushed her against a concrete wall with a Jeep."

"Ouch."

"Not ouch enough. They told me she was still alive when they took her away."

"Still alive? What happened to her?"

"No idea. When they told me I hadn't killed her, I went straight out and got passed-out drunk. No one ever told me what they did with her and I never asked. I only hope they put her where she'll never get out. I still have nightmares about that bitch."

Eric sat there for a moment, taking these things in. It was a lot to swallow, but given all that he'd already seen, why not add a secret, supernatural organization and a real-live witch to the mix? He had no reason to doubt that these stories were true. "So how is it you know so much about *me*?"

"I don't know anything about *you*, per se. I told you my job was to gather information. Well, my last assignment was to gather information from the cathedral. We only knew as much about the place as was absolutely necessary, of course. As always, it was all on a need-to-know basis. So all we knew was that there was something at that location that was of interest to Saulkin's employers. There were three of us there that night. I was keeping an eye out, so I didn't go in. The other two did. Neither came back. That was when I decided that maybe I wouldn't come back either. I'd known for months that the only way to leave was to die or vanish, so I vanished. Eventually, I ended up here. And as far as I know, they still think I disappeared with my partners that night."

"So that's how you know there's nothing but death waiting for anyone who goes inside the cathedral."

"That's right. That…and the gas station attendant told me."

"The gas station attendant?"

"Yeah. I expect you'll meet him a little farther up the road. Little guy. Kind of funny. Acted like he knew me. Knew about where I'd been. Told me I'd be smart to never go back there, which of course he never had to worry about. He never said it outright, but he managed to *suggest* that I'd be safe if I kept to the fissure, that no one *bad* would ever find me again."

"And it was around that time that you came across the church?"

"It was, actually."

"Nice."

Father Billy nodded. "I know. It may not seem like much of a life, but at least I'm alive. Thanks to him."

"You really think they'd have killed you? The people you worked for?"

"Definitely. Still will, if they ever find out I'm still alive."

"Which is why you shoved your gun in my face instead of shaking my hand when I showed up."

Father Billy gave him a grin that was almost charming. "Couldn't let you die out there. God wouldn't like that. But I couldn't chance you being one of *them* either."

"Understandable. But how did you know I wasn't one of them?"

"I could see it in your eyes. It takes a certain kind of person. You don't accidentally get mixed up in their business."

Eric had no idea what that meant, but he thought it was something akin to a compliment.

"Anyway," Father Billy went on. "The gas station attendant told me about the cathedral. He said that it would always reject those who came looking for its secrets."

"Including me."

"Including you. It's happened before. He told me that the

cathedral sometimes calls to people in their dreams. They're drawn to it, compelled to go there or else be driven crazy."

"That definitely sounds like me."

"Everyone dies there. That's all there is to it."

"So my choice is madness or death?"

Father Billy sighed. "I can't, in good faith, let you go blindly into that cathedral. But I also can't stop you and leave you to the insanity of the dream. What I *can* do is make sure you know what your options really are."

"I understand."

"The choice is yours to make."

Eric nodded.

"But right now, we have to deal with the golem."

"Right. That thing. What is it, anyway?"

"In Jewish folklore, it's an animated creature made of inanimate matter. Like if you made a man out of clay and brought him to life, for example. These aren't the same things. The guy who told me the story gave it the name. I doubt there are any *real* golems by that exact definition. I don't think these things have anything to do with Judaism, for starters. And I don't know *what* they're made of. But the basic principle seems to be the same. It's not a living being, but a creation of some kind, brought to life for the sole purpose of ambushing passers by."

"Which explains why it can be stopped by breaking its focus," Eric realized. "Limited intelligence. Limited attention span."

"Exactly. And that's the problem we've got right now, isn't it? Finding a way to break its focus before it kills one of us."

"So far, driving a tractor into one and dropping another off a four-story roof has done the trick. But I'm guessing you don't have a tractor and I know this church isn't tall enough."

Father Billy contemplated this for a moment and then rose decisively to his feet. "I think I might have something that'll be just about as good. Wait here." He turned and stalked across the room, leaving Eric to sit and watch after him.

At the far end of the church, he opened a door and disappeared into what might have originally been the church office.

Eric stood up and returned to the homemade peephole in the front door. The box was still there. Wooden, not much larger than a microwave oven, it was easily the most ominous object he'd ever seen in his life. Was there really a monster hiding inside? It was hard to imagine anything so terrifying emerging from such a small package. But then again, the warped dimensions of the wardrobe monster had not been remotely related to the physical size of its home. It had poured out of that wardrobe like a spring-loaded snake from a novelty peanut brittle can, its terrifying bulk filling the cramped bedroom before clawing its way through the hallway and chasing him to the front door.

He recalled the second golem, the resort monster, and its spongy green and black flesh that vaguely resembled tree bark. Maybe they weren't so different from the golems of Jewish folklore after all. Perhaps the myth had a very real origin.

One never knew.

Looking out at the yard, he realized that he'd forgotten to snap a picture of the corn creeps. That would've been a good one to show Karen. He had no idea how he was going to describe that particular oddity.

He glanced back in time to see Father Billy step out of the church office and lean two shotguns against the wall beside the door. He went back inside and returned a moment later with a holstered pistol on his hip, carrying an assault rifle and a small duffel bag.

Apparently, the good father had turned the church office into an armory.

"I thought you said it was safe here at night."

"Doesn't hurt to be prepared. Never know when some dumbass is going to show up with a golem or something."

"Fair enough."

"Way I heard it, there was a guy out there somewhere who could make these things. Caused all sorts of trouble. You can probably imagine."

Eric thought he just about *could* imagine it. How many hapless people could one of these things kill before someone figured out how to stop it?

"This…'foggy man' of yours apparently knows the same trick."

"Apparently."

"The problem here isn't necessarily breaking the golem's focus. I think I might be able to handle that. It's that goddamn box. Even if we find an adequate distraction, it'll just return to wherever it's tethered. That first one went right back to the wardrobe. The second one…you said it crashed through a door?"

"Yeah. From outside."

"I'm guessing whatever it was hiding in was sitting just outside the door. Maybe even a box just like that one out there. You would've tripped it as soon as you came close enough. And that's where it returned after you knocked it off the roof."

Eric considered telling him that the creature fell off the roof of its own accord, but decided it was unimportant.

"It stands to reason, then, that this one will always return to that box. Meaning I'll be attacked by it every time I go out my fucking door."

"I'm starting to see why you don't care much for company."

Returning to the front doorway, Father Billy placed the assault rifle on the chair next to the one that dropped the three corn creeps. Turning to face Eric, he reached into the duffel bag and withdrew a stick of dynamite and a coil of fuse.

Eric actually took a step back at the sight of the stick. "Do I want to know how much explosives you keep back there?"

"I doubt it." Father Billy cut a short length from the fuse and fitted it to the stick of dynamite.

"Grenades too expensive?"

"Yes, actually. And they're harder to acquire without drawing attention to yourself." He held the prepared stick out for Eric to take. "This is for you."

"What? No. I don't know anything about dynamite."

"You know you don't want to be right next to it when it goes off, don't you?"

"Well, yeah."

"Then you know something about dynamite. In fact, you know more than enough to do the job I'm about to give you. You see, my theory is that if you destroy the container a golem is tethered to, you'll get rid of it for good."

"Sounds reasonable," guessed Eric. "Either that or they'd just be free to go where they please."

"That's also a possibility," Father Billy admitted. "I'm going out there and I'm going to get its attention. Then I'm going to run like fucking hell. You're going to watch for it to chase me out of sight and then you're going to light the fuse, run out there and drop this in its box."

"No way. I don't want anything to do with that."

"You'd rather be the bait?"

Father Billy made an excellent point. Reluctantly, Eric took the dynamite.

"Come on. Let's get this over with."

"What if it doesn't work?"

"Obviously, I'll be fucked. Now let's go."

Father Billy didn't wait for him to protest further. He slung the duffel bag onto his back, shouldered the assault rifle and picked up the weapon he'd used to greet Eric. He then slid open his homemade peephole and surveyed the yard on the other side. Nothing had changed. The box remained where it was. Neither the foggy man nor the corn creeps had returned. He slid the panel closed and pulled a lighter from his pocket. "Take this. Light the fuse as soon as it comes out of the box. When it's followed me around the side of the building, run out and drop it into the box. Then run like hell. If I'm right, it'll either vanish or it'll return straight to what's left of the box, so you don't want to be anywhere near it."

Eric nodded. He didn't like this. But at least there *was* a plan. He hadn't had a plan all day. He was flying by the seat of his pants. And he couldn't keep relying on dumb luck to save his ass.

Father Billy, who was no father to anyone, opened the door and stepped out into the gloom.

Eric closed the door behind him and watched him through the

peephole.

Nothing happened at first. Father Billy made his way slowly across the yard, his body tense, ready to spring away.

But step-by-step, nothing happened.

Eric began to think that the golem would ignore anyone but him, that others could walk right up to the box without disturbing it. He had just begun to wonder if this plan was doomed to fail when something enormous exploded from the top of the box

A great, howling visage burst upward with the speed and force of an automobile airbag inflating in a collision. It swelled into the sky, raining down broken branches from the massive trees as it rose higher and higher. Two stories tall, it dwarfed Father Billy in its shadow. Massive teeth bristled from a long, fleshy snout and terrible eyes the size of tractor tires blazed like molten rock. Long, coiling tendrils unraveled themselves from the creature's body and snaked across the sky.

It was a huge mass of pale gray flesh against the dark canopy of branches, but somehow its body resisted any attempt he made to grasp what it looked like. It was more than just a great ball with a gruesome face rising into the sky, but that was as close as Eric could come to describing the thing. Whatever made up the lower half of its massive torso seemed to be too strange for his limited, human mind to comprehend.

Father Billy was moving in an instant, across the yard and around the side of the building.

Not surprisingly, he was also swearing like a longshoreman.

Eric lit the fuse to the dynamite. The instant it caught, the object became even more frightening than he ever imagined. In just a short amount of time, this unremarkable brown stick was going to detonate with catastrophic force, blowing itself to dust and taking with it anything in the immediate vicinity. If the fuse burned before he could deposit it into the box, it would, at the very least, blow off his hand.

He tossed aside the lighter and looked out one last time to make sure they had gone. He saw the creature's long, fleshy tails sliding across the rocky ground, away from the now empty box.

Bracing himself, he opened the door, stepped over the corn creep carcasses and ran as fast as he could go toward the foggy man's murderous gift.

He could hear the golem howling behind the church and hoped Father Billy was okay. It was by far the largest of the three monsters the foggy man had left for him. He doubted even the world's largest bulldozer would faze it and it appeared to be free-floating, obviously leaving it immune to falling. He would be lying if he said he wasn't relieved that he didn't have to find a way to break its focus all on his own.

He was sure something would happen to try to prevent him from completing this task. It was far too simple. Surely he could not be so lucky. Yet nothing attacked him and nothing blocked his path. He ran to the box and dropped the dynamite inside without any trouble. Relieved, he turned and ran back toward the safety of the church.

He only made it halfway back before he spotted the golem. It was rising up into the air behind the church, its crazed eyes shining down at him.

Father Billy was screaming something he couldn't make out from this distance. But he didn't need to understand the words. He knew perfectly what was going on: It *knew*.

Somehow, the thing knew what he had done. By tampering with its box, he'd managed to divert its attention from Father Billy to himself.

It simply didn't seem fair.

It was coming for him, clambering right over the church roof, tearing up shingles and knocking aside the already-leaning steeple. Pieces of it rained down between him and the door.

Booming gunshots rang out as Father Billy tried to draw the monster's attention, but it seemed to know which one of them it wanted.

He stood frozen with fear, trying to decide what he should do. He could still make it to the church. It wasn't that far, but he'd never survive. The building wouldn't protect him from something this big. This thing would only tear the small structure to pieces searching for him.

Behind him, inside the box, the dynamite fuse continued to burn.

A tone rang out from his front pants pocket, alerting him to a text message. Numb with fear, hardly realizing what he was doing, he pulled his phone out and glanced down at it. One word stared up at him from the little screen: RUN!

Chapter Nineteen

Eric ran for the woods and the golem followed.

The thing howled, its terrible voice rolling across the clearing like slow, rumbling thunder, filling him with bone-chilling dread. Beneath this awful howl were the sounds of splintering wood from the church roof, the booming echoes of the rifle and Father Billy's bellowed curses, all mingling into a single, chaotic din at his back.

Almost as soon as he entered the woods, he could hear the thing tearing through the heavy branches directly behind him.

How long did it take a stupid fuse to burn?

Seconds dragged on as he ran for his life. He wove between the trunks of the massive trees, hoping to slow the creature down, but he could hear the thundering crash of these same trees smashing to the earth behind him, some of them startlingly close.

Finally, he heard the explosion. A great, hollow concussion that struck his ears like a crack of thunder. At the very same instant, the golem cried out in a dreadful, howling shriek that might have been agony or rage or even simply despair. It was difficult to know for sure.

The howling stopped. A hush fell around him.

He dared a glance back over his shoulder, hopeful that the ordeal was already over, and glimpsed one of the forest's massive trees crashing down from above him, shattering branches in its path as it hurtled toward him.

Eric bolted out of the way. He felt the ground tremble with the force of the impact. A great gust of air rushed past him and dust and debris rained down around him. He was not sure how close he came to being crushed, but he strongly suspected that he had missed certain death by mere inches.

High above him, the golem howled again.

So much for getting rid of it by blowing up its box.

He ran as hard and as fast as he could go, but it didn't seem to be enough. Somewhere in the nearby woods, another tree crashed to the ground close enough to rain splinters onto him. He couldn't keep this up forever.

As he shoved his way through some dense underbrush, something scraped his left arm, drawing blood and wrenching from him a frustrated curse.

He had no idea how he was going to survive this. There was nowhere to go. The thing was obviously perfectly happy to spend the rest of the day pulling up every massive tree in this forest in search of him. How could he even *hope* to break its focus?

Another tone rang out, the sound of the cell phone, still clenched in his left hand, alerting him to another text message. He glanced at the screen.

LEFT

This was new and surprisingly bossy behavior for his cell phone.

But given that he was out of ideas and terrified for his mortal life, he found it hard to turn down freely given advice. Since he was only running blindly through these woods anyway in hopes of not being crushed to death or eaten whole by a two-story monster, he humored his phone and turned left.

Another reverberating crash from behind him.

Another blood-curdling howl.

Eric crested a hill, descended the other side and emerged from the woods into the oldest and creepiest cemetery he had ever seen outside of a horror movie.

"Really?"

Sure. Go left and into the creepy cemetery. That's what he got for listening to a stupid phone. *Now* what was he supposed to do?

Glancing over his shoulder again, he saw another tree crash to the ground and the massive, looming face of the golem floating after him.

Nowhere to go but among the headstones, he ran out into the cemetery.

"Sorry!" he breathed as he trod across graves of people long gone from this world. "Really sorry! Don't mind me!"

Behind him, the golem was far less polite. Another tree came crashing down into the cemetery, crushing several headstones and making enough noise to…well…

After all that he'd been through today, Eric would not have been remotely surprised to see the dead bursting from the hard, rocky earth and loping after him. Or simply screeching at him to keep it down. But surprisingly enough, they kept to their coffins and left him to the golem.

Making his way across the cemetery, he glanced back again and found the monster floating after him, howling its grizzly howl and glaring down at him with its enormous, red eyes. Its long, fleshy snout was unrolling itself from its gruesome face, crooked teeth as big as elephant tusks emerged and bristled outward as it reached toward him.

It was almost on top of him. He couldn't outrun it much longer. His legs were beginning to ache. He could feel a pain forming in his sides. And he still didn't have any idea how to break its focus.

Then Father Billy was there, running toward him. He had several more sticks of dynamite in his hands, all of them lit, all of them with troublingly short fuses.

"Keep going!" he yelled as they drew close to each other. *"No matter what, just keep going!"*

The golem howled thunderously.

Father Billy ran past him, toward the monster, swearing at the top of his voice at it.

Eric did as he was told and kept running.

He heard shouting. Unearthly howls filled the air.

As he entered the forest again, a brief series of enormous booms rocked the cemetery and all fell silent but his own frenzied fleeing as he tore through the underbrush.

He dared not look back for fear that he would find the creature right behind him still, just waiting for him to turn and look in its molten eyes before snatching him off his feet and grinding him to pulp between its countless, massive teeth.

But no such fate awaited him.

He climbed to the top of the next hill and passed into a thicket of smaller trees. The gloom lifted. The chill receded.

He found himself in a clearing behind a barbwire fence.

The sun was shining brightly again.

He climbed the fence before allowing himself a look behind him. He was alone. Father Billy's explosive, head-on attack had finally done what the single stick of dynamite in the thing's box had failed to do.

Eric leaned against the fence and allowed himself a moment to catch his breath.

It was over.

Once more, he had survived.

But now he couldn't help but wonder what had become of Father Billy. Had he survived the attack? Or did he sacrifice himself to break the golem's focus? He hoped the good father was okay.

His cell phone rang.

Apparently, he was home again.

And he was still clutching the phone in his hand for some reason.

Looking at the screen, he found with no surprise at all that it was Karen.

He hesitated to answer for a moment as he wondered where those text messages had come from, the ones that advised him to RUN and go LEFT.

He pushed the question to the back of his mind and answered the phone.

"Where are you now?"

"Cow pasture."

"Hope you're watching where you step."

"I am."

"You sound out of breath."

"You know how it is. Staying in shape."

"Right. My husband the fitness nut."

"Have to keep those buns nice and toned."

"Right. Where've you been? I've been trying to call for hours."

Eric recalled the untimely call that almost got him caught and eaten by the corn creeps. He thought about pointing out the danger she had put him in with all her calls, but decided better of it. That seemed like a good way to start a fight, especially given that *he* had not called *her* even once today to assure her that he was still alive.

Besides, if he'd been smart, he would've turned the stupid thing off.

Instead, he focused on what she'd just said: "Hours?"

"Yeah. It's been like three hours. You're making me a nervous wreck."

"What time is it now?"

"It's almost five."

According to Eric's watch, it was not yet two o'clock.

"I'm losing time."

"What?"

"It hasn't been that long for me. Time isn't consistent in and out of the fissure."

"That's not possible, Eric."

"Of course it is. It's a well-known scientific theory that time can be distorted, though it's usually on cosmic scales. Black holes, light speed..."

"Every third or fourth episode of *Star Trek*?"

"Well...yeah..."

"Whatever. If you say so. What's going on in Wonderland?"

"Right, well, after I got off the phone with Paul... Wait... If it's been three hours, did Kevin ever get there with the PT Cruiser?"

207

"He got here a while ago. Gave me back my key, had some cookies and then Damien came and picked him up." Damien Glowstern was Kevin's best friend. He was practically a member of the family.

That was one less thing he had to worry about, at least.

"I don't know where Paul is."

"Paul's in the fissure," he told her.

"He's *what*?"

Eric turned away from the fence and started walking again. He didn't care to stay in one place very long. That seemed like a good way to invite trouble.

"He called me right after we hung up last time. Told me he was poking around. He'd already found his way through the barn."

"Oh my god… Is he in any danger?"

"Yeah. I think he is. But he might be all right if he doesn't do anything really stupid."

"That's really not at all reassuring."

"I know."

"You haven't heard from him since?"

"I just got my reception back when you called. I haven't checked messages."

"Great… Now I have to worry about both of you."

"I told him you'd be mad."

"Good."

"I threatened to cut off his cheesecake privileges."

"That would serve him right."

"I know. Anyway, I hung up with him and then promptly ran into the corn creeps."

"Corn creeps?"

"Ugly things. Mean. Lots of them. They chased me to this old church. I got to spend some quality time with Father Billy."

"A priest?"

"No."

"Oh…"

"Long story."

"I see."

Eric noticed that his arm was bleeding and recalled that he had gouged himself on something while running through the woods. Fortunately, it didn't look that bad. Next to the claw marks on his arm, it hardly warranted concern. "We had a visit from the foggy man while I was there. He left a present for us. Another one of those monsters."

"Scary."

"Yeah. But we took care of it."

"How'd you do that?"

"Dynamite."

"Sounds effective."

"It was. Eventually."

"Well, I'm glad you're okay."

"Me too." He didn't bother telling her in detail just how narrowly he'd managed to remain okay. Maybe once he was back home and safe, but not now.

"Do you think you're getting close?"

"I hope so." He was making his way across the pasture now. There were a few dozen cows at the far side of the field, but none seemed remotely concerned with him. Still, he kept his eyes open for anything that might like to eat him. After all that he'd seen, he wouldn't have been entirely surprised to see those very cows stand up on their hind legs and start stumbling toward him, clutching knives and forks.

"How's the dream coming?"

"I think I missed something. The corn creeps weren't supposed to chase me to the church."

"Really? That's what they're called?"

"I didn't come up with it. Father Billy did. And he seemed a little touchy about it, to tell the truth."

"Oh. Sorry."

"I think I was supposed to stay on the road. I think there was somewhere else I was going to go. Now I think I've missed it. I'm not entirely sure, but I have a feeling I might've gone around it instead."

"Do you think you'll need to go back?"

"I don't think so. I feel like it's more important to get to the cathedral. But I'm not sure anymore. Father Billy thinks I need to stay away from the cathedral."

"Maybe he's right."

"Maybe. I don't know. He saved my life back there. Twice, actually."

"I like him already."

"Yeah... I lost him, though. I'm not sure what happened to him."

"You think he might be dead?"

"It's possible. I don't know. I hope not."

"Me too."

"Whatever happened, it's done now. I can't go back. He told me to keep going. No matter what. He's not the kind of person you care to disobey. And who knows if I could get back there even if I tried. The path might not lead back there anymore."

"That's so weird to think about."

"I know."

"Are you going to be okay?"

"Yeah. Just... Tired."

"I should let you catch your breath."

"Yeah."

"And you should call your brother."

"I should."

"Call me back and let me know he's okay."

They said goodbye and hung up. Eric made his way to the far side of the field and climbed another fence. There, he stepped onto another dirt road and found that it was familiar. He'd been here in his dream. He was back on the path.

He wondered what he missed by taking his detour by the church. Hopefully it wasn't anything important...

He dialed his brother's number and continued walking.

Paul answered on the first ring.

"Where are you?"

"I'm at that Gold Sunshine place."

"Still?"

"Yeah, still! I'm hiding in one of those little cabins."

"From what?"

"I don't even know! Absolutely no idea! Damn thing came out of the corn! Looked kind of like a little bitty rhinoceros..."

"Rhinoceros?"

"Lots more teeth, though... Funny little legs, too. No bigger than my dog... Came charging right at me! *Mean* little bastard! Bit me! Tore my pants leg all to hell..."

"Are you all right?"

"I'm fine. Just a few scratches. But I almost didn't make it to this cabin! You didn't tell me about those things!"

"Mutant mini rhinos are a new one to me."

"Grunting and snarling… Scared the holy hell out of me!"

"I warned you it wasn't safe. Should've listened to me."

"I know."

"Is Kevin on his way to pick you up?"

"Not yet. Him and Damien were still looking for this place when I called him."

"And you haven't worked up the guts to go back out so you can make a break for the driveway?"

"Can't! Stupid thing's standing guard out there!"

"Really?"

"Yeah! I'm looking at it right now, through the window! It's just sitting there, dozing in the grass, *waiting* for me! Little freak!"

Eric laughed. He couldn't help it.

"It's not funny!"

"It's exactly what you deserve."

"It's still not funny!"

"Well it's got to go away sometime."

"You'd think…"

"Well, as long as you're safe…"

"Safe, yes. Free to leave this smelly old cabin, not so much. Hot as shit in here, too."

"Should've gone home when you had the chance."

"I know…"

"Keep an eye out for Taylor. He was there when I went through.

Maybe he can help you out with your little…rhino-thing."

"I haven't seen anybody all day."

"Well keep your eyes open."

"Right."

"Could be worse."

"I'm sure it could."

"At least it wasn't corn creeps."

"Corn creeps? What the hell's a corn creep?"

"About a hundred times scarier than a mini-rhinoceros."

"I'll have to take your word for that."

"Yes, you will. Did you get a picture of it?"

"About twenty of them. Not much else to do in here."

"Send it to Karen. Let her know you're safe. She's worried about you."

"You told her I'm here?"

"I did. She's pretty pissed."

"Well, shit."

"I told you."

"Yeah, yeah."

"Let her know."

"I will."

"I'll check on you again later."

"Okay. Chances are I'll be right here. Stupid…whatever the hell it is…"

Eric hung up and stuffed the phone back into his pocket. He had to admit, it gave him a chuckle to think of Paul being held prisoner in one of those little cabins by a pint-sized rhinoceros.

He gazed around at the surrounding pastures. No dwarf rhinos were charging him. No corn creeps were stalking him. There weren't even any coyote-deer watching him. He seemed to be alone except for the cattle, and so far they seemed to be nothing more than ordinary cows.

Hopefully it would stay this way for a while. He needed a break.

He kept wondering about Father Billy. Was he okay? Had he escaped the golem? He hated to think that his untimely arrival had brought tragedy to any man, much less one with such a unique relationship with God.

His phone rang again.

When he checked the number to see who was calling, he found it blank again, like it had been when he received the broken call in the church. Curious, he opened the line and pressed it to his ear. "Hello?"

"Eric! I think I finally got the hang of this! Sorry I cut off before."

"Who is this?"

"It's me, silly. Isabelle."

Eric stopped walking. He was shocked. "*Isabelle?*"

"Yeah! I got out!"

"Away from Altrusk?"

"Yeah! Well… Sort of… I mean I'm definitely well away from Altrusk. He'll never find me now. But I'm still kind of stuck."

He couldn't believe it. He'd honestly believed that he'd never hear the girl's voice again. "How?"

"Remember that room I told you about? The one with the door I was afraid of?"

"Yeah?"

"Well, I did it. I went in. It didn't let me out, like I'd hoped. And it hurt really bad…but it sent me somewhere else. Apparently, there's lots of places out there like Altrusk's house. And I guess I can move between them."

"That's…kind of cool."

"I know, right? After you left, Altrusk was insanely mad. He couldn't really hurt me—he's already done all he can possibly do to me—but I decided I had to do something. So I went to that room with the door and I just went for it."

"That was very brave of you."

"Thanks. But…I have you to thank for that."

"Me? I didn't do anything."

"Yeah you did. You were my friend. I needed a friend. Plus… Well, this is kind of weird, but do you remember how I told you I had that connection to my family? I could feel them? I was in their thoughts?"

"Yeah?"

"Well, after you left, I realized I have that with you now, too."

"You do?"

"Yeah. So I'm kind of in your thoughts now."

"Oh. That's…"

"Weird and kind of creepy? Yeah. I know."

"I wasn't going to say that."

"I know you weren't."

"Okay, yeah, it's weird and kind of creepy."

"I know. But hey, I may not be able to get back to my family, but I can at least move around. And I found out I can talk to you."

"Yeah. How exactly are you doing this?"

"I found a way to hop into the phone lines. And since I'm in your thoughts, I know your number. I'll be able to talk to you any time I want, as long as you have a phone. *Any* phone."

"That's…cool," he replied. And he meant it. After assuming she was lost, it was incredible to actually be able to talk to her again.

"In fact, even without a phone, you can always talk to me. I'll always be able to hear you. And I think I can help you, too."

"Really?"

"Yeah. I've learned a lot after all these years of being stuck in Altrusk's house. I have all that he knows, for starters."

"You do?"

"And the knowledge of all the other people trapped in that house. Plus, I think the house itself gave me an intimate connection to the fissure. I could even feel Father Billy a little bit. I'm not sure if it was because he's in the fissure or because he was with *you*, but I could see where he was and how to guide you back to him."

"Wait… So that was *you* sending me those text messages?"

"Yep!"

"How did you—?"

"I'm in your head, remember?"

"Right. That's useful. Thanks."

"By the way, Father Billy's fine. He might've lost some of his hearing, but he's definitely not dead."

"That's good news. I was worried."

"I know."

"This you-being-in-my-head thing is a little weird."

"I know that too. Sorry."

"It's okay. I'm just happy you're safe."

"*I'm* just super excited to be able to talk to you!"

"Me too. Where are you? You said you could go to other houses like Altrusk's?"

"I can. And not all of them are super-scary. This one's kind of nice. It's in Australia."

"Australia? Really?"

"I know, right?"

"So there's a fissure in Australia?"

"There're fissures all over the place. They're not all well-defined. And they don't all connect to nightmare worlds like the one you're in. Like I said, it's nice here."

"Cool."

"But I should go for now. You need to concentrate on the path. I'll call you later, okay?"

"Sure."

"Oh. And can I call Karen?"

"What? Oh. Yeah. I guess. You can do that?"

"Of course. I can call anybody now."

"Even your parents?"

Isabelle paused. "Um. Yeah. I can. But…"

"What would you say?"

"Yeah. They'd think it was a cruel practical joke. And that wouldn't be cool. But Karen's a real nice person. And she already knows about me. I'd like to talk to her."

"Knock yourself out."

"Thanks!"

"But she's going to be a little surprised to hear from you."

"I know. But she'll be cool with it. I'm sure of it."

"Me too."

"I'll talk to you later. Bye-bye!"

"Bye." Eric hung up the phone and stared at it for a moment. That was probably the single strangest telephone conversation he'd ever had. But it was also very likely the happiest.

Smiling to himself, he continued on.

Chapter Twenty

The road carried him past more pastures and a *lot* more cornfields. There was even a soybean field. That made for a nice change of scenery.

Yet the usual peacefulness of the rolling farmland was gone. He was constantly watching these fields, waiting to see something dark and green rise up above the corn stalks and peek at him. And of course, if there were such things as corn creeps, why not soybean creeps? Cow creeps? Hay creeps? Or even just another pissed off monkey.

The sun had begun to sink in the western sky, but he still had a few hours left before dusk. The temperature had not even begun to drop yet. He considered what Father Billy told him about the corn creeps not coming out at night and wondered if it would really be safer after dark, or if those horrors would only give way to even more dangerous creatures.

He had a feeling that, regardless of the time of day, there would always be something in the fissure to fear.

For the time being, however, the only threat seemed to be

sunburn. His arms and neck had grown noticeably hot from his time in the August sun. It was going to be an uncomfortable night. But at this rate, he'd count himself lucky if he lived long enough to suffer through it.

He was also starving. He'd now missed both breakfast and lunch. If he was stuck out here much longer, he might find that he'd gladly go a round with Furious George for a McDonald's drive-through.

In the dream, he recalled making his way along this path. He also began to recall something else. An injury. His arm was bleeding. It wasn't bad, but in the dream he kept looking at it. It burned.

Looking at his right arm now, in the waking world, Eric saw no sign of the injury, of course, but he could remember it vividly. It looked like teeth marks.

During the time he was off the path, taking his unplanned detour through Father Billy's church, he was supposed to be continuing along the road, across that wooden bridge. Because he hadn't gone there, the memory of that part of the dream never came back to him like it did in the other places he'd visited. Only vague snippets recurred to him.

He wondered why he'd been able to recall perfectly the details of the rooms back at the resort building without entering them. Merely standing in the doorway and looking toward those rooms had brought back vivid recollections of the dusty, empty spaces behind those doors. Similarly, he realized that he'd remembered much more of the grounds surrounding Altrusk's house than he had actually seen. He'd even used the memory to save himself the trouble of searching for the path leading away.

Perhaps it was his proximity. After all, he recalled getting as far as the wooden bridge, though he never saw that structure during his flight from the corn creeps.

Maybe it had to do with straying so far from the path he took in the dream.

All he could recall was some sort of building. A house, he thought, but he couldn't quite be sure.

A series of incoherent images rolled around deep in his mind. A porch. A driveway. A decorative well. Something strange about a tree… Something watching him…? Noises. Panic. Running.

He couldn't make any of it come together. It was no use.

But somewhere along the way, he'd been bitten. And the shape of the teeth marks in his arm was almost human…

He couldn't even tell himself that it was only a dream.

But at least he hadn't been seriously harmed. He'd continued on, little worse for the wear, meaning that Dream Eric had *still* probably ended up with the preferred path. He had only traded a bite mark on his right arm for a painful scratch on his left.

Around him, the fields were quiet. These were mostly fallow, empty, allowing him an unobstructed view all around him.

Nothing stalked him here.

But perhaps farther out, beyond where he could see clearly…

He walked and he watched for unnatural things, until at last he crested a hill and looked down into the next valley. A large building waited there for him.

It appeared to be an old factory of some kind. Several smoke stacks rose from one end of the facility. Several large storage tanks stood at its back. A large loading dock with six bays stood empty and silent. A single stretch of blacktop led away from the building and off through the open hayfields.

An old sign still stood out by the road. Half of it had blown off long ago—likely in a storm—so that it was impossible to read the name of the company, but its logo was still visible. It appeared to be a Canada goose.

Standing at the top of the hill, looking down at the sprawling structure, his only thought was, *What now?*

He closed his eyes and recalled the dream. Two days ago, the Eric who would never have met Father Billy set off down the hill toward the silent factory. Today, the Eric who was never bitten did the same.

He had barely begun when his phone rang again.

"I just had the strangest conversation of my life," Karen announced before he could even say, "Hello."

He didn't have to ask who this conversation was with. "Isabelle's a sweet kid, isn't she?"

"Very sweet, yes. Also kind of spooky."

"Well she *has* been trapped in a psychotic, inter-dimensional house for the last thirty-six years."

"That's going to take some getting used to."

"I've dealt with harder things to accept today." The foggy man's three golems were not the least of these things.

"I guess you probably have."

"She looks really good for someone old enough to be your mother."

"I couldn't believe it when she told me who she was. Not just that she got out of the house, but that I was even talking to her. I mean I believed you…"

"You *sort of* believed me," Eric challenged. "You didn't entirely believe me. You never did. You *couldn't* have. It's too much to accept. *I* didn't even entirely believe it. I'm still not sure I do."

"I guess so. But it was like when you sent me those first pictures. Those things from the barn… It was such a shock."

"I know. If it's even remotely the way I felt when I *saw* all those things, when I *experienced* them, then I'm amazed that any part of you believed me at all."

"I've known you too long to doubt anything you tell me. I trust you. It would be impossible for me to *not* believe anything you say to some degree."

"That's good. Because I'm racking up some mileage over here."

"You are," she agreed. "She's really taken with you, you know?"

"What?"

"Isabelle. She adores you. She went on and on about you."

"That's…sweet…I guess. I didn't do anything though. I just stumbled into the house. She was the one who rescued *me*. I wouldn't be here now if it wasn't for her. I would've vanished into that house just like she did thirty-six years ago if she hadn't appeared in that hallway and led me to her secret room. I was nothing but trouble for her."

"Well, *she* doesn't think so. She thinks you gave her the courage to get out of that monster's house. It's kind of adorable. I think she might even have a little crush on you."

"That's awkward. I've never been into older women."

"Thinking about it now, I kind of like it. You're her hero. And she's ours."

"She's definitely mine. In fact, I seem to be collecting those today." He recalled Grant's timely intervention with his tractor and Father Billy courageously taking on the freak-in-the-box.

223

"I'm just happy you're running into so many helpful people."

"I'm not sure how *helpful* most of them really are. No one wants to tell me exactly what it is I'm expected to find in the cathedral."

"Hopefully they all know what they're doing."

"No kidding."

"So where are you now?"

"I'm heading toward what looks like an abandoned factory way out in the middle of nowhere."

"That sounds lovely. I can't imagine it possibly going wrong."

"I know. What do you think? Another of the foggy man's golems or a nest of ravenous monsters?"

"Maybe it's where you'll have your epic showdown with the foggy man, himself."

"Nice. I can't wait."

"Isabelle promised me she'd watch out for you."

"That was nice of her."

"I'm really glad someone is."

"You've done a fine job watching out for me yourself."

"Me?"

"Yeah. If it wasn't for you, I'd still be standing around at that dock, trying to figure out where to go next."

"You'd have figured it out on your own. Eventually."

"I'm not so sure of that."

"*I* am. You're pretty slow, but you usually get it in the end."

"Thanks. You're too kind."

"I know."

"Did Paul call you?"

"He did. He's in a real mess, isn't he?"

Rushed

"It's pretty damn funny, isn't it?"

"Kind of, yeah. Did he send you a picture of the thing that won't let him out of the cabin?"

"No."

"I'll have to send it to your phone. It's almost cute."

"Doesn't sound like Paul's thinking about bringing it home."

"No. It doesn't."

"At least he's safe in the cabin."

"I know. Hopefully Kevin can get to him before too long."

"I hope so."

"Oh, I've got to go. Toni's here for the cake."

"That's okay. I've got to go get the living hell scared out of me by whatever's waiting in this factory."

"Have fun."

"You know I will."

"Eric…"

"What?"

For a moment, Karen was silent. He could tell she was frightened. Between all the pictures he'd sent her and now talking to the undeniably real Isabelle, it was becoming harder and harder to dismiss all these things with a joke and a smile.

"Be careful," she said at last.

"I will."

"I love you."

"I love you too."

"Bye."

Eric said goodbye and hung up the phone. He didn't like hearing so much worry in her voice. She was usually much stronger than that.

He could tell that she was ready for him to come home.

The factory loomed ahead of him.

It was silent.

The overgrown lawns and crumbling parking lots confirmed that this was not merely a day off. No one had worked here in a very long time.

Glancing down at his phone again, he saw that he was beginning to lose his signal. The factory was on the edge of the gray zone. He recalled his dream. This was like the lake. He wouldn't be able to go around. The only path was *through* the facility.

Had the fissure always been here? Surely a factory could not have been built in such a place without someone noticing it. Perhaps the fissure was always growing. Perhaps it had spread to this place only after the facility was built. Or maybe it was like the resort and someone chose this place specifically because of the fissure, with intentions that went well beyond manufacturing American-made products.

He crossed the parking lot with its weed-choked cracks, following the same path he recalled taking in his dream, and found himself walking toward a heavy, steel door with peeling, green paint.

The lock was broken. The door remained closed only because it happened to be weighted so that it rested closed. He recalled this from his dream. He also recalled the darkened hallway behind the door, the eerie silence that had settled with the dust.

Now he climbed the steps and pushed open the door, trying to prepare himself for whatever terror must await him in the darkness.

The hallway was brightly lit.

He stood in the doorway, confused, as a tall man in business casual clothes and a white hairnet walked from a doorway on the right-hand side of the corridor to a set of stairs on the left and ascended out of sight. At the end of the short hallway was a door with a scuffed plastic window. The room beyond was well-lit, too. As he looked on, someone walked briskly by.

A heavyset woman in a pair of bright yellow coveralls came down the stairs and entered what appeared to be an office without glancing at him.

Where was the darkness he remembered? Why were these people here?

In the dream, there had been no one. The entire building had been bathed in gloom so deep it was difficult to see anything. There had been no signs to indicate that anyone had been here in a very long time.

He stepped through the door, letting it bang closed behind him, and entered the room where the yellow-clad woman had gone. This room was open and empty, filled with dust, but brightly lit. There was another door in the far corner, but the room behind it was unlit.

He peered into this darkness and found only another empty room. There were no other doors. Where had the woman gone? And where had she come from? He hadn't seen any cars outside.

There was no furniture in this darkened room. No desks, no chairs, no office equipment filled the empty space.

He took a step back, away from the disconcerting darkness, confused, and turned around.

Walking toward him was a very large man in the same yellow coveralls the heavyset woman had been wearing. In his meaty hands, he lifted a heavy-looking shovel into the air and swung it at Eric's startled face.

Chapter Twenty-One

Eric closed his eyes. He stood there, his back to the wall, cringing in anticipation of the blow. But it never came. When he dared a peek, the large man and his shovel were gone.

A tall man was standing in the middle of the room instead, studying a piece of paper.

"What just happened?" he asked, but the man merely turned away and walked out of the room.

"Excuse me…"

Eric followed him into the hallway, but he was gone. Instead, an attractive woman with dark features was walking toward him from the door at the end of the hallway. She was carrying a clipboard under her arm and pulling her long, black hair out from under her hairnet.

"Can you help me?" he asked, but the woman ignored him so completely that he had to step quickly out of her way to keep from being pushed aside.

"The hell?"

His cell phone chimed at him, announcing a new text message, and when he pulled it out of his pocket, he again found a single word staring back at him.

LISTEN

He frowned at the word. Listen to what? The place was silent.

Then it occurred to him. It *was* silent. *Utterly* silent. There was none of the noise a factory should have been making, even before its machinery began running. It wasn't even the polite hush of a quiet hospital wing. Even the footsteps of these people were perfectly silent.

Duh.

He'd been so distracted by the shock of finding people working here that he hadn't noticed how unnaturally quiet they all were.

Beginning to understand, he turned and peered into the room where the big man had swung the shovel at him. There, on the wall directly over where he'd been standing, was a metal rack, exactly the sort of place someone might hang such tools when they were done with them. The man hadn't been trying to brain the hapless intruder at all. He was merely hanging up his shovel. If he hadn't closed his eyes, he might have seen it pass right through him.

Or simply disappear.

Turning around, he found a very short, rotund woman moving toward him from the door at the end of the hall. The door wasn't swinging as if someone had just passed through it, and he very much doubted it that it would open so soundlessly.

This time, he stood his ground and the woman faded away just before she could collide with him.

Residuals.

Completely harmless, Grant had assured him, but deceptive. The foggy man left them to trip him up. The first lured him into a trap. The second had been put there to try to deter him from staying on the path, likely in hopes of making him either give up or try to find another path, which likely would've resulted in straying too far into the other world and becoming lost forever.

So what was the point of *these* guys?

He closed his eyes for a moment and tried to remember what he did in his dream.

It had been dark. Very dark. But he'd had a light.

Why did he have a light? He wasn't carrying a light now.

Then he remembered. He used the cell phone.

Dream Eric was pretty smart.

He'd poked around these offices without finding anything. Then he made his way through the door, which he recalled now was not at all quiet, but instead extremely noisy when pushed open in this deep silence. Using the light from the phone's digital screen, he began to explore.

Eric didn't need the phone to light his way today. These rooms were brightly illuminated. But as he looked up at the fluorescent lights in the ceiling, curious about why they were on now and not two days ago, he realized that they were unlit. The light didn't seem to be coming from those.

This was new. Apparently the foggy man could even manufacture residual lighting.

How the hell did that even work?

Too tired to contemplate such a thing, Eric pushed open the door, wincing at the loud screeching of its hinges, and stepped out onto the factory floor.

If this were a real factory, the noise would be deafening, the air would be stifling and the very floor would be rumbling beneath his feet. But in spite of the dozens of people bustling around, the thrumming of the machinery, the conveyor belts clattering, there was not the subtlest noise to be heard beyond his own shallow breathing. The air was stale and cool, musty-smelling. His ears and nose detected the truth. Only his eyes saw the lie.

He stood in the middle of the walkway, gazing around at the silent chaos, wondering what the foggy man was doing here.

A young man walked past him, appearing no less real than Eric, and he reached out to touch his arm. It was as if he had only imagined him there. As soon as his fingers came close, he was gone without a trace. He did not fade. And he did not disappear, exactly, if that made any sense. He was just gone, as if never there in the first place, as if he vanished not before his eyes but even for a second or two in his very memory.

This was insanely weird.

And after all he'd seen today, that was saying a lot.

To his left was some kind of office. It was dark beyond the door. No residual lighting had been used there. Farther to his left, a corridor led into another room where it was also dark. But to the right, another area of the factory was lit up. It seemed that the foggy man hadn't bothered to animate the entire facility.

But why?

Eric looked up at the overhead lights. Like the ones in the hallway, they were dark. Looking down, he realized that he did not cast a shadow here, suggesting that the light he was seeing was just like the people: of another time.

His cell phone rang.

No name.

Isabelle.

He put the phone to his ear and immediately heard her sweet voice say, "That foggy guy's good."

"This is definitely quite a trick," Eric agreed.

"Residual lighting, huh? That's a new one."

"What's he up to?"

"No idea. I can't feel him. Even when you were looking at him from Father Billy's church, I couldn't see him. It's like he's not really there, like *he's* residual, too."

"He can't be residual. He causes too much trouble."

"True. But I can't feel him anywhere."

Eric looked around at the silent workers. It looked like they were manufacturing some kind of food, but he couldn't tell what. Like the sound, the product itself was missing. Though the production lines were running at full-speed, there was nothing on the conveyors. It was like the rooms that remained dark. The foggy man had simply left it out.

"Snack foods," said Isabelle.

"What?"

"They made snack foods here. Potato chips, cheese puffs, pretzels. That sort of thing. Some specialty organic brand."

He kept forgetting that Isabelle could read his thoughts. That was going to take some getting used to.

"Did something bad happen here? Like at the resort?"

"I don't think so. In this case, I think the factory just closed. But that doesn't mean nothing bad *ever* happened here."

"Are all these people dead now?" he wondered, studying the busy workers.

"I don't know that, either."

Eric didn't think they were. Not all of them. Maybe not any of them. None of them had hair or clothes that looked very dated. These were people who probably worked here no earlier than the nineties.

If so, these weren't ghosts at all. They were merely glimpses into the past.

"Why is he even here? Why isn't he looking for the cathedral?"

"You're not that far away," Isabelle informed him. "Given the head start he had, he should've been there and gone. I really don't know why he's hanging around. But it obviously has something to do with you."

"Obviously."

"Sorry I can't be more help."

"You're more help than anybody else I've met today."

"I'm glad."

"And unlike everybody else I've met, you've stayed with me. That's a little reassuring. By the way, how is it you can call me when I don't have a signal?"

"I'm not sure. I use the phone lines in this house to call you, so I really shouldn't be able to reach you when no one else can. So I guess it can't just be the phone. Maybe the connection has more to do with us, something about the way I'm in your head now."

"Huh. Well I'm just happy you're here."

"Me too!"

"So what do you think I should do now?"

"What did you do in your dream?"

Eric tried to remember. "I went right," he realized.

"I think that's your best bet."

He nodded. At least that way, he could let Dream Eric lead the way for him.

"I'll hang up so you can watch for trouble. I'll text you if I need to tell you anything."

"Sounds good."

He disconnected the call, but kept the phone clenched in his hand. He wanted to read anything Isabelle had to say to him immediately. And he wanted it at the ready in case the lights went back out, which didn't seem at all unlikely, given the special nature of the light source.

The next room was mostly empty. An office of some sort sat in darkness on the other side of a door to the right. To the left was another corridor. It, too, was dark, but the room at the far end was brightly lit.

In his dream, he had wandered around the open rooms, trying his best to see the far ends of these empty spaces. There was no machinery in the dream. It was all residual, just like the people and the light. The factory had been cleaned out long ago.

He recalled peering into several offices and storage rooms, but ultimately he made his way down the left corridor.

As he turned around, a skinny woman with a remarkably unattractive face hurried past him and vanished halfway across the room. A moment later, a very fat man materialized from thin air just a few feet from where the woman disappeared and laboriously strolled out onto the production floor Eric just left.

A few short hours ago, that would've blown his mind.

He remembered being jumpy. In the dream, he'd been mostly

calm throughout the day, sometimes in stark contrast to what he felt here in the waking world. He was never attacked by the wardrobe golem. He never saw the coyote-deer while trying to cross the gut-wrenchingly scary bridge. Nothing terrifying waited for him between the resort and Altrusk's house. He'd even crossed the lake without encountering Furious George. Dream Eric had been surprisingly lucky. But whatever he encountered during the part of his dream that he could not quite recall had frightened him as badly as any of the things he'd encountered today and the result was that he was nearly sick with fear as he wandered these dark, deserted chambers in search of the way forward.

This did not in any way help him feel any calmer now. If anything, a worried Dream Eric made the situation much worse. He felt as though he would remember something bad happening any moment, at which point the bad thing would happen here and now, with no time to defend against it.

Yet as he made his way down the corridor, nothing terrible happened to either Eric.

Although there were bright lights at both ends of the corridor, he found that very little of it seemed to reach beyond the doorways, so that he found himself illuminating the floor before him with the cell phone's digital display to ensure against any unforeseen hazards.

The next room was a great, empty space, likely a large storage area of some kind. Once upon a time, forklifts probably prowled up and down the corridor, moving things around, keeping the production lines running. But now the room was empty. Three men stood in the middle of the room. Two of them wore hair nets. One of them was talking, yet he made no sound.

His phone chimed.

SOMETHING SEEMS WRONG

"No kidding," he told the phone.

BE CAREFUL.

"I will."

Dream Eric had wandered around this empty room, exploring, searching for the path that would carry him forward. Eventually, he made his way to the far corner, where a set of steps led up to the second floor.

Now, the Eric that was running two days late walked past the three men and headed for the stairs.

Something felt wrong, but he couldn't put his finger on it.

He glanced back one last time at the three men conversing silently in the middle of the room and then ascended the stairs and entered a long, dark hallway.

In his dream, he peered into each room, probed it with the light from his phone and moved on. Now he used the returning memory of the dream to avoid these rooms. He was not at all eager to step through a door and find himself face-to-horrible-face with another golem.

And if he were to be completely honest with himself, this seemed like the perfect place for a golem, as far from any of the outer doors as possible, completely lacking in places to run and hide, plenty of dead ends in which he could find himself cornered.

Apparently, the residuals weren't restricted to the illuminated rooms. His light fell on a man and a woman carrying on a silent conversation in the middle of the hallway, then an older man carefully examining a wall where a bulletin board must have once hung.

He followed his dream self down the hallway and into another large, empty room, his eyes wide open, his cell phone illuminating dreadfully little of the space before him. The fear he'd felt in the dream became contagious. A sick feeling began to spread outward from deep in his belly.

Yet nothing happened.

He made his way deeper into this dark room, past a young man busying himself with invisible work, through another door into another hallway and finally down a narrow set of stairs into yet another unlit room where he found a pretty young woman who looked as if she might be flirting with someone, except whoever she was chatting with was not there.

From here, another darkened corridor led to an illuminated room that he quickly recalled was the same room where the three men were talking.

But when he returned, only two of the men were standing there. The one without the hair net had either wandered off or vanished.

In the dream, he returned to the first production floor he'd found and made his way down the other darkened corridor.

Sometimes the dream came to him in bursts, giving him ample time to see what awaited him. Other times, he was forced to relive the events of his dream as they occurred. It seemed to be particularly stubborn in revealing the secrets of this factory to him.

It was weird recalling the dream when so much looked so different. It was distracting.

He made his way back to the production floor and looked around at the dozen silent workers busying themselves with the empty line, going through the motions they went through ten or twenty years ago, oblivious to the fact that this factory would one day replay their actions for a stranger in torn and bloody clothes.

His cell phone chimed again.

I FEEL SOMETHING

Eric glanced around him at the room. He tried to recall everything he saw in his dream, but too much had changed between then and now. Thanks to the foggy man, it was almost impossible to know what was real and what wasn't, much less tell if something had changed.

I DON'T THINK YOU'RE ALONE

Swearing louder than he'd intended (he kept forgetting that the only sounds in this place were those he made), Eric turned and scanned the room.

In the dream, he'd continued on to the left. But he hesitated to go in that direction now. Was it another golem? How would he deal with it this time? He had neither a tractor nor any dynamite. And he didn't know how to get to the roof. No foul-mouthed father was here to help him. All he had was a cell phone and a little girl in Australia.

Residual remnants of people who hadn't been here in years walked silently past him, carrying on their endless business as if he wasn't there. Because he *wasn't* there. And they weren't here.

It was strange being all alone in a room filled with people.

"What am I supposed to do?" he wondered.

A young woman walked away from the line for no apparent reason and vanished into the doorway through which he'd entered the production floor. A middle-aged man simply vanished from his work station and a much younger man appeared a few feet to his left, silently nodding as if spoken to, though no one was talking to him. Farther away, a grumpy-looking woman with curly blonde hair escaping from under her hair net hurried around the machinery as a heavyset man strolled thoughtlessly along the isle straight toward her. The two came within a fraction of an inch of colliding and then both of them abruptly vanished, exactly as they did when he touched one of them.

They didn't match. It seemed they weren't all from the same point in time.

By the far wall, a man in a hard hat was working on one of the machines, oblivious to the fact that the machine currently appeared to be in operation.

A thin man without a hairnet entered from the next room and strolled silently toward him, looking as if he was on his way home for the day.

From the darkened corridor to his left, where Dream Eric had wandered in search of the way out of here, a security guard strolled into the room with his flashlight, apparently going about his rounds in the dark after hours.

Taking a deep breath, Eric set off toward the darkened half of the factory.

He passed a very tall man with a very thick mustache, but found no golem.

At the end of the corridor was a large, empty space. Another corridor led to another illuminated area far to the right. Between here and there was only more darkness.

He stood against the wall for a moment, remembering the dream, letting it reveal the room for him.

Phantom workers walked past him, some of whom he'd seen before in other areas. There was the heavyset woman he followed into that first office. And the large man who had nearly swatted him with his shovel. He watched them as he recalled wandering around this room in his dream, revealing nothing of interest before setting off down the next corridor.

Eric continued on as well and soon found himself in what appeared to be the packaging area of the plant. Here, silent machinery thrummed and immaterial workers prowled the lines, tending to invisible product.

Only about half of the machinery had returned here, however. The conveyor belts abruptly began and ended over an empty floor.

Eric walked up to one of the conveyor belts and watched it run. It looked so real. And yet no machine in the world could run so silently. He reached out and tried to touch it. The entire line was gone just like the people he'd tried to touch.

A woman who had been standing beside the machine continued working, unfazed by the disappearance of her workstation.

He looked around the room. He recalled peering into the corners, probing the vacant darkness. Again and again, nothing was here.

Another corridor went on into the darkness ahead. He turned and walked toward it.

He was ready to be gone from this place.

What was the foggy man up to here? What was the point of bringing back all these people and machines? Was he trying to hide something? There had been more than enough opportunities to spring a golem on him. If the purpose was simply to ambush him, why bring back so much of the factory?

A young man in a black tee shirt and dark jeans with no hairnet was walking toward him from the next corridor. He recognized him. This was one of the three men standing together in the storage room where he ascended the stairs to the second floor a short while ago, the one who had disappeared by the time he came back around.

Perhaps he was some kind of supervisor. There might be offices down here, where hairnets didn't have to be worn when the factory was up and running. He didn't like the wide open spaces of the factory floors, but the idea of searching dozens of smaller rooms was no improvement.

No longer concerned with avoiding the residual people, he passed within a few inches of the young man and had taken a couple steps before it occurred to him that he felt a breeze as he went by.

Startled by this realization, he turned to take another look at the young man.

Before he could face the stranger who walked among the ghosts, something struck him in the side of his head and the world swam away.

Chapter Twenty-Two

The world spun chaotically around him, swirling through his clouded mind as he struggled against the sleep that dragged him down into the darkness.

Pain filled his head. He couldn't think.

Eric had a vague sense of being dragged across the floor by his feet. But that didn't make any sense. He was terrified, though he couldn't seem to remember why.

A door rattled loudly open. The noise seemed thunderous.

Sunlight flooded over him, stabbing at his eyes when he tried to open them.

He fell. He landed hard on the ground and pain exploded from his head and shoulder. The world swam briefly into focus.

Blacktop before his eyes.

He tried to move, but he felt so heavy. He squinted up, trying to see where he was.

A pair of legs.

A voice. Someone said something, but he couldn't understand the words. He still couldn't think.

Then something struck the ground in front of his face.

Darkness came again, chasing away the sunlight, washing away the pain, leaving only peaceful sleep.

Chapter Twenty-Three

The pain came back.

Eric awoke to a harsh buzzing noise that sent jagged shards of pain deep into his brain.

He opened his eyes, squinting into the blinding sunlight, confused.

What happened?

Where was he?

What was that awful noise?

Gradually, his eyes focused and he found himself on the ground, looking at his cell phone, which was lying on the asphalt next to his face.

It was vibrating.

Grimacing at the pain, he reached out and picked it up. Immediately, it quit ringing and chimed at him.

He had a new text message.

Groaning, he sat up and looked at the screen.

THANK GOD!

As soon as he had read the message, the phone chimed again and the message changed.

THAT WAS SCARY!

"What happened?" Eric asked.

Again the phone chimed.

YOU WERE AMBUSHED

"Who? The foggy man?"

WHO ELSE?

Who else indeed? Eric rubbed at the swollen knot on the side of his head. Slowly it came back to him. The factory. The residuals. The young man in the black tee shirt and jeans.

A real person hiding among the residuals...

He felt as if he should've known. But he'd been expecting more than a sucker punch. He thought he'd find a golem. He never expected to be attacked by a mere human.

The phone chimed again.

I DIDN'T SEE HIM IN TIME

"That's okay. Me neither." Eric realized that he had begun talking directly to Isabelle. The phone did nothing but relay her messages to him. Even from the other side of the world, she could hear him. If his head wasn't pounding, he might have found this unbelievably surreal.

YOU OKAY?

"I think so. I have a pretty hard head." He rose shakily to his feet and groaned. "Good thing, too. What the hell did he hit me with?"

I DON'T KNOW

Looking around, Eric found that he was outside one of the factory's loading docks. The door was rolled up behind him. He recalled being dragged across the floor. There was a metallic rattling noise that must have been the door opening. Bright sunlight. Falling. Landing on the hard asphalt.

The bastard tossed him out the loading dock door.

When he first looked down on this factory from the hilltop, it was standing amid hayfields with an old, paved road leading away from it. But he could see no hayfields or roads from here. A rocky valley stretched out before him. Tall pine trees stood scattered across the terrain. Once again, he appeared to have been transported out of Wisconsin and into a distant mountain range.

He recognized this area. Eventually, he had found these doors in his dream. He'd continued onward from here, along the valley. He was back on the path.

Why the hell would someone club him from behind and then drop him off right where he'd wanted to be in the first place? What was the point?

"Any idea where he went?"

I THINK HE WENT ON AHEAD

Eric gazed forward. An odd-looking lizard was slowly making its way through the weeds where the broken blacktop gave way to hard earth and rock. It was at least twenty inches long and bright red. It had a long horn protruding from the top of its head. He couldn't recall ever having seen anything like it before. It likely existed solely in the fissure.

It didn't seem concerned with him. Hopefully it was as harmless as the coyote-deer and the mutant livestock.

Again, Eric rubbed at the knot on his head. He recalled seeing someone standing over him while fighting for consciousness. Was it the foggy man? Or was it someone else? He didn't recall seeing that weird illusion of invisible fog. But then again, he hadn't seen much of anything. "I guess we should keep going."

BE CAREFUL

He nodded and began walking, circling well around the red lizard.

Just in case.

The pain receded a little, but only a little. His head continued to pound, his shoulder throbbed. He ached all over. But he was slowly regaining his focus.

Making his way through the valley, he checked the cell phone, but still it had no signal. Only Isabelle could talk to him without a signal.

He also saw that his battery was starting to run low. This surprised him a little, since he'd never had to recharge it after only a single day. But then again, he'd never used the stupid thing this much.

He hoped it lasted long enough to see him through the rest of this odd journey. As much as he hated the phone, he'd grown accustomed to having some connection with the world outside the fissure.

Besides, without the phone, he couldn't talk with Isabelle.

He returned it to his pocket and glanced up in time to see a hawk soar overhead.

The pine trees grew denser, the terrain flatter, the ground rockier. Then, just as quickly, the mountain terrain gave way to hayfields again.

His cell phone signal came back.

He'd missed only seven calls this time.

Among these missed calls, Karen had sent him the picture Paul took of the creature that chased him into the cabin. It really did look like a little rhinoceros, except that it appeared to have legs more at home on a greyhound, though much shorter, and teeth similar to a boar's tusks, though much bigger.

He'd almost forgotten about his brother's sticky situation.

The next time he talked to Isabelle, he'd have to remember to ask her where Gold Sunshine Resort was located so that he could send directions to Kevin if he needed them. But even as he made himself a mental note, his cell phone received a new text message.

I ALREADY TEXTED KEVIN DIRECTIONS

Right. She could read his mind. He kept forgetting.

"When did you do that?"

WHEN YOU WERE TALKING TO PAUL

"Oh."

FORGOT TO TELL YOU

SORRY

"It's fine. So you talked to Kevin, too?"

I JUST SENT HIM DIRECTIONS

"You didn't tell him who you were?"

I SAID I WAS A FRIEND OF YOURS

"Cool." Kevin probably wouldn't have thought much about such a message. He would have even dismissed the curious way Isabelle's messages were always fast-tracked straight to the screen, never bothering with those YOU HAVE A NEW TEXT MESSAGE notices. He would've just thought it was an odd glitch with his phone.

At least he knew Kevin was on his way. Now he only had to worry about Paul remaining safe until he could arrive. He would have to call him soon. But for now, he might as well wait for Karen to call. It wouldn't be long now.

And it wasn't. Within a few short minutes, the phone rang.

"Aren't you there yet?" she asked him.

"Not yet."

"This is taking forever."

"I know. Some idiot keeps leaving weird stuff in the path. How'd Toni like her cake?"

"Loved it."

"I had no doubt. How did you decorate it?"

"Clown."

"Oh. I don't like clowns."

"I know you don't."

"They're creepy."

"Mine wasn't."

"I'll bet he wasn't. Your clown would be cute and cuddly."

"*Very* cute and cuddly."

"That's your thing."

"It kind of is."

"I don't know what it is. You see a clown on television, he's fine. You see one on a street corner, he's scary as hell."

"Toni said good luck, by the way."

"You told her about all this?"

"Just that you'd been having some disturbing dreams and now you're out trying to clear your head."

"That's a nice, clean summary."

"The thought of trying to explain the whole thing to her was just way too exhausting."

"I know what you mean."

"So now where are you?"

"The usual. More fields."

"How'd it go at the factory?"

"Exceptionally weird. And painful."

"What happened?"

Eric told her about the residual factory workers and its one not-so-residual resident.

"Are you okay?"

"I'll live."

"Why would he hit you and then just dump you back onto the path?"

"I don't know. It doesn't make any sense. It's like he just decided he wanted to go out of his way to hit me upside the head."

"Well, there *are* days when I can relate."

"Ha-ha."

"I'm just saying."

"I can't figure out why he doesn't just go to the cathedral, find whatever's there and leave. He had a huge head start. Why does he feel the need to come back and torment me?"

"Maybe he can't get at whatever's in the cathedral."

Eric considered this for a moment. "That's not a bad theory," he decided.

"Maybe he's already been there, but he can't get to it, or else can't find it, so he's trying to slow you down."

"That would make sense. Except why just knock me out? Why not kill me? He definitely had the opportunity."

"I don't know. But I'm definitely glad he didn't."

"You and me both."

"Be careful out there."

"Definitely. Hey, have you heard from Paul?"

"He called a while ago and said Kevin and Damien were on their way to pick him up at the resort."

"Good."

"He said a friend of yours sent Kevin directions. Isabelle?"

"Yeah. She's pretty awesome like that."

"She is."

"I should call and make sure he's still okay."

"You should."

Eric said goodbye and dialed Paul's number as he scanned the fields around him. He seemed to be alone for the moment, but the foggy man couldn't be far.

Paul answered on the second ring.

"You okay?"

"No, I'm not okay! The stupid thing still won't let me out!"

"Still?"

"It's just lying there! Sleeping!"

"Did you try sneaking out while it was asleep?"

"It jumps up and charges the door! Last time, I think I heard the wood crack."

"Patient little freak, isn't it?"

"No shit!"

"Have you heard from Kevin?"

"He called a few minutes ago. They should be here any time. But I don't know what we're going to do when he gets here. I'm guessing the stupid thing isn't going to let them out of the truck."

"You'll figure something out."

"I guess we'll have to."

"Just remember, I told you not to follow me."

"I know! Don't be a shithead."

"Oh, I definitely reserve the right to be a shithead."

"You would."

251

"Yes. I would. You're lucky that's all you ran into. It could be a lot worse. The thing in that biggest building would be just as relentless, but it would've ripped the roof off that cabin and kept coming."

"Got it. Thanks."

"Any time."

"I'm going to hang up now and keep waiting for the cavalry."

"Good luck."

"Thanks."

Eric hung up and chuckled. "Serves you right."

Chapter Twenty-Four

Eric continued on. Time passed. The fields gave way to a rocky, brush-strewn hillside and the path began to wind down into another wide valley. Again, the land took on that deeply shadowed look, though the sky remained clear and bright. And the stifling summer air was suddenly cut by a cool wind, as if a storm were approaching.

He scanned the area all around him, alert for any sign of movement. Something he had never seen before would likely be appearing any moment and he was sure it wouldn't be anything as benign as the curious but harmless coyote-deer or a few mutant chickens.

He wasn't sure how much more of this his poor heart could stand.

The ground grew rockier as he reached the bottom of the valley. And as he followed a narrow stream around the base of a hill, he found himself descending into a deep, rocky canyon. Everything his eyes fell upon came back to him from the forgotten memory of the dream, as vivid in his mind as it was to his eyes in the present.

The shadows grew even deeper as the rock walls rose on either side of him. He had no idea how far the canyon went. He couldn't see the far end. That peculiar chill in the air grew even colder. The sickening dread that had filled his belly since he first discovered the barn at the far end of Annette's field began to burn hotter within him. He caught himself holding his breath as he gazed up at the high walls that held him prisoner on this path, unable to go anywhere but forward and back, and back was apparently not an option.

Something was wrong here. He couldn't recall exactly, but he sensed that something in this place had frightened him in his dream.

But so far he remembered nothing but these same sheer walls and this winding stream.

He tried to make himself relax. There was nothing here. He was alone. Being jumpy would not help him avoid hidden dangers. It would only make things worse when they finally revealed themselves.

One step after another. Eyes wide open. Aware and alert. This was clearly the path. The dream told him so. He needed only to keep moving.

But then he paused as a memory finally surfaced. Though nothing appeared now, he suddenly remembered that he *had* seen something in his dream, something high up on the ridge, looking down at him, a hefty, menacing shape.

In the dream, he had begun to hurry. And he hurried again now.

He scanned the canyon walls, looking for the shape from his dream, but it was not here. Not yet.

For the time being, at least, he seemed to be alone.

But just two days ago, something had been prowling this canyon.

He stepped through the narrow stream, unconcerned with

keeping his shoes dry. (They were still damp anyway from his trek through the swamp.) He made his way between the rocks, clambering past boulders and trying to watch both the walls above and the ground where he put his feet.

A broken ankle would do nothing to help him survive whatever hunted here.

In his dream, the creature had disappeared. He had no idea where it went. He prayed that it had simply slunk away.

Here in the waking present, he felt a deep, rising dread inside him as he realized that the dream was about to become a nightmare.

He considered turning back, but at this point he was already too far within the canyon to see where he entered. It might be quicker to continue forward. Besides, the creature in his dream had already seen him. It might have seen him this time, too. It might be stalking him even now. Turning back might only bring him face-to-face with the beast even sooner.

He needed to trust the dream. That's what he had been told. The dream had always shown him the correct way. The dream didn't take him into Altrusk's house. The dream didn't take him to the wardrobe. He only experienced those awful places because he left the path laid out for him in his dream, the path he would have taken if he'd arrived before the foggy man, safe from his nasty tricks.

Many of the things he'd seen today were not to be found in his dream. Two days ago, he never spotted a coyote-deer. He never ran afoul of Furious George with his terrible teeth. But there had also been things in his dream that weren't here today. There was the thing swimming in the swamp, for example. It never showed itself to him today as it apparently would have two days ago. Maybe this would prove to be the same.

He scanned the walls on either side of him, watching for a prowling shape.

The dream continued to unroll in his mind, revealing itself to him as it would have happened. He was afraid in his dream. And he was afraid now. Something lived in these rocks. And he was sure it was still here somewhere. In both times, it remained nowhere to be seen.

He followed a bend in the stream, where the canyon floor grew narrow, and peered up into the crack of sky above him. The walls were at least sixty feet high now. There was no way out but back and forward.

A lone hawk was circling high above.

He glanced behind him as the previous section of the canyon was obscured by the crowding walls, and recalled that he'd done the same in the dream.

In the dream, he glimpsed a shape bounding along a high ledge, following him.

His fear swelled, both in his dream and now, though he saw no such shape today.

It was not his imagination. Something was here. It had been here two days ago and it was here now.

"Isabelle?"

Immediately, his cell phone chimed a message.

I'M HERE

"Are you seeing this?"

I AM

"What is it?"

I DON'T KNOW

He turned in a circle, scanning the rocks all around him, looking for some sign of something watching him, but still there was nothing.

I DON'T REALLY UNDERSTAND THE DREAM, BUT I KNOW IT'S REAL. WHATEVER YOU SEE WOULD HAVE BEEN HERE TWO DAYS AGO

"What should I do?"

I DON'T KNOW

"Yeah. I don't know, either."

DON'T PANIC

"Right."

In his dream, he'd begun to move faster. He did the same now.

Weaving between the rocks, following the stream, splashing through the water, Eric made his way deeper into the canyon, his eyes wide open for the slightest indication that he was no longer alone.

BE CAREFUL

Eric thought that went without saying.

He glanced back. Still there was nothing.

He'd glanced back in the dream, as well, and something was peering back at him from behind a boulder, watching him with fierce, yellow eyes.

Only two days ago, there was a monster in this canyon. Where was it now?

His dream began to unravel faster. He hurried onward, weaving around the rocks, looking back and forth from the unending path before him to the danger behind him. He saw the creature slip lithely from behind its rock and stalk after him. It looked like a cat, a mountain lion, perhaps, but it was a deep shade of speckled red and appeared to have very long hair.

Dream Eric did not linger to appreciate the cuteness of a fluffy killer cat. He began to run.

In the present, Real Eric began to run as well, his eyes wide open. No such cat was visible today, but the terror of his dream fueled him. He could not make himself believe that the same cat was not here at this moment, already preparing to pounce.

He remembered the beast charging.

He came to a stop as the memories came flooding back to him, and stared at the rocks ahead of him. That was where it happened. Where it *would have happened*. He'd run for his life. He'd leapt over that boulder, but the cat was faster, more agile.

It was on him in seconds, knocking him to the ground. It dug painful gashes into his right arm as it pinned him to the ground.

Now, Eric seized the same arm, wincing. He could actually feel the pain as the memories overwhelmed him.

He tried to defend himself, but the cat was so strong. It snapped at him. Its teeth were so big, much bigger than any cat's teeth. And its ears were wrong for a cat. They were long and floppy. And something about the nose wasn't quite right either, but he couldn't recall it exactly. He'd only had a moment to take these things in before the beast that wasn't quite a cat bit off half of his right hand.

Eric looked down at his hand, the same hand, trying to grasp the absurdity of remembering this hand without three of its fingers, without half the palm.

So much blood.

He couldn't breathe.

He remembered. God, he remembered it all, every excruciating detail.

He'd clutched for something—anything—to fight the monster off. It slashed him with its claws. It nearly tore his ear off!

Its back claws dug into his legs, holding him down.

He was going to die.

Eric pressed his hands to his face, trying to force away the image of those horrible, blood-covered teeth snapping at him, but it wouldn't go away. The dream was going to reveal itself and he had no choice but to watch.

The pain was excruciating, but still he struggled.

His cell phone chimed again. He looked down at it, numb with shock at the things he was seeing.

GOD, ERIC…

Still, the memory unraveled. Somehow, his left hand fell on something. A rock. His fingers wrapped around it. He swung it. He missed. He swung again and clipped the beast's bared teeth. It roared at him.

In the present, Eric opened his eyes. There was the rock, lying right where he'd found it, unmoved because he never actually came here that day, never had to face the hell cat.

He remembered thrusting the rock upward. His aim was true. The narrow end of the rock struck the creature in the eye. It roared with pain and leapt off of him, shaking its head.

He scrambled away from it, his eyes searching the ground for a better weapon. He found another rock. One with a sharper tip.

He could see that rock too, lying near the base of the canyon wall.

Dream Eric stood up and faced the cat, threatening it with the sharp rock.

He could see himself, his mangled hand dripping blood, more

blood running down his arm, down the side of his face, down his legs, soaking his shirt and pants.

The cat-thing seemed to consider this weapon. It wasn't impressed. It moved closer and he thrust the rock's tip at it, aiming for its eyes, though he wasn't quite close enough to reach.

The creature stopped. It eyed him carefully. It almost seemed to *calculate* the situation. Then it began to back away.

Even in a state of shock, Dream Eric had realized that it wasn't over. The cat wasn't stupid. It hadn't managed to kill him, but it wasn't over. There was no reason to risk being struck by the rock. Its prey was badly hurt. It wouldn't be much longer.

It retreated back into the canyon from which it came, but it didn't go far.

Eric's eyes scanned the walls. He could still see no sign of the cat, but this was an excellent hunting ground. He had no doubt that if it wasn't here now, it would soon return.

Isabelle sent him another message: GET OUT OF THERE!

He paused long enough to retrieve the pointed rock from the dream. If the cat put in an appearance today, he'd at least have something to jab into its eye from the start. Now armed—though he'd much rather have one of Father Billy's assault rifles—he moved on, still shocked by the horrors he'd just recalled. And still the memories continued to play out in his mind.

Wounded, bleeding profusely, nearer to death than he'd ever been in his life, the Eric of two days ago had continued on, desperate to get out of this canyon before he collapsed and became an easy meal for the clever cat.

He recalled using his shirt to slow much of the bleeding, but he couldn't stop it. Not all of it. Death had become a grim probability.

Now, two days after that encounter with the cat that never actually happened, Eric followed the stream along the canyon floor, his eyes scanning every rock, every crevice, searching for the beast he knew would try to kill him because it had already happened…even if it hadn't actually come to pass.

All this insanity was beginning to make his head hurt.

As he rounded the next bend, he came upon a pool of blood beside the water and bent to examine it.

He was no hunter or tracker, but even he could tell that something had been badly wounded here recently, probably within the past couple hours. Maybe sooner.

In his dream, he'd stumbled through this area, watching the rocks above him, occasionally catching sight of a dark, red shape moving along the rim above him, watching him, waiting for him to collapse and serve himself politely up for dinner.

He saw no blood in his dream, except of course for his own, which he left in frightful quantities.

Perhaps today the cat had found another meal. Perhaps one of those coyote-deer had wandered through the canyon, or even an *ordinary* deer. If that was the case, then perhaps the cat was fed and napping, unconcerned with Eric's trespass.

That would be a stroke of luck.

He followed the trail of blood along the stream and around the bend, cautiously peering around each rock. The last thing he wanted to do was walk up on the thing and surprise it during its meal.

A dreadful thought occurred to him suddenly. He imagined turning a corner and finding the beast snoozing among the carnage of its last kill. Among that carnage would be his own face, inconceivably dead even as he stood staring at himself.

It didn't even make sense, yet the image was so profoundly terrifying that it nearly paralyzed him.

After all, he could hardly expect that anything was really impossible after all he'd seen and done today.

But as he made his way around a pair of fallen boulders, he found that there was nothing left to fear. The trail of blood led him directly to the still body of the cat itself.

Things had happened so quickly in his dream that he didn't get a really good look at the beast. Now he saw that it was at least as big as a full-grown tiger. It had an extra-long, bushy tail and paws the size of a grizzly bear. It was amazing the thing hadn't killed him instantly in his dream.

But then again, if it *was* a cat, perhaps it liked to play with its food. It was a gruesome idea, but one that might explain why Dream Eric still lived.

The beast lay collapsed on its side, its eyes glazed and staring up at the rock walls of the canyon. A drying pool of blood had spread around it.

In his dream, he'd kept going, managing somehow to remain on his feet, all the way to the canyon's far end. He hadn't seen another predator.

What could have killed this thing?

But then it came to him. What was here that wasn't here in his dream?

Isabelle answered the question for him: THE FOGGY MAN

Yes. The foggy man. And given that he'd just put in an

appearance back at the factory, it was obvious that he didn't have that big of a lead on him. He would have only been by here in the past hour.

The foggy man had dispatched the cat that would have nearly killed him had he arrived two days ago when he was supposed to. Had the foggy man, then, just saved his life? That would be an ironic twist in all this.

But the three golems had been more than proof enough that the foggy man wasn't here to protect him. Likely, the cat had merely inconvenienced him as he passed through. The foggy man was probably sure enough of himself that he didn't feel the need to let the cat finish him off.

Still clinging to the pointed rock, just in case, Eric left Fluffy where he lay and continued on.

Above him, the walls began to recede and withdraw and the rocky ground gave way to soil and trees. Soon, the canyon began to give way to a forest where he recalled making his way from tree to tree as the cat prowled along behind him at a distance, watching him, waiting for him to topple over.

His cell phone began to vibrate in his hand. It was Isabelle.

"That was terrifying!" she announced as he lifted the phone to his ear.

"I know."

"I'm sorry I couldn't warn you. I've never heard of anything like that in the fissure before. I had no idea it was out there."

"Don't worry about it. I can't expect anyone to know everything. Not even you."

He kept looking around, still expecting to see something stalking him among the rocks. Fluffy's mate, perhaps.

Brian Harmon

In his dream, he struggled to keep going, staggering, fighting to remain conscious. He was beginning to think he was about to recall every detail of his own, gruesome death.

But it wasn't long after the last remnants of the canyon were out of sight that he came across a paved, two-lane road. And there, about a hundred yards to his right, stood a small gas station.

"I see something," he told Isabelle.

He remembered stumbling toward this station in his dream, somehow still on his feet, desperate for help.

He also remembered what Father Billy said about being helped by the "gas station attendant" and that he would likely meet him later in his journey. Clearly, coming across this place was no coincidence.

"That's an odd place," Isabelle observed.

"What?"

"There's something strange about that place. What is it?"

"It's just a gas station."

"Weird… I couldn't quite tell. It's different."

"Different from the other places in the fissure?"

"It's different from *anything* I've ever seen."

"I don't understand."

"It's hard to explain. I don't really get it. It's just dif—"

The phone went silent.

"Hello?"

But Isabelle was gone again, apparently cut off.

But he *always* had a connection to Isabelle.

Uncertain what this meant, Eric pocketed the phone and looked around. Miraculously, he still seemed to be alone. Nothing had tried to kill him yet.

He made his way along the shoulder of the quiet road. At the same time, his memories unraveled and he saw himself bleeding and weak as the longhaired beast tracked him from the cover of the trees.

He remembered thinking that his only chance was to find help at the gas station. If no one was there...

He shuddered at the memory. It was so vivid. Every emotion, every throbbing pain, as clear as if he were feeling it right now.

He kept looking down at his hand. He could see it as it was, intact and strong. And he could see it as it would have been, wrapped in his tee shirt, blood dripping through the fabric, so much smaller than it should have been.

He felt sick.

The gas station was deathly silent. The building was in need of paint, the parking lot needed repaved. But the place had a clean look that the deserted buildings back at the resort and the farmhouse lacked.

There was an old, white limousine backed into the woods next to the building. It was badly rusted around its wheel wells and the paint was blistered on its roof and hood. It looked like the sort of thing the owner of a place like this might have as a side business, except that he doubted anyone would want to rent a junky limousine. That pretty much defeated the purpose.

As he drew closer, movement in the trees caught his eye, startling him. But no danger lurked in the branches. Instead, a large hawk flexed its wings and stared down at him.

He wondered if this could possibly be the same hawk he'd been seeing all day. Ordinarily, that would be preposterous. There were likely thousands of hawks out here. The countless acres of fields made for ideal hunting grounds. But the idea of being followed all this way by a single hawk didn't seem so unlikely given all that he had seen.

Eric walked past the pumps to the door. He knocked. At the same time, he remembered knocking in his dream, pleading for someone to come to his aid.

Both then and now, the door opened and a broadly grinning man only the size of a ten-year-old boy stood staring up at him.

Chapter Twenty-Five

"Running a bit late, aren't you?" said the man.

Father Billy had described the gas station attendant as a "little guy" and had not been exaggerating. He did not possess the stout, dwarfish stature associated with most little people, but was instead perfectly proportional. He was simply quite small.

Eric stared down at him, distracted. In his dream, he recalled this man taking him by the arm and leading him inside. Instead of, "Running a bit late, aren't you?" he had instead said, "Aren't you in a sorry state."

Not sure what else to say, he rubbed tiredly at the lump the foggy man left on his head and replied, "I'm sorry."

"Well, come on in."

The gas station office was small and cluttered. The little man moved a box from the seat of a dusty chair and invited Eric to sit, which he did. Immediately, he recalled sitting in the same chair in his dream, except he'd been on the verge of passing out.

His eyes drifted to the large window that offered a view of the pumps. In his dream, he recalled seeing the beast out there, crouching among the trees on the other side of the road.

"You look remarkably whole. I half-expected you to come in missing a limb or two."

Eric stared at him, surprised. What was that supposed to mean? His eyes dropped to his hand, the vivid memory of his missing digits in the dream left a burning knot deep in the pit of his stomach.

Opening an old refrigerator, the little man said, "Here, have a Coke," and promptly passed him a can.

Eric felt numb. The can was cold against his hand. His mouth was dry. He *was* thirsty. He hadn't had a thing to eat or drink since he left home early that morning. Although he'd promised Karen he would stay caffeinated, he never stopped for coffee. He hadn't felt the need. He was wide-awake. "Thanks," he said weakly. He opened the can and took a long drink.

The gas station attendant walked around his desk and sat down. He didn't say anything. He merely peered back at him with that constant smile.

"I'm sorry," Eric said. "I'm just…"

"Overwhelmed by whatever you've just remembered in your dream, I'm sure."

"My dream. Yeah. How do you…?"

He waved his little hand as if to say, "Forget about it," and smiled. "Don't worry. Just sit and take it in. You've got time. You've earned a break."

The little man fell silent and Eric looked around. He'd seen all this before. In his dream. It wasn't vividly clear, like other parts of the dream. He was in a lot of pain. He was *dying*. But the gas station attendant fixed him up. He bandaged his wounds, stopped his bleeding. He gave him something for the pain. Something strong.

It was a dream. It wasn't real. But...

He looked across the desk. "If I'd shown up here badly injured... Say, mauled by a big cat..."

The man's eyes lit up and he opened his desk drawer. He removed a small box and laid it on the table. He recognized the box at once. There were syringes inside. "Morphine."

"Morphine would probably do it," Eric agreed. He didn't ask what a gas station attendant was doing with a supply of morphine in his desk. Given the grim details of his dream, he didn't dare complain.

The memory of the dream was breaking up as he recalled weaving in and out of consciousness beneath the apparently surgeon-like hands of the small attendant. He recalled snippets of images as the little man bustled busily around his chair, which at some point had apparently reclined so that he was able to lie almost horizontally.

Eric glanced down at the chair, but could see nothing to indicate that it had such a feature.

It was as if the little man had transformed the dirty office into an operating room, disinfecting his wounds, stitching him up, stabilizing him. He thought he even recalled seeing bags of blood and an IV hanging from the shade of the lamp in the corner.

But surely that had been a traumatic hallucination.

Yet the morphine was real...

"What's happening to me?" Eric asked.

"What's happening is you were called upon to make a journey to the cathedral, a journey that could only be made by walking along the path of the fissure. The calling came to you in your sleep and in the form of a premonition that manifested as a dream. No doubt, you awoke from that dream with an overwhelming urge to get up and go, but you didn't remember the dream itself."

"That's right."

"Given that I was expecting you two days ago, I'd guess you resisted the urge that night and the next."

"Yeah. I did."

"That can be good or bad. Things change from day to day. Some of the things that weren't there two days ago will be there today and things that *were* there two days ago will be long gone now. But you already know that, don't you."

He did, in fact, know this. None of this was information he hadn't already worked out for himself.

"I'm guessing by the fact that you're still in pretty good shape but look like you've just seen the reaper, that your most recent memory showed you something you're glad you missed."

"Yeah. Big cat."

"Fluffy thing? Might be cute if it wasn't so terrifying?"

"That's it all right."

"Yeah that'll do it. I take it you survived long enough in the dream to make it here."

He had the strangest feeling that the little man already knew very well that he did, that he had known it long before he arrived. But he responded anyway: "I did."

The little man smiled broadly again. "And I'll bet that, until now, the trip you took in your dream was much less burdensome than what you've been going through."

Eric nodded. With the sole exception of the strange bite-mark he'd obtained in the area he missed while detouring through Father Billy's neck of the woods, Dream Eric hadn't run into anything truly terrifying. "Can you tell me what I'm doing here? What am I looking for at the cathedral? Why do I have to go through all this?"

Still, the gas station attendant smiled at him. "Frustrating, isn't it?"

"Yes. It is."

"All right. There's something hidden in the cathedral, something you have to retrieve."

"Why? Why me? Why not you?"

"It's on a high shelf."

Eric stared at him for a moment.

"A joke," the little man assured him. "The truth is simply that you were chosen."

"By who?"

"By powers far beyond your understanding."

"*All of this* is far beyond my understanding."

The little man laughed, but Eric wasn't joking. How was he supposed to accomplish anything? He wasn't even sure yet if he'd survived all this in his dream. "What *is* the cathedral? Grant told me it was at the exact point where two worlds meet. A singularity."

"That's right. The cathedral surrounds that singularity. The conflicting energies, as you've been experiencing them as you've made your way through the fissure, come to a pinnacle in that one spot. Everything changes there. All that you know ceases to exist as you approach that singularity. That makes it the perfect place to hide something no one should ever find."

"So there's something hidden there? Something *real?*"

"Actually, there are two things. *One* is hidden in the singularity.

271

The other... Well... Somewhere *else*. Both are actually quite useless on their own. One requires the other."

"Okay... So then what's the point?"

"The point is that somebody, somewhere, has found the location of the *other thing*. And it would be apocalyptically bad for the same people to locate *both* things. That's why you're here. Your one job is to make sure it doesn't get found. Even if it means claiming it for yourself."

"But what makes me special enough to have whatever's hidden in the cathedral?"

"You were chosen to find it. *That's* what makes you special enough."

Eric fell silent as he tried to decide if this made any sense.

"Trust me. You have all you need to succeed at this. I mean, look at you. You're faring much better than you did in your dream."

That was true. He could still type. He could still hitchhike ambidextrously. He could still flip a double-bird when a single wasn't enough to express just how he felt. And he could still play cowboys and Indians with imaginary twin forty-fives. Eric looked across the desk and said, "Father Billy... He said the guy he used to work for was in the business of finding things. He was after what's in the cathedral, wasn't he?"

"Yes and no. Technically, he was only investigating whether something existed there. He didn't find it. But the organization that he works for is persistent. They're the ones who've located the... *other thing* we were talking about."

"You're not going to tell me what these things are, are you?"

"Nope."

Eric sighed.

"All things in their time."

"Right."

The two of them fell silent for a moment. Memories from his dream passed before him. He saw the little man tending to him, telling him many of the same things he was telling him now, about the thing hidden in the cathedral, about the people who wanted to claim the thing and its mysterious counterpart. But in the dream, he told him all these things without being asked. Dream Eric was in no shape to ask any questions.

He recalled the pain. It was surprisingly vivid. He kept rubbing his right hand.

Looking across the desk again, Eric said, "What am I supposed to do with this thing? If these guys who are looking for it already have the other half, what's going to stop them from just hunting me down and taking it from me?"

"First of all," replied the little man. "I never said they *had* the other one. I only said they had located it. As long as they don't have *this* one, the other one is useless to them. They'll never expend the energy and resources to retrieve it."

"So it's pretty safe wherever it is?"

With his broadest smile yet, the little man replied, "You'd be amazed."

"I see."

"*Secondly*, they won't come to take it from you. I can assure you that. They won't know you have it."

"How can you be sure?"

"Trust me."

It was strange, but Eric found that he really did trust this man. There was simply something about him. He was special somehow. *Meaningful.* If that made any sense.

"Directly behind this station is a narrow path. It's little more than a game trail. Follow it and it'll take you to an old salvage yard. There'll be scroungers there, but they shouldn't bother you if you don't get too close."

Scroungers? That was good. He was worried there wouldn't be any more freaky creatures to deal with.

"Edgar will meet you there. He'll show you the final road, the one that'll take you to the cathedral."

Eric sat there, staring at his nearly empty coke can, pondering all that he'd heard. The attendant did not rush him. He sat patiently behind his desk, continuously smiling.

He recalled the dream. Like now, this man had told him all these things and sent him on ahead. His head fuzzy with morphine, still weak from loss of blood, Dream Eric had barely understood everything that he was told. Specifically, he realized, he'd neglected to ask the only question that really mattered. So he asked it now: "If I make it to the cathedral…will I survive?"

For the first time since they met, the little man's smile disappeared. He stared back at Eric with an expression that was actually quite sad. "That'll be entirely up to you," he said.

"Father Billy said that you told him no one who enters the cathedral ever leaves alive. You told him it would claim anyone who went looking for its secrets."

"I might have said something like that once, yes."

"Then how is that up to me?"

His smile returning, the gas station attendant replied, "It's *always* up to you."

Eric didn't understand. But he clearly wasn't going to get any more than this. He drained the rest of his coke and glanced around for a garbage bin. There didn't seem to be one.

"Just leave it anywhere. I'll toss it in the recycling bin next time I go out."

Eric placed it on the corner of the desk and stood up. "Thank you," he said.

"You're quite welcome." Then, leaning forward, the little man added, "For *everything*."

Though it seemed impossible, Eric felt certain that he was referring to the events of his dream, when the little man saved his life.

Chapter Twenty-Six

Eric left through the front door, just as he did in his dream. In both time frames, no big, floppy-eared cat waited to tear out his intestines.

He glanced up and down the narrow blacktop road—not one car had driven by since he arrived—and walked around to the back of the station. There, he found the narrow game trail, just as the little man had promised.

Suddenly, it occurred to him that he never asked the man's name.

He considered going back, but decided to simply keep walking. If he survived his journey to the cathedral, maybe he'd see him on his way out. If not, what did it really matter whether he knew the man's name?

Pushing past the overlapping branches, he made his way along the narrow trail, down a long and shallow hill, across a densely forested gully and up over the next rise.

His cell phone rang. It was Isabelle.

"What happened?" he asked.

"I have no idea."

"It's like we got cut off. But I didn't think that could happen."

"I didn't either."

"Did you catch all that weirdness back there?"

"Some of it. But it was weird. It was like you were in a cave or something. I could barely reach your mind."

"Strange."

"Very."

"You were saying there was something odd about the gas station before we got disconnected."

"I was. I don't know what it is, but there's something very *different* about that place. I don't think it's a part of the fissure."

"Then what is it?"

"I don't know. It's just… Odd."

"Well, it's behind me now."

"It is. I should hang up. Karen'll be calling you soon."

"I'm sure she will."

"Bye."

Eric disconnected the phone, but didn't bother sticking it back in his pocket. Now that his signal had returned, he saw that he had eight missed calls. Karen had already been trying to reach him. And sure enough, within five minutes the phone began to buzz again.

"Where are you now?"

"I'm in the woods."

"How's the dream coming along? Remember anything interesting yet?"

"Interesting? More like *disturbing*. Apparently, two days ago I would've been mauled and almost killed by some kind of freaky cat."

"*What?*"

"Crazy scary, right?"

"What happened?"

Eric told her about his trip through the canyon and the disturbing memories that churned up as he made his way along the stream. He then told her about his visit with the diminutive gas station attendant and his curious smile.

"So weird... Who do you think he was?"

"I have absolutely no idea. I guess he's like the old folks. A caretaker of some sort."

Karen considered this for a moment. "Could be. But he sounds more important than a caretaker."

"He does. Maybe he's the head caretaker. The guy in charge of it all."

"Maybe."

"I couldn't even begin to guess. This is all way over my head."

"The cathedral is starting to sound like a crazy scary place."

"Believe me, I know."

"What did he mean when he said everything changes there?"

"You keep asking me like I'm going to have an answer for you."

"Sorry."

"It's okay. I'm just saying that this is seriously beyond my field of study."

"You didn't take that class in theoretical dimensional compression physics? How irresponsible of you."

"I know. It's days like these when those fluff classes really come back to bite you."

"Slacking never pays."

"It really doesn't."

Both of them fell silent for a moment as Eric made his way deeper into the forest.

"Are you all right?" Karen asked finally.

"I'm fine. I'm just a little shaken."

"That sounded like a hell of a nightmare."

"It was. It was so vivid. I can't figure out how I managed to get up and walk out of the gas station in the state I was in."

"Well, it *was* only a dream."

"No. I'm pretty sure it wasn't."

Karen sighed. "I guess it wasn't."

"It wasn't real. But it *was* real, too. It's…"

"Totally insane."

"Yeah."

"Yeah."

"I think I see something up ahead. I'm going to hang up for a little bit again."

"Okay. I'll call you later." Apparently, she was done even pretending she could count on him to call her back in a timely fashion.

"Sure. Bye."

Pocketing the phone, Eric pushed through the dense foliage and stepped out into a wide field where tall grass and weeds struggled for real estate with seven impressively long rows of old and rusting automobile carcasses. An old, red Firebird, half hidden in the tall grass, stood facing him. The yellow bird painted across the vehicle's distinct hood stared back at him.

This was obviously the salvage yard the gas station attendant told him to expect. But it clearly hadn't been used in many years. The newest vehicle he could see was a seventy-seven Chrysler.

There didn't even appear to be an obvious driveway by which any of these vehicles might have arrived here. It had long ago become overgrown with brush to the point of vanishing into the trees, so that these cars looked as if they had simply dropped out of the sky.

Cautious and alert, Eric made his way deeper into the salvage yard.

It only took a few minutes before he heard the first unnatural sound. Something rustled in the grass between two rusty Chevrolets. Only a moment later, something moved in the next row. He stopped and scanned the area, but he could see nothing.

Then he glimpsed movement in the grass.

Scroungers.

The gas station attendant warned him there would be scroungers. He hadn't bothered to tell him what a scrounger was, and Eric hadn't bothered to press the little man for the information, assuming—and rightfully so, it seemed—that he would see for himself soon enough.

The little man *had*, however, assured him that there was nothing to be feared from these creatures, assuming he did nothing stupid to provoke them. But he couldn't help but feel that he must make a very tempting target standing out here in the middle of all these rusted-out vehicles, isolated from the rest of the world.

He turned away from the noises and made his way up the row, away from the unseen scroungers. He slipped between two long-silent trucks and made his way toward the middle of the field.

Several more times he heard something moving in and around the vehicles he passed. Once, something scurried away almost underfoot and he barely resisted the urge to cry out and jump around like a frightened little girl.

Yet the things manage to remain frustratingly out of sight.

While he honestly didn't care to see any more strange and unusual creatures—he'd seen enough already to last him a lifetime—he found that he didn't care much for not being able to see what was moving around him. Without his eyes to size up the beasts, he was left with only his imagination to fill in the blanks. And his imagination had become vastly more frightening since he began this journey. All sorts of horrid visions passed through his head, from giant, venomous snakes to great, bloated cockroaches, his mind was more than happy to churn out one horror after another to guess what awful surprises crawled unseen in the grass at his feet.

And his dream did not help soothe his curiosity. As the memories unraveled themselves, he recalled himself moving through this field in a mental fog, his mind numbed to the horrors of unseen creatures scurrying around him.

Awake and in the present, Eric continued on, trying to ignore the dream. He didn't want to see the dream now. It wasn't doing him any good. In the dream he kept looking at his hand. It looked so small. So *wrong*.

It made him feel sick.

As he passed an old Chevrolet pickup truck, something hissed at him from beneath the hood, urging him to step faster through the high grass.

"They're mostly harmless."

Eric turned to find an old man with a bald, sunburned head walking among the ruined automobiles. He wore stained bib overalls over a flannel work shirt that looked far too hot for August.

"But you'd better trust me when I say you don't want a closer look at them."

Eric looked around, wondering where the old man had come from. He was sure there hadn't been anyone out here when he first entered the field. "You're Edgar?"

"I am. And you?"

"Eric."

"Eric," repeated Edgar. "You're a damn idiot, Eric."

Caught off guard, Eric could only think to say, "I'm sorry?"

"You must be. To still be here, pushing on, after all you've been through already."

Eric did not reply. He was not insulted, really. Given all that he had been through, given the horrors his dream had recently revealed to him, he found that he was inclined to agree.

Edgar strolled between two of the old vehicles, his eyes washing over them, a sad sort of expression on his face. "A goddamned fool…"

Eric's cell phone chimed. He pulled it from his pocket and glanced at the screen.

CHARMING GUY

Looking up from the phone, he said, "I wanted to turn back at the farmhouse. Grant Stolyen talked me out of it."

"Goddamned fools, the both of you."

Again, the phone chimed.

RUDE!

"You think I should leave now?"

"You won't quit now."

"I won't?"

"If you haven't quit by now, you ain't going to."

"Then what's the point in telling me what an idiot I am? I mean, if you know nothing you say will change my mind…then you're just insulting me."

The old man shrugged. "Just stating my opinion. I'm entitled to one, aren't I?"

"I expect you are." Eric caught a glimpse of movement to his left and glanced over in time to see something dark and scaly crawl out of the engine of an old, hoodless Ford and drop into the tall grass below. "We're *all* entitled to our opinions. Even us fools."

"True."

"I, for instance, am of the opinion that you're something of an asshole."

This time, when his phone chimed, it said simply, LOL!

The old man smiled a little. "That so?"

"All of you," Eric continued. "You and Grant and Taylor, even that crazy-ass Annette. You're all here just to tell me what you think I need to hear to keep me moving."

Edgar cocked a hairy eyebrow. "I thought I was telling you to go home."

"But you just told me that you know I won't."

"Because you're an idiot."

"No. Because I know by now that I need to see what's waiting for me in the cathedral. I know it just as well as you do."

Edgar moved on to another vehicle, his crooked fingers sliding over the rusty metal, almost lovingly. He pulled open the door and peered at the ruined interior as if reminiscing about the days when this car would have been brand new and sitting on the lot, that new car smell wafting from its upholstery. He did not respond.

"Is there even a chance I would've come here and needed you to encourage me to go on? Or was I always going to have resigned myself to this by now?"

Edgar turned and looked at him now, his expression serious. "There's *always* a chance. For everything. You should remember that."

Eric stared at him for a moment, at the softness of his eyes, the blemishes on his skin, the creases in his face. Every detail was so vivid. "How long have you all been dead?"

WHOA…

Edgar sighed and turned away. Again, he placed his bony hand on the car. "I'll have been gone fifty-three years this winter."

Fifty-three years. That would've been around the winter of sixty-one.

"And the others?"

"Nearly as long."

"I see. And you're all stuck here? Just waiting on someone like me?"

"Not someone like you. *You. You're* the one we've all been waiting for, the reason we carry on with our lives the way we lived them when we still lived, tending to things. And waiting, of course."

"But why?"

"We all lived our whole lives along the fissure. And we all *died* along the fissure. A lot of things don't work right here, you've seen that for yourself. Death comes here just like it does anywhere else. A fatal heart attack is just as final in any world. But what comes next…well, that's a little different."

"Are you stuck here forever?"

Edgar shrugged. "Couldn't tell you. Haven't been here forever yet. I sure as hell *hope* I'm not. I *hope* we get to move on when *you* finish what you came to do."

"If I succeed."

"If you succeed."

Eric stared at the man as he moved on from one vehicle to the next. It was difficult to grasp the idea that he was speaking to a ghost, even more difficult to believe that Taylor, Grant and Annette had all been nothing more than spirits. They had all seemed so real, so tangible. But now that he thought about it, they'd all appeared as if out of nowhere. Though they had each interacted with their environments in some way—Annette had her laundry, Grant his tractor, Taylor his tools and Edgar these long-discarded vehicles—he hadn't touched any of them himself. Not one of them had offered to shake his hand.

One thing bothered him, though.

"What about Ethan?"

Edgar sighed. "Annette's still waiting for him to come home, isn't she?" He lifted the hood on an old Chrysler and peered in at the long-rusted engine. "But he never came home. Took a turn for the worst. Died in the middle of the night while she was asleep at home. Couldn't accept it. She died just a few months later, still refusing to believe he wasn't coming home, and that's how she exists now, always waiting for him to come back home to her. She just couldn't handle it. She couldn't take losing someone again."

Eric recalled the way Annette talked to him about her father's death, as if he weren't a complete stranger. It wasn't hard to imagine how difficult it might be to keep losing people you loved so much. "But why isn't Ethan here with her?"

"Because he died in a hospital bed, some twenty miles away. She died in her home, here in the fissure. He moved on. He escaped while the rest of us were trapped. And poor Annette ended up trapped twice. Once here in the fissure and once inside herself."

THAT IS SO SAD!

It *was* sad. It was probably the saddest thing Eric had ever heard in his life. He felt terrible for poor Annette.

Edgar stood and silently stared at the rusted engine of the Chrysler as a scrounger wormed its way up and over the fender. It looked like a cross between a lizard and a bug, about thirty inches long, with six frog-like feet on very short stubs of legs. It had no tail and no neck, only a snake-like head with a wide, toothless mouth and great, blank eyes that, like the rest of its body, were a muddy brown.

The old man watched the creepy creature flop gracelessly into the grass. "They ain't got no teeth, but you still don't want to get bit by one. Their saliva's toxic. Might not kill you, necessarily, but it'd feel like your skin was on fire. You'd have terrible hallucinations and there's a good chance you could go blind."

Now Eric's skin was crawling. His eyes swept the grass around him, alert for dark shapes creeping toward him.

Edgar grinned. "Don't worry. They rarely bite people. They mostly eat bugs and rodents. You'd pretty much have to step on one to goad it into biting you."

Eric still wanted to get out of the salvage yard and as far away from the scroungers as possible.

His cell phone buzzed inside his pocket, but he chose to ignore it. He did not like the idea of further dividing his attention in a field full of venomous scroungers. His luck today wasn't the worst it could have been, seeing that he was still alive, but it also wasn't the kind he'd want to take on a weekend in Vegas.

"So you'll be heading for the cathedral now, I take it."

"I don't see any other alternative. I keep hearing that the dream will drive me crazy."

"It might. Or it might not. That would be up to you, I guess, whether you're strong enough to take it. But for sure, the only way to make it stop is to go to the cathedral. You do that and one way or another you won't have that dream again."

"One way or another... Nice."

"You wanted me to be truthful."

"I did."

Edgar lowered the Chrysler's hood again and began walking between the isles of long-forgotten vehicles. Eric walked with him. "Straight ahead is the old driveway. You can just make it out. About half a mile ahead, it'll clear out and you'll find yourself on a dirt path. Don't even think about turning around. Try to follow the road back to here and you'll be lost forever in the other world."

"One way road. Got it." After all he'd seen he did not doubt this to be true for even a second. "By the way, how far have I gone now?"

"You're in the extreme northwest of Wisconsin now."

That was a long way from where he started.

"By the time you get to the cathedral, you'll be somewhere in northern Minnesota. No one's sure exactly where it is. You technically can't even get there from here. The only way to reach the cathedral is to walk the entire length of the fissure, starting at Annette's house."

Annette's house. That was where the dream began...

Eric nodded. If he'd been told he was in the Congo, he'd have little reason to doubt it.

"Like the others, I'll be leaving you to go on alone."

Eric turned and looked at the old man. "There's something else, isn't there?"

Edgar looked back at him. He did not wear any question on his expression. He did not even pretend ignorance. He only waited.

"You and the others. You're not just random, are you? It's no coincidence that you all lived and died in the fissure. You have a connection to the cathedral."

Edgar did not lie. "We do."

"Are you at least going to tell me what it is?"

Edgar considered it for a moment. Eric didn't think he would respond, that this information was simply not for him to have. But he was about to be surprised.

"This thing you're looking for, the thing that's hidden inside the cathedral…we were the ones who put it there. Nearly a hundred years ago."

This caught Eric off guard. "You put it there?" He'd assumed that whatever was at the cathedral had simply always been there, or at the very least that it had been there for untold ages. He never even considered the possibility that someone had walked this path before him.

"I had a dream just like yours once. We all did. Except there were six of us. There was me and Taylor, Grant, Annette and Ethan. We were the five who survived the trip. And we all stayed here to make sure what we left there remained safe. Only Ethan moved on when he died. The rest of us are here still."

"And you're still not going to tell me what it is you put there, are you?"

"Can't. We never knew what it was. We weren't allowed to see it.

We all followed our dreams and we all ended up in the same Illinois hayfield, gathered around a curious little clay pot. Each of us knew somehow that we weren't allowed to open the lid and look inside."

"So the six of you carried it north. All the way to the cathedral. And one of you died along the way."

"Ben."

"His name was Ben?"

Edgar nodded.

Eric started to ask what became of him, but he found he did not want to know. Somehow, he felt that knowing what happened to Ben would only make the task ahead of him harder.

Edgar was staring at him now, studying him. "How have you done in your dream? Are you better today than you would have been?"

Eric remembered his mangled hand. His head fuzzy with morphine, he never learned Edgar's secrets in the dream. He'd only learned the way forward and stumbled blindly on. He recalled the three golems, the foggy man. But he also recalled Father Billy. Isabelle. "I'm definitely better off today," he replied.

"Good. Our dreams were different, too. Some things were better. Some things were worse. To this day, I'm not sure which was better."

The two of them reached the edge of the salvage yard and stopped. Eric could see where the old drive used to be by the gap in the trees, but the brush and branches had crowded it until it was barely recognizable. If he wasn't careful, he could easily wander off the path and get lost forever.

"Off you go," Edgar said. "Might as well get on with it."

Eric nodded. He considered asking if he should expect to run into more creatures between here and the cathedral, but decided he was better off not knowing. As long as he remained aware of the possibilities, he was as prepared as he was ever going to get. "Thank you," he said, but as he turned, he found that Edgar had already turned away and was walking back toward the salvage yard. Like the others, he did not disappear. He simply walked away like a man still of flesh and blood. He lifted a hand in a silent wave.

Finally, Eric understood his apparent fondness for the cars. They were just like him: long forgotten.

Pulling the phone from his pocket, he snapped a picture of the old man, just to see what would happen. He examined the picture and then watched as Edgar strolled off between the vehicles.

Turning away and pushing into the brush that had overrun the driveway, Eric wondered if he, too, would eventually become one of these many forgotten things.

Chapter Twenty-Seven

Eric had only walked about a hundred paces beyond the edge of the salvage yard when his cell phone rang again. It was Paul.

"How's the standoff?"

"Over," replied Paul. "Stupid thing ran off as soon as it heard Kevin's truck."

"Anticlimactic."

"No shit. It would've been nice if it'd stuck around long enough to make it look like I wasn't just *imagining* the damn thing."

"You got pictures at least."

"I did... But pictures can be faked. I would've rather had Kevin run the little freak over. Then I'd have *real* proof."

"Someone would've argued that it must be endangered. Then there'd be hell to pay."

"I guess. But it bit me! How do I know I don't have rabies or something?"

"I don't think it was rabid."

"You don't know that."

"I'm pretty certain."

"Fine. Can't believe I wasted almost my whole day sweating in a stupid cabin."

"Well I told you not to go."

"I think we already covered that."

"Just making sure I made my point."

"You made your point."

"Good."

"What about you? Where are you?"

"Northern Minnesota, somewhere, I think." Technically, he was most likely still in Northwestern Wisconsin, since he'd only just left Edgar behind. But at any moment he could jump forward.

"Damn, you're moving."

"I know."

"Do you know how much farther you have left to go?"

"I should be arriving at the cathedral soon…"

"Then what?"

"No idea. I'm flying by the seat of my pants here."

"You're doing considerably better than I did."

"Well, I *was* chosen for this."

"Oh aren't you special."

"Apparently I am."

"Right."

Eric grinned. "I'll probably be something of a legend around here… You'll be the dumb brother who got chased by a mutant baby rhino."

"Nice."

"Over time it'll probably evolve, like legends do. I'll be all buff and manly, spouting cool one-liners as I battle all the monsters with my bare hands. Instead of a cabin, you'll be hiding in a tree. Crying. It'll make a great bedtime story."

Paul chuckled. "That sounds like just my luck."

"I may start the tree rumor myself."

"Shithead."

Eric laughed. It was a humorous thought. He could almost imagine that all those epic heroes of literature were really only awkward people like him who stumbled along strange paths just like this one.

Paul laughed too. It was hard not to. It had been such an odd day for them both. "I'm going to hang up and try to sleep a little. I'm exhausted and I still have to drive my truck home."

"Lucky. I'm going to go find this probably terrifying cathedral and try not to die."

Paul didn't find this funny. "Be careful," he said.

"I intend to."

"Let me know you're okay."

"I will."

Eric said goodbye and hung up. It was a relief knowing that Paul was no longer in the fissure. It was one less thing for him to think about as he made his way through the trees toward his goal.

The cathedral.

He kept thinking of Father Billy and his prediction that he would "die screaming in the festering asshole of the almighty cathedral." It was funny how the most vulgar of descriptions were the ones you remembered most clearly. And Father Billy had obviously possessed a talent for turning vulgarity into poignant honesty.

He claimed that no one who entered the cathedral would survive.

He said the gas station attendant told him that it would claim anyone who went looking for its secrets. And the gas station attendant had admitted to saying as much.

Yet he was still urged onward, a lamb to slaughter.

Eric pushed on, ignoring the hot dread he felt growing deep in his belly.

The cell phone rang again. It was Karen.

"Are you okay?"

"I'm not dead so I can't complain."

"Don't even joke about that."

"Sorry."

"Hey, I did a search for Taylor Parlorn in some family tree databases and I got a hit in the same county as Gold Sunshine Resort. It might be a relative."

"Let me guess, the guy died in the sixties?"

"Um… Yeah. How did you know?"

"It wasn't a relative."

"I don't understand."

Eric told her about Edgar and the revelations that their conversation had spawned.

"Wait… So you're telling me these people were all *ghosts*?"

"I'm pretty certain of it."

"That's crazy. You don't even believe in ghosts."

"I *didn't*. Now… Well, things change."

"Maybe they were lying to you. Maybe it's all a trick."

"I don't think so."

"How can you be sure?"

"I took a picture of Edgar before I left."

"Really...?"

"I'll send it now."

"Okay."

Eric hung up and sent the picture to her. A moment later, she called him again.

"That's so weird. Is that where he was standing?"

"It was." The picture showed clearly the salvage yard and the dozens of rusted vehicles. But where Edgar had been walking away from him, there was nothing more than a faint blurring, as if the lens had been dirty.

"But that picture of Isabelle wasn't like that."

"Isabelle isn't dead. She's... Well... Something else."

"I guess so..."

"You don't really believe it."

"I do," she argued.

"Not really."

"I... Well... I don't know. It's hard. It's all so..."

"Weird. Yeah. I got that."

"I'm sorry. It's hard. But I don't *not* believe you. I know you're not lying to me."

"Well that's a start."

"I just..."

"I know. The alternatives aren't very appealing. Either I'm telling you the absolute truth and it's going against everything you've ever believed possible, or it's all a lie, in which case either I'm completely insane and making this all up as I go, or somebody's totally screwing with my head. Believe me, I've considered the possibilities."

"I don't think you're crazy."

"That's good."

"I just wish you were home already."

"Me too. But it looks like I've got one more stop to make."

"The cathedral."

"Yeah. It's up ahead somewhere. And I'm sure I'll be losing my connection soon."

Looking around, he realized that the landscape was already changing. The brush was thinning out, the grass beneath his feet quickly thinning to bare earth. The trees were receding, the terrain growing rocky again.

"I'm going to have to go. I doubt you'll hear from me again before I get to the cathedral."

"I'm scared," she confessed, finally letting out the words that she'd been bottling up all day.

"I know. Me too. But there's literally no way back." He glanced over his shoulder and realized that the brush he'd just pushed through was far less overgrown. The path that lay behind him was not the same path he'd just walked. Like Edgar told him, this was a one-way road.

"Please be careful," Karen begged. Her voice crackled. The connection was nearly gone.

"I will. I promise. Now I've got to go."

She said something else, but her voice was lost in static. He did not dare try to back up to find the signal again. Instead, he just said, "Bye Karen," and hung up the phone.

Before him, an earthen path wound through the familiar rocky terrain of the fissure. The trees thinned away until there were none standing before him and he was climbing a steep hill in a mostly barren landscape.

He remembered climbing this hill in his dream. He was afraid. His mind was cloudy. His mangled hand throbbed ceaselessly.

He still couldn't remember what waited beyond the crest of the hill, but there was a sick dread creeping up from the depths of his gut.

His cell phone rang.

That could only be Isabelle.

"The cathedral is just on the other side of that hill," she warned him. "You're almost there."

"Can you see everything I see?"

"Not *see* it, exactly. I just know it's there. I can feel what you feel. And right now you feel like you're walking into the gates of hell."

Eric had to admit that her ability to read his feelings was dead-accurate. The gates of hell made a perfectly adequate description.

"I just wanted you to know that I'm with you. And I'll stay with you. No matter what."

Eric smiled. "Thanks, Isabelle. That *does* make it feel a little better."

"I know," she replied. "I can tell."

"In my dream, I was almost killed back in that canyon."

"You were. You lost most of your hand."

"I did. But in the dream, I arrived before the foggy man. He wasn't here. I never had to run from his golems. I didn't get my shoulder torn up on the roof of Altrusk's house."

"That's right."

"I also never found *you*."

"I'm glad you didn't come two days ago."

"Me too."

Eric was halfway up the hill now. Soon he would have his first look at the cathedral. He hoped the sight alone wasn't going to be enough to kill him, but after all he'd been through, he wouldn't be a damned bit surprised.

"Listen," Isabelle said. "I know you're scared, and I know you're not sure you can do this, and you're right to not feel confident. This fissure…it's really messed up. The other world, the one that's smashed up against ours, it's a bad place. It's the worst kind of nightmare you can imagine. And whatever you find in there, it's probably going to be even worse."

"You think so?"

"I do. The fissure is concentrated there. The two worlds are so smashed together that it pervades reality. It takes the bad from that world and it magnifies it."

"Sounds like a blast." Eric was breathing harder now. He was growing tired. This hill was steeper than it looked.

"And the foggy man will be there somewhere, too. He'll be waiting for you. You need to be careful of him."

"No kidding."

"Seriously, Eric. He's bad news."

Eric stopped walking. "Did you figure something out about him?"

"No. Not exactly. I felt something back at the factory. Something disturbing. It took a while for me to figure out what it was. But now I think I get it. It's not *him* I was feeling. *He's* not what you have to fear. He's no devil. But the people he works for… I can't really explain it, but there's something terribly *wrong* about them. And he's afraid of them. He's going to be desperate not to fail them."

Moving forward again, Eric said. "Is he already in the cathedral?"

"I don't know for sure. But I *am* sure he's nearby. You need to be very careful."

"Believe me, I intend to be."

"Good."

"But can I really hope to beat something as bad as that?"

"There's always hope. And I've realized something since I got away from Altrusk."

"What's that?"

"I've realized there's a thread of order in the universe, a thread that connects us all, and one that's way too intricate to be there by accident. We're not alone. And I really don't think you're here just to die."

"I sure hope not."

"Do more than just hope, Eric. *Believe*. I need you to look back on all that's happened today. Every detail. You have to realize that there's more to all this than a bunch of creepy ghosts and a wonky dream. There's a reason you're here today and not two days ago. I'm part of that reason. That cat was part of that reason. The foggy man is also part of that reason. I think it's the same reason *you're* the person who had the dream and not some Olympic athlete or super-genius."

"Thanks, Isabelle. You're right. I have to believe I'm not just here to die."

"Don't forget it. Not even if it all seems lost."

"I won't. I promise."

"Good."

Eric approached the top of the hill. He felt so tired. It was as if he'd just hauled himself up the side of an enormous mountain.

"You helped me escape from Altrusk, Eric."

"It was you who helped *me* escape."

"But I'd still be there if I hadn't met you. You saved me. And I can never repay you for that. I…" She trailed off, the words lost before they crossed her lips.

"I know. And I promise you, I won't go down without giving everything I have."

"You'd better not."

"I swear."

"Good."

Eric reached the crest of the hill and surveyed the land before him.

"You've seen it…"

"It's…"

"Apocalyptically terrifying."

That was about as perfectly as he could have ever described it. Before him lay what looked like a lifeless crater at least four miles across. At the very center was the cathedral. He'd expected some kind of grand architecture, towering spires, a gothic monolith, perhaps. Instead, it was nothing more than an enormous hole in the ground.

"This is where I let you go," said Isabelle. "Don't forget what I said."

Eric was staring into the black abyss at the center of the barren crater with his mouth agape. Now, at Isabelle's words, he drew himself up. She was right. He didn't come all this way to die. "Thank you," he said.

"You're welcome."

He took a deep breath.

"Bye," said Isabelle.

And then Eric stood all alone.

Chapter Twenty-Eight

Eric made his way down the slope of the crater. No plants grew here. The earth lay crushed beneath his feet, the soil barren. It was no explosion that formed this crater, nor any falling celestial object. The earth had not been forced into this shape in an instant, but instead over billions of years. The weight of two worlds pushed down on him, literally driving him against the ground so that every step was a labor. Even the air here felt heavy.

Inside that hole at the crater's center was the point where the two worlds met. A singularity, the denizens of the fissure had called it. This was what happened where worlds collided. He could actually feel the pressure against his skin.

No creatures roamed the crater and Eric did not blame them for keeping their distance. It was uncomfortable here. His ears felt as if they were about to pop. He couldn't quite catch his breath.

There was also no sign of the foggy man. Not since he came across the carcass of the floppy-eared cat had he seen any evidence of the mysterious figure shrouded in nothingness. He hadn't left any more traps.

It didn't make sense. The foggy man had almost a full-day's head-start. He clearly had nothing to fear from the creatures in the fissure. Why, then, had he not simply come straight here to the cathedral? Why go to all the trouble of leaving those golems? Why reveal himself the way he did at the church? And why go to all the trouble of ambushing him at the factory, only to toss him back out onto the path?

What was his plan?

Feeling as if he suddenly weighed as much as a full-grown horse, Eric made his way slowly across the rocky floor of the crater to the stadium-sized hole at its center. Even as he approached the rim of that mysterious abyss, he expected something more. Surely a structure of some sort stood waiting for him inside the hole. Or perhaps he would find that the hole itself was a cathedral, with an ornate stairwell winding downward among marble columns and gorgeous glass lamps. But as he peered over the edge, he found nothing but shadows and gloom.

Even Father Billy's dilapidated old church was more of a cathedral than this. How did the word "cathedral" ever even come to mind with this place? To Eric, it seemed like the exact opposite of a cathedral. It was as if he were gazing into one of the deepest and darkest pits of hell.

Several sets of wooden steps led down to a walkway that circled the rim of the hole and gave access to two questionable-looking staircases that descended along the inner walls on opposite sides.

Eric walked carefully down the steps, half-expecting to fall under the burden of the crater's strange gravity. He crept gingerly to the aging railing and peered down into the darkness below.

It was like a bottomless pit. Even with the sun still shining overhead, the light only reached into the hole a short distance. The rest was utter blackness.

There was such a wrongness about this place that Eric had to steel himself against the urge to turn and run away. Surely whatever madness the dream would plunge him into would not be nearly as bad as whatever awaited him down there.

That heaviness was even stronger here. He could feel it crushing down on him as he peered down, threatening to push him into the abyss.

He had no idea where he was going to find the courage for this.

"Frightful, isn't it?"

Eric jumped and turned. There, standing at the railing only a few feet away, peering down into the same blackness, was the foggy man.

But he wasn't foggy now.

He was just a man.

Eric was certain there was no one here when he approached. There was literally nowhere to hide.

"You."

"Me," the stranger admitted. Without his mysterious shroud of invisible fog, there wasn't much about him that was even remotely frightening. He wasn't very big. In fact, he was rather scrawny in his dark jeans and black tee shirt. And he was barely more than a child, at most only twenty-one, with tousled black hair falling over a round and youthful face.

He turned away from Eric and strolled along the railing, still staring down into the darkness below them. "Fascinating. I've been to a lot of strange places, but this is definitely the most intense. Can you feel it?"

Eric remained silent. He didn't have to ask what he was talking about. He *could* feel it. There was a strange energy about this place. It was more than just the heaviness. He couldn't quite describe it.

"It's terrifying, isn't it?"

Still, Eric did not reply. But he did agree. This place *was* terrifying.

The young stranger stopped walking and placed both hands on the rail. "What could be down there?"

That was the question of the day, wasn't it? What was hidden at the bottom of this hole? What could possibly be worth all this trouble? Eric wondered that himself. He also wondered if the answer was remotely worth the very likely mortal cost of finding out.

"There's more than one fissure leading away from here, you know. Another one stretches out over Lake Superior. Another into Canada. At least two run west from here. There are other singularities, too, each with its own fissures snaking off it. There are places like this all over the world. But only *this* fissure is so well-defined that you can use it to travel all the way to its singularity."

Now he turned to Eric, his intense eyes fixed on him. "Why is that?"

Sensing that his time for remaining quiet was over, Eric replied, "I wouldn't know."

The no-longer-foggy man stared at him with those piercing blue eyes, studying him, considering.

Eric stared back. He wasn't sure what this mysterious person wanted him to say, but he had no intention of playing along. This was, after all, the man who left three monsters to kill him and then clubbed him over the head and threw him out a loading dock door. He would have liked to walk over there and knock the stupid kid on his pompous ass…but of course that brought him back to those three monsters. Punching anyone who could do such a thing simply seemed like a very dumb idea.

Finally, the young stranger turned and looked down into the darkness below them again, as if deciding that Eric really didn't have an answer for him. "I've never come across anything like this place before. It's wrong. It scares me."

"It's a scary place," Eric reasoned.

"I know about scary places. I've been to a lot of them. Just a few months ago I was in Mexico. There are these caves there…" He trailed off and stared down into that darkness for a moment, his eyes distant, distracted, haunted. Then he blinked it away and smiled at him. "Four men went insane and ate their own hands."

Eric couldn't make himself hide his revulsion. He didn't know what was worse, the idea of men devouring their own hands or the fact that this psychopath could relate such a thing with a smile on his face.

But perhaps the smile was nothing more than a mask. Perhaps that haunted look that had passed over his eyes a moment before had revealed some shred of his humanity.

He hoped so, at least.

"But this…" The man gazed down into the darkness again. "This feels so wrong… No matter where I am, the wrongness of this place doesn't go away."

Eric had no idea what this meant, but he didn't bother saying so.

"My tricks don't work here. Why?"

Eric actually glanced around, expecting to find someone else here with them. But they were alone. The question was obviously for him. "What?"

There was no smile this time when the stranger turned his eyes on him. He glared. "I can't shift here. Why can't I shift here?"

"Why would I know that?"

"Don't play games with me."

"I'm not playing games," Eric replied calmly. "I don't have a clue what you're talking about. I don't even know what you mean by 'shift.'"

For a moment, the young man continued to glare at him silently. He seemed to be trying to decide if he was being lied to, but Eric had no idea why this person would think he had any answers for him.

"Who do you work for?"

Eric stared back at him. "What?"

"Answer me."

"Creek Bend High School."

This seemed to catch him off guard. "What?"

"I'm an English teacher."

"I told you not to play games with me."

"And I told you I'm not playing games. Just who do you *think* I am?"

"I don't know. FBI maybe."

"FBI…? Really?"

"Maybe."

Eric chuckled. "Right. I'd make a *great* FBI agent, wouldn't I? Stumbling around here like an idiot, nearly getting myself killed. *Repeatedly.* Cursing at that ape-thing that was throwing rocks at me back at the lake. That was *very* professional. Even better, I should join the CIA. Become a secret agent."

The foggy man, still missing his fogginess, considered him for another moment.

Eric considered him back. Did this guy actually think he was some kind of government agent? It seemed ridiculous that anyone could mistake someone like him for something so grand.

"You weren't carrying a gun at the factory," the stranger recalled. "Or a badge."

"I don't sound like a very responsible federal agent. And while we're on the subject, let's talk about you hitting me over the head back there, why don't we?"

"I want to know who you are."

Apparently, Foggy didn't care to discuss that matter at the moment.

"I'd rather talk about who *you* are."

"Answer me."

"I don't *have* any answers," growled Eric, beginning to lose his patience.

The young man stared at him, apparently still trying to decide if he was playing dumb or legitimately stupid.

"How do you do it, anyway? How do you make the golems?"

Again, the stranger lowered his face and stared down into the darkness. Eric didn't think he would answer, but like so many other times today, he was wrong. "I don't know, honestly. I just can. I find a container. A box, a closet, the trunk of a car, anything. And then I... I just...*funnel* some part of myself into it."

"A part of *yourself*?"

"It's difficult to explain. It's like a kind of energy deep inside me." He glanced up from the empty abyss beneath them and met Eric's eyes as he said, "I'm not sure...but I think it might be my soul."

"Your soul...?"

"I'm not sure," he said again, as if afraid that the man he'd three times tried to kill might think he was bugshit crazy for saying such a thing.

Now it was Eric's turn to gaze down into the darkness and ponder. His soul? Really? He could hardly deny the possibility that a man could utilize his own soul to make monsters, certainly not when he'd already been attacked by three such beasts in only a few short hours. But there was something profoundly unsettling about using one's own soul to create such foul abominations.

The man went on: "I funnel that energy out and into something...*incredible*. And I make it live. That's a grossly simplified description, but it's as good as I can explain it. They don't make words for what I do. Not in any language."

Eric had no doubt. "And the fog?"

"Fog?"

"That half-disappearing thing... Where you look like you're standing in an invisible fog."

"Huh. Never heard it described like that before."

"So how do you do it?"

"I shift back and forth through physical space."

"How does that work, exactly?"

"It's complicated."

"I'm sure it is."

"You have to grasp the concept that there are things beyond our world."

"I really don't think that's going to be a problem for me today."

The foggy man shrugged and said, "Reality is layered. It's a spectrum. The world exists across most of this spectrum, but most life on earth only exists within a small portion of it. Humans, in particular, only exist within a narrow band of it. I can slide along that spectrum, out of that narrow band, effectively disappearing from this world altogether. Or I can shift to the very edge of that band and only *partially* fade away, if I choose. You wouldn't think only partially leaving this plane of existence would be useful, but it turns out it scares the shit out of people."

"It *is* exceptionally frightening to see."

The man grinned. He seemed quite proud of himself.

"So then, can you move between these two worlds without using the fissure?"

"No. The two worlds here are completely separate. All the worlds in all the fissures are. They each have their own spectrums. I can shift along the spectrum in any world, but I can't just jump between worlds. That's pure science fiction."

"Right. What was I thinking?"

Again, he gazed down into the abyss. "But it doesn't matter in this place. Nothing works here. And I don't know why."

"Neither do I."

"I don't believe you."

"Believe what you want. I don't know why you can't work your voodoo here. I could *guess* it's because the singularity screws everything up."

The foggy man stood at the railing, contemplating this in silence.

Eric stared at him. "Have you tried going down there yet?"

"No."

"Why not?"

"Because I'm afraid."

"You? Afraid? Maker of golems? Traveler of strange worlds?"

"I didn't survive this long, doing this job, by being stupid. I can tell when things don't add up. And this place is seriously *wrong*."

"So you work for *them*, then? The people Father Billy told me about?"

The man looked up at him, surprised. "'Father Billy?' *Really*?" He laughed. "That's a bit of a stretch. But yeah. *Them*."

"Bad people."

"Good, bad, what's the difference? They pay good. It's a fun job. Speaking of fun, wait until I tell *them* I found William Lonneskey hiding out in an old church out here."

Eric glared at him. "Just leave him out of it."

But the young man ignored him. "That should be interesting."

"What's your game?" Eric asked, eager to move off the subject of Father Billy. "What are you trying to accomplish? You try three times to kill me and then at the factory you just sucker-punch me and leave? Now you want to have a heart-to-heart? You beat me here. You had almost a whole day's head start. Why didn't you just take whatever's down there and leave before I even arrived?"

"I already told you, it's wrong down there."

"It's been wrong everywhere I've been today!"

"It's *extra* wrong down there. I arrived yesterday evening and stood right here, looking down into that darkness. Immediately, I knew I couldn't just go down there. All my tricks failed me. I couldn't sense anything. It was like looking into absolute nothingness. I climbed back up into the crater, where my tricks still worked, and I looked for somewhere in the spectrum where this place was safe, but no matter where I went, it was always the same. It was *death*."

If this man could do his "shifting" thing in the crater, then that explained why Eric never saw him as he approached. He was likely shifted as he approached the cathedral. The better to catch him off guard.

"So how did I fit into it all? How did you even know I was coming?"

"I didn't. I have a few rules that keep me alive in my line of work. The first one is always watch your back. Jobs like these, I leave golems covering my trail, just in case someone decides to follow me. When one of them is disturbed, I know about it immediately. They're a part of me, as I've said. I also instantly know the results of those confrontations. I know when my golem does its job and I know when someone manages to get away. So I knew you were following me. I knew you managed to beat the first two golems. But then you never found the third one that I left at that village."

"Village?"

"I went back and found out you took a little detour. Visited Lonneskey at that church instead."

The village must have been what he missed. He'd recalled a building or two, but because he circled so far around it, that part of the dream never recurred to him in enough detail to reveal what he'd found there. Now he knew.

"I saw you there, saw who you were with. I don't know what business you were up to. I didn't care. I just needed you both gone. So I left another golem. And I made sure you saw me leave it."

"I didn't have any 'business' with Father Billy. I left the path because I was chased by a bunch of corn creeps. He was a good enough man to not let me die on the lawn of his church."

"Lonneskey is hardly a good man."

"People change."

"No. They don't."

"How did you get back to us if you were already here? Some of these paths are one-way. It's impossible to go backward."

"The fissures create disturbances in the spectrums. I can feel them. I can see the paths. All of them. Including the ones that lead backward."

"Convenient."

"It is."

"So then what was up with the factory?"

"After I left that golem at the church, I realized something."

"What's that?"

"I realized that it probably wasn't a coincidence that you were here. I realized you were probably looking for whatever's hidden here. That's also when I realized that I might need you. Lucky for me, you managed to survive a third golem. But then I had to keep you alive long enough to meet you here. The problem with that was that I left a particularly nasty golem in the factory."

So there *was* another golem at the factory.

"My second rule is always remain flexible. I had to distract you so you wouldn't stumble across the golem and finally get yourself killed just when I needed you."

"The residuals."

"Residuals? Yeah. I suppose so. I can't really take credit for that trick. I learned that one from an old friend. Just before I killed him."

"Your mother must be so proud. So you put the residuals there to hide the golem from me?"

"That, and to spy on you. I wanted to know what was so special about you, how it was that you defeated three of my golems. I saw you talking to someone... But after knocking you out, I couldn't make that device work. It looked like an ordinary, cheap phone."

It figured that someone would knock him over the head just to get a closer look at his stupid phone. "It *is* an ordinary, cheap phone."

"You weren't using it like a phone. You were talking to someone. They were feeding you information."

That's right... He was talking to Isabelle. And he wasn't simply talking on his phone. He'd been talking *to* it. Isabelle was sending him text messages, warning him that something seemed off in there. And he hadn't sent any texts back to her because she didn't need him to. She could get into his thoughts. To someone who didn't know about Isabelle, it would seem that his device was communicating with him independently and despite the lack of a signal.

But this man had already threatened Father Billy's life. He had no intention of letting him know about Isabelle.

"*Someone* was talking to you," the foggy man insisted.

"Yes," admitted Eric. "The crew of the Enterprise. They'll be beaming me up shortly."

"I don't care for sarcasm."

"I don't care for pompous, murderous little pricks."

The young man shrugged. "Fine. I dragged you safely around the office where I hid the golem and I sent you on your way. Even gave you your phone back. Didn't want to risk you not making it here for our little talk."

"You're a real saint."

"I also took care of that cat for you. I'll bet that could've ruined your day."

"You have no idea."

"What?"

"Nothing."

Eric met the young man's stony gaze. For a moment, they both remained silent.

This man didn't seem to know anything about his dream, or about the old folks who had helped him along the way. He was under the impression that he must be some kind of government agent, specifically sent to either confront him or beat him to the prize in the cathedral. And his peculiar use of the cell phone only reinforced that fantasy. It was clear that he didn't trust him, but the irony was that he would never in a million years believe the truth.

And if he was really lucky, that would give him just a sliver of an advantage.

Finally, Eric asked, "So what now?"

"Now, we're going to go down there. And you're going to lead the way."

"That's not going to happen."

"Isn't it?"

"No. I've heard enough. There's nothing scary about you. You're just a rotten kid who needs his ass kicked real good. I'm not playing your game. You can go to hell."

The foggy man, no longer foggy at all, barely even a man, pulled a handgun from under the back of his tee shirt and pointed it at Eric, instantly regaining his full attention. "One more rule: I never rely solely on my talents."

Eric stared into the barrel of the gun. "How prudent of you."

Chapter Twenty-Nine

The foggy man's pistol pointed at his back and an ominous darkness waiting below, Eric descended the wooden stairs into the black depths of the cathedral.

Nothing about this situation gave him a good feeling. All things considered, the gun was probably the least of his worries at this point. (But it still pissed him off to think that the little bastard had so completely taken control of the situation.)

He promised Isabelle he would be careful, yet here he was, in a very vulnerable position, shepherded into this nightmare hole in the ground at gunpoint, his very fate in the hands of the enemy and his odds of making it out alive dwindling with each passing second.

He was ashamed to admit that he had let his guard down a little. Discovering that the foggy man was no longer foggy, that he no longer had his ghostly tricks at his disposal, made him careless.

Karen would be so disappointed in him.

The sun still shined overhead. Eric could still feel it on the sunburned skin of his arms, neck and face. Yet there was also that peculiar chill in the air, the cold from that other world as it crushed down on him. The duality of the fissure was distinctly noticeable here. He felt as if he could feel both worlds at once, their opposing forces at work on him, the hot and the cold, the light and the dark.

He felt as if he were growing heavier with each step. His ears popped. His eyes felt dry and heavy, like they did when he rose with too little sleep. His head ached. His feet hurt.

Miserable, Eric descended deeper and deeper into the darkness.

He looked up at the sky, expecting to find that it had grown black, but in spite of the gloom that was quickly enveloping him, it remained clear and blue.

Lowering his eyes to the steps before him, Eric found that the cathedral's rock wall had inexplicably turned into huge stone columns that appeared to run all the way up to the rim of the hole, yet there had been no such columns there when he stood at the top looking down. The walls had been nothing but rough stone.

And he found himself not entirely surprised by this transformation. The columns were familiar. They had been in his dream. As he carefully descended the steps, his thoughts muddled in a fog of pain and morphine, he had marveled at these same massive columns, his weary mind struggling to recall whether they had been here all along.

Soon the gloom thickened, his sight reduced to a few yards and then only a few feet, a few inches…

Eric stepped carefully, willing himself not to stumble beneath his inexplicably increasing weight.

He could no longer see anything in front of or below him. All he could see was the sky above, still blue and bright, but utterly unaffecting the shadows of the cathedral. He gazed up into that blueness, but had to lower his eyes. It was unnervingly alien to see something like this. His mind couldn't quite wrap itself around the concept. He felt like he would go mad if he kept trying.

But navigating these steps in the dark was almost as unnerving. He kept expecting the steps to end without warning and spill him screaming into the black emptiness beneath him.

He considered turning around and making a move for the gun now that the light had gone, but he didn't quite dare risk it. He couldn't be sure the young man didn't possess unnatural night vision in addition to spectrum-shifting and golem-conjuring.

Besides, he would probably only end up getting himself shot as he fumbled awkwardly in the dark. He was hardly James Bond. The foggy man, in his curious line of dark work, would almost certainly have the advantage over him in any confrontation.

The foggy man... He'd grown tired of that. Over his shoulder, he asked, "Do you have a name?"

"Yes."

"You going to share it with the rest of the class?"

"Wasn't planning on it."

Eric shrugged and faced forward again. Foggy it was, then. "So what is it we're looking for down here?"

"No idea," replied Foggy. "You tell me."

"How the hell should I know? You're the agent of darkness. Don't you know what you came here for?"

"Nope."

"What did your bosses tell you to find?"

"I was just told to find what's here and bring it back."

"But they didn't tell you what it is?"

"They didn't say. I didn't ask."

Eric recalled Father Billy telling him that his old bosses paid him to not ask questions. It seemed that Foggy here worked under the same contract. "Sounds like information I'd demand to have before I took a job like this."

"You don't *demand* anything from the people I work for."

"Who *are* the people you work for?"

"I don't know, exactly."

"You don't know who you work for?"

Foggy fell silent.

"Right. If you say so."

"It's a need-to-know kind of thing."

Just like Father Billy said. "And you don't need to know. It's only your ass on the line."

"Just shut up and keep walking."

Clearly, Eric had found a touchy spot. If he had to hazard a guess, he'd say that Foggy wasn't too happy about the lack of information he was given. But he was far too stubborn to admit that he was nothing more than someone's loyal little, waggily-tailed lapdog.

He didn't push the subject. He had no doubt that Foggy would kill him if he grew tired of his mouth, but he was beginning to agree with Isabelle. The people this man worked for were bad. It was unsettling to know that there was an organization like this out there somewhere.

Although it would tickle the hell out of the conspiracy theorists, he imagined.

Abruptly, the light began to return. The sky above never changed, but suddenly the sun's rays were able to reach them again. Eric's visibility grew from a few inches to a few feet to a few yards. But with the visibility came unsettling things.

The columns were gone again. Only smooth bedrock covered the wall. But far more disturbing than that was the fact that the wall had inexplicably changed sides. It was now on their right, and they were spiraling down into the darkness counter-clockwise, in the opposite direction, with no memory of having turned around.

Eric stopped, forgetting about the gun at his back. "Are you seeing this?"

"I am."

"Good. Just checking."

"Keep going."

"You do realize that if you kill me you'll be all alone down here, right?"

"If I have to take my chances, I will."

"Suit yourself." Clearly, he wasn't going to reason his way out of this.

The cathedral was silent but for the sounds of their footfalls on the steps, and even that noise was eerily hushed within these walls. The wood did not creak, despite its obvious age, and there had been no echoing of their voices when they spoke.

Nothing down here seemed to be working quite like it should.

Darkness fell again.

Darkness went away.

Things changed.

Openings appeared in the walls here and there and Eric peered into great, cavernous chambers where shadowy things seemed to stir in the stillness. Odd shuffling noises rose from beneath the steps. Sometimes strange lights seemed to flicker through the darkness at the far side of the hole.

The wall was on their left again. Then it was on the right and Eric was sure he'd only imagined that it had ever been on the left. Without being aware of exactly when the steps ended, he was walking on a flat surface, stumbling blindly through the darkness.

Were they at the bottom already?

Had only a few minutes passed? Or had it already been a few hours?

The sky above remained blue and calm.

Were the walls moaning at him?

Was that a face peering at him from the gloom?

Pressing his hands to his eyes, Eric tried to force himself to focus. Something was terribly wrong here. Nothing made sense. It felt like his *mind* was breaking.

The dream was broken here. Everything came back to him in jumbled pieces and out of order, compounding the confusion. He couldn't recall if he saw something scurrying past his feet or merely heard it. And that shape that scuttled overhead… Was that from the dream? Or did he see it just a moment ago? And that scream? Was it real or imaginary? Now or then? Here or there?

He was beginning to remember why the dream had always filled him with such dread.

The light went and came without any warning or reason.

"Are you feeling this too?" he asked as the shadows lifted and revealed a forest of stone columns rising up into the sky.

But Foggy did not answer.

320

"Where are we? What's going on?"

When silence met him again, Eric turned to face his unwanted companion, only to find that he was utterly alone.

Where had he gone? How *long* had he been gone? How long had he been down here?

Nothing made sense.

He turned around, his eyes rising up to the towering columns.

What was going on?

He continued down the stairs, descending several of the steps before thinking to wonder where these stairs came from and when, exactly, he began this descent. But he immediately began to wonder if he'd ever *stopped* descending the stairs, if he had only imagined walking on solid, horizontal ground among those massive columns.

It was becoming difficult to keep up with where he was. The cathedral was doing something to his mind. The two worlds… They overlapped. Two realities. Trying to occupy this one space. The distortions grew stronger as he neared the singularity. He couldn't tell one from the other, couldn't even distinguish reality from his dream.

When he looked back, however, the foggy man was still gone.

He was still alone.

The bizarreness of the cathedral must have allowed them to get separated.

Apparently, Foggy's skills were no match for the otherworldly nature of the cathedral. He'd failed to keep track of his prisoner.

Eric knew that he should take advantage of this. This was his opportunity to beat the foggy man to the prize. But he still had no idea what he was doing. And it was hard to ignore the fact that there was now a likely pissed off psychopath running around down here with a gun.

He peered up into the blue sky that hung over him. Night had not fallen up there, but perhaps night never fell up there. It would not surprise him. Nothing here would surprise him. This place defied all manner of logic. But there remained a few certainties. The first of these was that there was no way back from here.

He was sure that if he turned around and tried to make his way back out, he would find himself turned back again and again, hopelessly forced to continue only downward, swallowed whole by this unearthly pit.

Closing his eyes, he made himself breathe. He tried to focus. It was hard. The morphine blurred his thoughts, dulled his senses even as it dulled the pain.

No. The morphine wasn't real. That was the dream.

It was becoming so hard to keep the two apart in his weary mind.

Noises behind him. He turned to look. But darkness had fallen over him again.

Somewhere far above him, he heard a scream.

Or was it a laugh?

Or was it only a memory from the dream?

God, it was so hard to tell anymore.

Never in his life had he ever been this afraid.

Turning back to the stairs before him, he tried to focus on taking one step at a time.

The light came back, revealing that the steps had turned to stone. It also revealed a vast, gaping cavern opening to his right. The floor of that cavern was alive with crawling things.

He closed his eyes and took one step after another.

He was so tired. He felt so heavy.

And the throbbing pain in his hand wouldn't stop.

Was that the sound of someone yelling? The foggy man, perhaps? Calling out for help? Lost in this hole? Lost in his head?

The stairs were gone again. Eric walked on solid ground once more, with no memory of when they ended. The columns were gone again as well. Only darkness surrounded him. Darkness, and that queer blue sky above.

He stared at his hand. So small, despite all those bandages. So much of it gone.

What was he going to do?

He closed his eyes.

He walked.

The weight of two worlds pressed down on him, threatening to crush him before he could reach whatever it was he was here to find.

Was he going to die here?

What was he even doing here? He tried to remember. The dream. All those miles in the PT Cruiser. Annette's house. The barn. The monster in the wardrobe.

Why didn't he just leave? What was he thinking?

The morphine was wearing off.

He couldn't take much more of this pain.

His shoulder hurt. The resort monster.

Altrusk...

Isabelle...

Isabelle. His hand went to his pocket. He felt the weight of the phone at his hip.

"I just wanted you to know that I'm with you," she told him as he approached the cathedral. "And I'll stay with you. No matter what." Her words. So clear in his mind. She made him promise not to give up. She made him promise to *believe*. Even when all seemed lost.

Now seemed a fitting time to heed her wise words.

He realized that he was trembling and closed his eyes.

He made himself breathe.

He was on the stairs again. The blue sky hung overhead, a reminder that he had not, in fact, descended all the way into the darkest pits of hell.

There was a light below him.

He was finally nearing the bottom of the cathedral.

Again he looked at his hand. The bandages were gone. It was intact. It had always been intact. Only in the dream had he lost it. The dream was infringing on reality as he struggled to separate the merged realities surrounding the singularity. After all, what was the dream but an alternate reality centered on him? Two physical realities colliding with two alternate time frames. It was no wonder he couldn't seem to comprehend what was going on.

Darkness fell one last time and Eric made his way to the bottom of the steps.

There, in an inky darkness, a brightly lit doorway stood before him.

Chapter Thirty

Squinting into the light, Eric stepped through the doorway and found himself in a sunlit room at the very bottom of the cathedral.

More than ever, he could feel the weight of the two worlds crushing down on him. He felt the air pressing against his skin, as if he were deep under water. His ears hurt. His eyes ached. His head throbbed. Even breathing was difficult. Claustrophobia washed over him, though the room was large and mostly empty. There wasn't even a ceiling. Above him, the entire cathedral towered overhead with the blue sky shining down on him.

Even though the sun could not be seen from this far down, and the rest of the cathedral had been gloomy at best and more often pitch black, this room remained bright and sunny somehow. Though darkness hung between the sky and this chamber, and there were no lights inside the room, it felt as if the sun were directly overhead.

Looking up through both worlds into that slowly darkening blue sky high above, with the entire pit opening overhead, he finally understood why this place had been called a cathedral. The one constant here was heaven. It was difficult not to imagine that some god or another must be gazing down from that enormous, ever-present sky, watching over him.

The foggy man was still nowhere to be seen, but Eric did not possess enough optimism to make himself believe that he had seen the last of him. He would need to complete this task quickly.

The walls were smooth and featureless stone, broken only by the door through which he'd entered the room. In stark contrast, the floor was an intricate display of handmade tiles, laid out in a complicated spiraling pattern that swirled inward to a single, golden disk in the very center of the room. There was no furniture, no pedestal, no shrine, nothing at all fantastic within this room. The only feature besides the crafted floor was a single ledge, about four feet high, built into the wall around the perimeter of the chamber. On this ledge, scattered throughout the room, were eleven clay pots.

Edgar told him that he and the others were once compelled by a dream much like his to find a clay pot and carry it to the cathedral. Clearly one of these was that very pot.

But which one?

With time ticking away, Eric walked around the room, examining the eleven pots, trying to determine which one was the one he came all this way to find. He was sure that opening the wrong one would put a quick and disappointing end to this long day. Yet he had no idea how he was supposed to choose the correct one.

He found himself reminded of the third *Indiana Jones* movie, in which Harrison Ford found himself forced to choose the Holy Grail from a large display of various goblets. There were considerably fewer pots to choose from here, but picking a wrong one would likely be just as disastrous for him as it was for that movie's villain.

And he wasn't half as smart or suave as Indie.

Think...

There had to be something here to tell him which one was the right one.

They weren't identical. Not by any means. One was green. Another was considerably larger than the others. A third had a chipped rim. Two of them had odd patterns painted on them. A sixth was smaller than the rest. A seventh had a red ribbon tied around it. Another had a black lid. He studied each of them as he made his way around the room. Here was one that was tall and skinny and stopped with an old cork. The next looked dirty and crusty. The last one had a rope tied to it for a handle.

Which one?

He recalled the lake. The two boats. Karen's words of wisdom. There was always a way. He just had to find it.

Isabelle told him the same thing. She said she'd discovered a thread of order in the universe since escaping Altrusk.

He had to believe.

He promised he would believe.

He closed his eyes and tried to recall what Edgar told him. He said there were six of them who arrived in that hayfield. One died along the way. Ben. They carried a clay pot all the way to the cathedral and then the five survivors spent the rest of their lives in the fissure to ensure it stayed there.

That was all he said.

How was it, Eric suddenly wondered, that the five of them came here and survived to see another forty or fifty years? According to

Father Billy, everyone who entered the cathedral remained there, never to be seen again.

He couldn't think about that now. Time was still ticking. Eric circled the room again, looking at each pot, examining it, trying to remember something. There must be something somewhere…

Taylor told him how to stop the golems. But he never said anything helpful about the cathedral. Grant educated him on the importance of sticking to the path. Not one of them told him anything significant about the cathedral itself.

Annette hadn't told him much of anything at all. She was far too lost in her own grief to have been any real help.

Again, he circled the room.

The foggy man wouldn't stay lost forever. And he was probably going to be pissed about losing him.

He had to calm down. He had to think.

Father Billy had only told him to stay away from the cathedral. Isabelle only knew what the other people trapped in Altrusk's house knew. The gas station attendant revealed plenty, but none of it helped him determine which of these clay pots was the one delivered by Edgar and company nearly a century ago.

The answer had to be with the ghosts. They were the ones who brought it.

He tried to recall the dream, but he had only stood there in the dream much as he was now, staring at the pots, trying to decide which one he should open.

This was getting him nowhere.

And he desperately needed to hurry.

He closed his eyes and tried to clear his head.

At the same time, he recalled doing the same in his dream. He recalled thinking about everything that had happened to him. Every detail. Every conversation.

It was difficult to think down here. The pressure was distracting. He wanted to leave.

His mind kept turning back to Annette for some reason, but she was the one who told him the least about what he was doing here. She was too busy talking about her dead father and the husband she pretended wasn't also long dead and gone.

Was that a noise he heard outside the door? The sound of someone approaching?

No.

But he didn't have much longer.

Hurry!

Again, he circled the room, practically darting from one to the next.

Which one was it?

Was it the tall one? The green one? The black lid?

Come on!

The big one? The red ribbon?

Eric stopped, his breath momentarily stolen.

Suddenly it occurred to him...

Annette...

Something she said between telling him about her dead father and that it was a long way to the cathedral. He'd nearly forgotten. It seemed so unimportant at the time.

"I gave him a red ribbon before he went in. That's good luck. Did you know that?"

Eric stared at the clay pot with the red ribbon tied around it.

He recalled something else that Edgar told him as well. While talking about Annette's tragic state, he said, "She couldn't take losing someone again."

He thought Edgar had been referring to the father Annette told him about, but now he realized that there had been another tragedy in her life. There was a third man she'd loved and lost.

He wondered before why it was that Father Billy was so sure no one had ever entered the labyrinth and lived to tell about it when Edgar claimed to have gone there with five others and then lived to a ripe old age. Now he knew the answer.

Edgar never told him how Ben died.

And because he didn't care to think more than necessary about death on this journey, Eric hadn't asked.

But now he knew.

Only Ben entered the cathedral with the clay pot.

And he never came back out.

"I gave him a red ribbon before he went in. That's good luck."

He thought she was still talking about Ethan. But she was giving him the most important message of all. She didn't give the ribbon to Ethan before he went in the hospital. She gave it to *Ben*. Before he went in the *cathedral*.

And Ben left it tied around the clay pot.

His heart broke a little for Annette.

Yet he had no time to dwell on her tragedy.

He stared at the pot with the red ribbon. He was finally here. He was at the end of his journey. The secrets were at last about to be revealed to him.

He reached out and grasped the lid.

In his dream, he recalled doing the same thing. Dream Eric had taken longer to piece it all together, but he got it in the end. And now the final memories of that dream were coming back to him at last.

He hesitated. He closed his eyes. He made himself breathe.

He remembered lifting the lid…

And then he remembered his death.

Chapter Thirty-One

Eric let go of the lid as terrible images returned from the depths of his memories and filled his mind with unimaginable horrors.

The dream that had once been his guide became the worst kind of nightmare he had ever experienced. Something awful reached out of the pot. It seized his hand and raced up his arm. Agony shot up to his shoulder and neck to his head and then enveloped his whole body.

Within seconds, he was alive with relentless, searing pain from head to foot. It consumed him. The memory was so perfect that he could actually feel it. His flesh crackled. His nerves were on fire. It felt like his bones were melting.

But it was more than mere physical pain. He felt himself being torn apart emotionally and mentally. Terrible things, indescribable things, filled his brain, shredding his very sanity.

Screaming in unspeakable agony, his final thought had for some reason been, *Don't open the pot!*

And then he had awakened in his bed, where his story began so long ago.

"I'll take it from here."

Eric turned, his face still contorted with fear, and found the foggy man's gun aimed at his head again.

Time was up.

"Come on. Back away."

Eric stepped away from the awful clay pot, his hands out to his sides, in clear view. They were trembling.

"I don't know how you got away from me back there, and I don't know how you got here before me, but I do appreciate you solving the riddle of the pots for me."

Clearly, Foggy had misinterpreted the fear on his face. He didn't realize that it wasn't the gun that had frightened him.

Eric didn't enlighten him.

He circled around the psycho with the gun, trying to force himself to relax, to shake off the horrors he had seen, but he couldn't stop himself from trembling. He couldn't make his heart stop pounding.

This was why he had felt such dread as he recalled the dream. Somewhere, deep inside, he'd known all along how it ended.

Now standing between Eric and the clay pot, preventing him from making a last ditch grab for it, the Foggy man swung the gun and struck him across the side of the head.

Eric dropped to the floor, cursing and clutching his face.

He was getting really tired of this guy hitting him.

"So this is the one, is it?"

Eric glared up at him. "No. It's the green one."

"Sure it is."

"The tall one, then?"

"Shut up."

"If you say so."

"I was watching you. It was this one. You were sure of it. I could tell."

Eric stared up at him, studying him. "I just like the pretty ribbon."

Foggy grinned. "I kind of like you. You're fun."

"I try."

He must have been watching from the door. When he settled on the one with the red ribbon, it would have been obvious that he knew it was the one. But he mistook hesitation for fear. From his perspective, as he crept up behind his target, it must have seemed that Eric let go of the lid because he heard his approaching footsteps. The fear in his eyes when he looked back was probably the same fear people had regarded him with for years.

It was ironic, really, that it would be his arrogance that ultimately destroyed him.

The foggy man shook his head in a mock display of regret. "But you're just not useful anymore."

"You don't know that. I have a lot of talents."

"Sorry. Nothing personal."

"How could I possibly take it personally?"

"That's the right attitude."

Eric *really* didn't like this guy.

"Now let's see… Should I kill you before or after I see what's so interesting about this pot?"

Eric glanced past him at the clay pot with the red ribbon tied around it. The memory of his dream still shook him. He couldn't get the horrors out of his mind. He had actually dreamed his own death. Looking back at the foggy man, he said as calmly as he could manage,

"I'd say the least you could do is let a beaten old man see what he almost had."

Grinning, the man formerly known to Eric as the foggy man stepped up to the ledge next to the clay pot and placed his hand on the lid. "It's something really powerful, isn't it?"

"Yes," lied Eric. "If you're really smart, you'll take it and disappear with it instead of giving it to your bosses."

"Maybe I will." Grinning, the foggy man lifted the lid off the clay pot.

Eric turned away and stared at the floor, unable to watch as the man who had once struck fear into his heart cried out in pitiful, wailing shrieks of terror and anguish.

He wasn't proud to have let the man die. But he would have killed him. There was no question about that. If the boy'd had more brains than ego, he would've killed him immediately instead of making him watch as he took the prize.

And he was going to get Father Billy killed, too. Eric couldn't allow that.

Still, no one deserved to die like this.

It went on for a long time. A *terribly* long time. And it happened just as he remembered it happening to him in his dream.

After all he'd been through, the dream he was following had been leading him to failure. If he'd arrived two days ago, when everyone here told him he was supposed to, he would have died.

Instead, he now remained perfectly alive *and* in possession of both of his hands.

But he never found what he was sent for, which meant he may still have to relive that violent death every night in his dreams. Except now he would remember every agonizing detail.

It was no wonder they said it would drive him mad.

Even after the foggy man stopped screaming, Eric stared down at the floor, unwilling to look at the body of the man he'd essentially killed. As he did, he realized that there was an image of a hawk etched into the golden disk in the center of the floor.

He looked up at the slowly darkening sky. The funnel opened up from this one point in the floor. Even the tiles had been arranged so that they spiraled into it.

Grant told him it was a singularity, the *exact place* at which the two worlds met. A single point in space.

Right at the bottom of this hole.

Right in the middle of this floor.

Birds. They'd been everywhere today, in some way or another, like signs. The eagle over the barn door. The birdhouses at the farmhouse. The totem pole at the resort. The Canada goose on the factory's sign. Even the symbol on the hood of the Firebird at the salvage yard. And then there were the *real* birds. He'd been spooking them out of brush and trees all day. The hawks. The crows. The ducks in the lake. Even the freaky chickens back in the barn and that giant bird coasting over the swamp. He'd thought that he'd seen them in the dream because they'd been so prevalent along the fissure, but they were more than that. The birds had been pointing to his true goal all along.

He felt around the edges of the disk and found that it was loose.

It was here. Hidden in plain sight. The clay pots were only a distraction from the true prize.

He pulled out the metal disk and found a narrow hole beneath it, barely large enough to fit his hand into. There was a wooden stick of some sort inside. He gripped it by its end and pulled it out, revealing it to be a four-foot long, wooden staff.

As soon as it was free and in his hands, Eric knew what it was, who it belonged to, what it was used for.

In fact, he knew a great many things.

He knew *too much*.

He closed his eyes and cried out as fantastic things flooded into his unprepared mind. Awesome things. Terrible things. *Powerful* things. This new knowledge shook him even more violently than the memory of his dream death.

He tried to let go of the staff, but he couldn't.

He rose to his feet and tried to walk, but he stumbled.

The things he suddenly knew...

Such information that he could scarcely fathom it...

He opened his eyes wide and stared at the staff he now held in his hands.

The hands that once held it... Hands so strong... Hands that had known *God*...

And he wasn't the first to hold this staff since those ancient times. Others had possessed this secret as well. Eleven of them. The last was entombed in a clay urn and deposited in an ordinary hayfield in Illinois. Not the secret at all, like Edgar and the others had believed, but merely a return of the last sentry into this tomb.

That was why there were six of them. They were the pallbearers.

He also knew that the staff was no longer important. Its power was spent, the knowledge it contained passed into him. It was time to put it back in its resting place.

Eric returned the staff to its hole and replaced the gold disk over the top of it.

His body still twitching with the power of the revelations he'd been given, he stood up on shaking legs and turned toward the door.

He didn't look to see what became of the foggy man. He was gone. That was all that mattered. He had no need to see what became of the body. It was better not to know.

He would likely never know who the man was. He never shared his name. And Eric didn't care to know it. He wasn't anybody, just a thug, another monster in the road.

Father Billy was right, it turned out. There was no reason to know a dead man's name.

Still trembling, Eric walked through the door and began the long ascent up the cathedral stairs.

Chapter Thirty-Two

The way out of the cathedral was far more treacherous than the way in. An ordinary man would never have found his way through the hellish labyrinth of darkness and shadows. He would have wandered aimlessly until something in the darkness ended his journey for him. But he was no longer an ordinary man. He knew the way out now. He knew how the cathedral worked. And he made the journey without thinking about where he was going. He merely climbed, his poor, exhausted mind still struggling to grasp the awesome things the staff had shown him.

He barely remembered the ascent.

Soon, he found himself standing in the crater, looking around, trying to recall where he was supposed to go next. But there was nothing to recall. The dream was over. And no one had bothered telling him what to do next.

He couldn't return along the same path that brought him here, and he had no idea which way would take him back home.

He sat down on the crushed earth and stared up at the sky for a

Brian Harmon

while. The sun had fully set. The first of the stars had come out.

It was so peaceful.

He felt so incredibly small.

"Magnificent view out here."

Eric lowered his eyes and found himself looking at the gas station attendant. He was standing in front of him, staring up at the sky above. He tried to remember how long he'd been staring up, but he was sure it wasn't long enough for the little man to have made his way across the wide floor of the crater without him noticing.

"Nothing to spoil it out here. No lights. No pollution. Just you and the stars."

Eric stared at the little man. "Are *you* God?"

Without looking down from the sky, the gas station attendant said, "Me? No. Not exactly."

Not exactly? What did that mean?

"But I can answer the questions you have for Him."

"Can you?"

The little man looked at him now. "Sure. Let's start with what happened down there, shall we?"

Eric stared at him. He felt so sluggish. He was like a computer that had used up all its memory. He nodded. "I found the staff. It... Showed me things..."

"It imparted onto you some very specific knowledge."

"That's what I said..." Eric replied drunkenly.

The little man laughed softly. His smile was so kind, so welcoming. And his eyes remained compassionate. "Some things are too important to ever be fully forgotten, but too dangerous to leave commonly known."

Eric thought about this for a moment, and then nodded. "This would definitely qualify."

"Definitely. These things you know...only one man was chosen to remember while all others were allowed to forget. When that man died, the knowledge lived on, stored in the living wood of that staff, waiting for another to come along and take the knowledge once more. In times when darkness closes in on this knowledge, a new man is chosen to take the information from the staff, leaving the staff itself empty in its cradle. Long after the danger has passed, and when the new caretaker passes on, the information returns automatically to the staff, waiting for the next to find it."

"So I'm the caretaker?"

"The latest in a long line."

"But you said the cathedral kills everyone who enters it."

"No. Technically, *you* said that Father Billy told you that I said the cathedral will claim anyone who comes looking for its secrets. *I* told you that I did, indeed, say something like that."

"So... How is that different?"

"The cathedral *does* claim all those who come looking for its secrets. But it doesn't kill those who deserve them. Eleven men have emerged just like you did. And they all returned in the end."

"Inside the clay pots."

"Exactly. To this day, they still protect their secret."

"So when I die, I'll go back there?"

"Only in body. The cathedral won't keep your spirit. I promise you that."

This was a relief. He *had* feared that he was now damned to a purgatory of hanging out on a shelf at the bottom of a deep hole somewhere in Minnesota for the rest of eternity, like a bored genie.

"You said before that there were two objects of interest. Is there another staff?"

"Not a staff, but yes, another object, another secret. If a man were to possess both, he would become very powerful."

"But with just one?"

"You are only blessed."

"Don't feel blessed. Feel like my head's going to explode. How can I be expected to live like this, knowing what I know? It's too much for any one man. What am I supposed to do? What do you do when you know the *true face of God*?"

"That's where I come in."

"You?"

The little man gave him the same, broad smile. "Yes. Me." He stepped closer to Eric and placed his small hands on his face. He looked deeply into his eyes and said, "I can take this knowledge and put it where it can't hurt you. I can put it into your forgotten dreams."

"My forgotten dreams…? Like the one that brought me here?"

"Yes. You won't have to remember it. You'll only know it when you sleep. It won't trouble you. It won't wake you. You'll know without knowing. The only difference will be that your sleep will be enhanced."

"Enhanced?"

"Deeper, more meaningful. You'll need less sleep and you'll recharge faster. You'll even heal faster when you sleep. Just a little."

"That's… Cool. I guess."

"*Very* cool."

Staring into the little man's eyes, Eric asked, "Why me?"

"Why not? You did magnificently."

"But wouldn't someone else have done just as well?"

"Maybe. Maybe not. But the right person *was* chosen. You can believe that."

"If you say so…"

"All done." The gas station attendant, who was by no means a mere gas station attendant, dropped his hands and stepped back.

Eric realized that he no longer remembered what he knew before. He simply recalled having once known something very significant, something life-changing.

"Come on. Let's get you home."

Eric stood up and walked with the small man across the crushed earth of the cathedral's crater. At the edge of the woods sat a vehicle he hadn't noticed before now.

As he walked, his cell phone buzzed against his leg.

It was Isabelle.

"You did so awesome, Eric!"

"Thanks. I couldn't have done it without you."

"Yes, you could've."

"No. I really don't think so."

"Aw… But it's over now. You get to go home."

"I do."

"And you still get me!"

Eric smiled. "I do, don't I?"

"You're stuck with me."

"I wouldn't want it any other way."

Somehow, he could tell that she was smiling on her end of the line.

"But wait… If you were there the whole time, did you see the secret too?"

"No. Only that you learned something very profound."

"Huh…"

"The secret must have only been for you. Not me."

"I guess so."

"I'll talk to you later, okay? Bye!"

"Bye." Eric hung up and stared at the phone.

"You've made a few great friends today," said the little man.

Looking up, Eric found that they had been joined by Edgar, Grant, Taylor and Annette. They walked with them, all of them smiling.

"Fantastic job, Eric," said Taylor.

"I knew you'd get the job done," Grant boasted.

Then both of them faded from sight. Eric stared after them, surprised.

"You came through for all of us," admitted Edgar. "We can't thank you enough." Then he was gone, too.

Annette smiled at him, tears spilling from her eyes. "I'm going to see my Ethan now!" she exclaimed. She pressed her fingers to her lips and then waved goodbye as she faded from sight. Again, he found himself alone with the gas station attendant.

"They've done their work. Now they're free. You did a great job today, Eric."

Ahead of them, he could see the vehicle that awaited them. It was the old white limousine from the gas station. As he watched, the door opened and Father Billy stepped out to greet him.

Eric was relieved. The last time he saw the man, he was running toward a towering golem with a double-handful of lit explosives. While Isabelle had assured him that he'd escaped the ordeal unharmed, it was nonetheless good to see him.

"It's not quite first class," said the diminutive gas station attendant.

"It's awesome," Eric told him. "I've never been in a limo before."

"Truth be told, neither had most of its parts before I put them there."

Eric laughed. "I'm still excited."

The little man smiled more broadly than ever.

Chapter Thirty-Three

Eric sat in the back of the old limousine, watching the trees pass by the windows, thinking about all that he'd done since he jumped out of bed that morning.

That felt like days ago instead of mere hours.

His shoulder still hurt, but not so bad. And with nightfall, his sunburned arms and neck had grown uncomfortable. But all things considered, he was simply thrilled to be alive.

His phone rang. It was Karen.

"Hey baby."

"What's going on? Are you okay?"

"I'm fine. I'm all done. I'm on my way home now."

"Finally! What happened?"

"I'll tell you about it when I get home. It'll be about… Actually, I'm not entirely sure. Hold on." Lowering the phone he called out to Father Billy, "How long will it take to get me home?"

"About eight hours, probably."

Returning his phone to his ear, he asked, "Did you catch that?"

346

"Yeah. I guess you got your walking in for the year, huh? Who was that?"

"Oh, that's Father Billy. He's driving me home."

"Oh. Okay."

"I'm his limo driver for the night!" Father Billy called back proudly.

"Oh. Wow. A limo, huh?"

"Yeah, I'm coming home in style," Eric boasted, grinning down at the torn upholstery and the stained carpet.

"Cool. No picking up girls, you two."

"Hey, no promises. If Father Billy wants to pick up some chicks, I'm not telling a bad-ass man of God he can't."

Up front, he heard Father Billy chuckle.

"I'm *definitely* going to pick up dinner, though," he warned. "I'm starving."

"I'll bet you are. You get yourself a treat."

"I intend to." His eyes drifted out the window as they passed a very familiar gas station. The pumps were gone, the door boarded shut. The lawn where the limo sat was overrun with weeds. It looked like no one had been there for decades.

Except that he glimpsed through the window a shiny new Coke can sitting on the corner of the desk, right where he'd left it.

"Huh…"

"What?"

"Nothing. Just tired. Listen, I'm going to have to go for the night. My cell phone battery is almost dead."

"Oh. Well, I guess I'll see you in the morning then."

"Yeah. Try to get some sleep."

"I'll try. If you've got any charge left when you get back in town, call and wake me up."

"I really don't think I'll have any charge left. Besides, I think I broke it at some point. It may be a lost cause."

"Oh no."

"Yeah. Anyway, I'd better say goodbye now."

"Okay. Goodbye. I love you."

"Love you too. Bye."

Eric disconnected the phone and stared at it. He had always hated these things. Stupid, annoying little devices that people took far too seriously. How ironic was it, then, that he'd had to rely on it all day long as a compass for this strange journey and a connection to those he loved?

A new text message from Isabelle flashed across the screen without waiting for him to answer.

DO IT!

Laughing, Eric rolled down the window and gleefully tossed the phone out into the night.

Keep reading for a preview of

The Box

Book One of
The Temple of the Blind

By Brian Harmon

Chapter 1

It was just a stupid wooden box.

But it was also a mystery. It was not just that Albert didn't know where it came from or how it found its way into his locked car while he was in class. It was not just the cryptic markings etched into its sides. It was not even that he still didn't know what was inside. It was the *sum* of all of these things. It was the fact that nothing about the box was obvious. It was an enigma literally locked up within itself…and that was *irresistibly* fascinating.

He had been studying it all afternoon. He'd already missed lunch and if he didn't watch the time he'd be eating dinner from a vending machine. He'd thought of little else since returning from his eleven o'clock class, and he didn't even know if there was anything to be learned from it. Yet each time he walked away, he soon found himself back at his desk, staring again at the box.

It was a ten-inch cube with no apparent seam to indicate a lid and no visible hinges. He had turned it over and over in his hands and could not determine how it was supposed to open. Yet there was something inside. Things rattled when he shook it. Also, on one side there was a lock, which indicated that the box did indeed open, but the revolving brass plate made a mystery of which end belonged up. The keyhole was about the size of a nickel, with a narrow slit suggesting that the key was very simple, perhaps just a narrow piece of flat metal, but he was unable to pick the lock with a pocketknife.

With the exception of a few small scars in the wood, there were no distinguishing marks on the keyhole side of the box. On each of the other five sides, however, someone had used a sharp object to carve into the wood. On three of these sides were written strange cryptic messages while the last two displayed something that appeared to be a sort of map.

He leaned back in his chair and tried to focus. He never before thought of inanimate objects as having personality, but this box did. He felt almost that it *enjoyed* being mysterious, that it mocked his ignorance. It was like a deeply intriguing character in a really good mystery novel. But in a mystery novel, the secrets are always eventually revealed. Whatever secrets this box held might never be relinquished, might not even exist, as far as he knew. And that made the mystery all the more exquisite.

Derek, Albert's roommate, entered the room and dropped his keys onto his desk. "You still staring at that thing?"

Albert glanced at the clock. It was already almost five. "Yep."

"I think you're making way too much out of this. Somebody probably got the wrong car or something."

Albert did not respond. It was a possibility he'd more than

considered. After all, it was only early September, just a couple short weeks into his first semester here at Briar Hills University. Having come from as far north as St. Louis, he knew no one and hadn't made more than a handful of acquaintances, none of whom knew him well enough to distinguish his car from all the others that occupied the parking lot the previous evening. Whoever left the box could very well have meant to leave it in someone else's car.

"I wouldn't stress about it."

Albert did not turn around. He could hear the familiar tones as Derek checked his cell phone for voicemail. He'd only been living with Derek Clarnet for three and a half weeks, but he already knew his every routine by heart. Every time he returned from class he would walk straight to his desk and drop his keys and wallet. Then he would always reach for his cell phone and check his voicemail. He never took it with him to class for some reason. If there were any messages that required a response, he would do so. And he would always play Solitaire while he talked on the phone. Every time, as soon as he was finished dialing, he would sit down at his computer and load the game. The moment he hung up, he would turn it off. It didn't matter whether he was losing or winning. Once he was done with that he would pocket the phone and leave through the bathroom to visit with Scott and David, their suitemates in the next room. He would return after a while for his keys and wallet and then disappear until later that evening, anywhere between eight and eleven, depending on how much homework awaited him. He would then sit at his desk and work until exactly midnight, when he would go straight to bed. He rose every morning at a quarter to seven and showered and shaved. He left for his first class right at seven thirty. He always ate lunch at eleven. He always ate dinner at half past four. He was, without a doubt, the most boring human being Albert had ever met in his life, and he was actually surprised at how annoying that was.

"'See Carrie,'" Derek read aloud.

Albert realized that he was reading the Post-It he'd left on his keyboard and sat up. "Oh yeah. Carrie from across the hall. She was looking for you while you were at dinner."

"Did she say what she wanted?"

Albert shook his head. "Nope." *And I didn't care to ask*, he thought. He'd recognized the girl as one of the four who lived in the suite across the hall, but he did not know her name until she asked him if he would tell Derek that "Carrie was looking for him." She was a very pretty brunette, petite, with shy mannerisms and a freckled face.

Derek said nothing more. He returned the phone to his desk and then stepped into the bathroom and locked the door. At six-foot-three, he appeared awkward at first sight. He was scrawny, almost geeky, but with his neat hair and piercing brown eyes, he was still fairly handsome. He was also very charming when he wanted to be. Albert had been sharing this room with him for only a short time, but it was already perfectly clear how they were going to get along. The two of them could coexist peacefully enough; their different interests made this room one of the only places on campus where they were ever likely to cross paths. Albert was a computer science major. Derek was a business major. Albert liked to read; Derek liked to go out. They would never be friends. In fact, Albert could hardly stand the guy. Besides his maddeningly boring routines, he was arrogant, self-centered, stubborn, closed-minded, cold natured and lacked any real sense of humor. Yet he was manipulative. He could suddenly become the most lovable human being alive when he wanted something, a tactic that Albert found dazzlingly obnoxious.

Albert had already noticed the time Derek was spending across the hall, trying his best to turn on the charm for Carrie and her suitemates. The names on their doors were Carrie, Danielle, Gail and Tanya. He was pretty sure that Gail was the heavyset blonde and now he knew which one was Carrie, but he still did not know which of the remaining two was Danielle and which was Tanya.

Derek returned from the bathroom, snatched his keys off the desk and left the room without speaking a word. A moment later his voice drifted back from across the hall.

Albert spent no time wondering about Derek or Carrie. He turned his attention back to the box and immersed himself again in its curious secrets.

He'd questioned everyone he knew about the box. He even called his parents and sister to see if they knew anything about it, half expecting it to be some sort of bizarre, belated birthday present, but no one knew anything about it. Everyone seemed to have the same opinion: that someone left it there by mistake.

He supposed he could just break the box open. He could smash it or saw through it. It was only wood. But he did not want to damage it until he'd had a chance to find the sender. After all, it might be important to somebody. Besides, he didn't want to destroy any of the markings before he could decipher them.

Each of the box's three messages was written using only straight lines roughly gouged into the wood. This left some characters frustratingly ambiguous. On one side, for example, there were ten characters arranged in three rows. To Albert, they appeared to read,

I Z

V I I

I O O S T

but it was difficult to be certain. It was impossible to tell whether some of these characters represented numbers or letters. The straight vertical lines could have been the number one or the letter I, for example. Or even a lower-case L. The S could have been a five. The two Os in the bottom line were drawn as squares, and could have been zeros instead, or for all he knew they could actually have been intended as squares. There was simply no way to know for sure, which made the clue that much more puzzling.

He had pondered over these three lines for hours now, trying to decipher them. The middle line could have been the Roman numeral seven, but with nothing else to go on, and no idea how to decipher the other two, he had no way of knowing for certain. It could be a V and an eleven. For that matter, the lines comprising the V were slightly crossed at the bottom. It could even have been a sloppy X.

Frustrated, he turned the box around.

Perhaps the most haunting of the messages was written on the side opposite the keyhole. Here there were five lines. The first four were complete words. From top to bottom they read HELP, COME, TOGETHER and YESTERDAY. The fifth line was not a word, but just three letters: G, N and J.

These lines were much easier to read than the previous three, even with their straight-line lettering, but with the legibility came a haunting feeling. Help. Come. It was as though someone were calling out to him for something. But what could yesterday mean? Was it literal? If so, he'd received the box the previous evening, so yesterday would have been two days ago. Or did it mean the past in general? Help come together yesterday. It made no sense. And how did the last line fit in? Perhaps it was someone's or something's initials.

The final side of the box was carved with only seven letters, scrawled across the surface diagonally from corner to corner, in larger letters than the other messages.

B R A N D Y R

He thought that he recognized these letters. It looked like a name. Brandy R. He knew a Brandy R. Or at least he'd *met* a Brandy R. Brandy Rudman was his lab partner in Chemistry. She was a sophomore, one year ahead of him and likewise a year older, nearly twenty, while he was barely nineteen, yet she could have passed as a sixteen-year-old high school student, small and girlish with a soft face and small, modest figure. She was very pretty. He had not expected to find a lab partner so quickly, but she was sitting in front of him on that first day and when the instructor told them to pair off she turned around, scanning the other students in the class until her pretty eyes fell on him. "You mind?" she asked simply, to which he replied a startled "Sure."

It was just dumb luck for him. He'd been attending classes for not yet a day and a half at a school where he recognized no one and instead of being the last lonely student standing around looking for a pair that would allow him to join, as he'd expected to be, he found himself paired off almost at once and with a very pretty young woman. And by even greater luck, she had so far turned out to be a very lovely person to know as well, friendly, kind, outgoing and fun.

His Chemistry lab was scheduled for Tuesdays and Thursdays at ten o'clock in the morning. Today was Thursday. That morning he stuffed the box inside his green backpack and took it with him to class, intending to see if she knew anything about it, but she was as ignorant of its origins as everyone else he'd spoken with, his last chance at an answer severed at its root.

"Must be another Brandy R.," she'd concluded, peering down into his backpack at the strange, wooden box. "I've never seen it before. It was in your car?"

"Yeah. All the doors were still locked. Nothing broken."

"Weird."

Weird was right. It was also disappointing. A part of him had hoped for an excuse to get to know Brandy a little better.

Albert turned and looked at the clock again. It was after five now. He needed to go eat dinner. He usually tried to go before Derek returned. The less time he spent with him the better.

He stood up and stretched. Some time away from the box would do him good. He was becoming frustrated with it again. Perhaps everyone was right, perhaps the box was never meant for him and he would never understand where it came from or what it meant. But that thought became like a looming darkness. He did not want to be left ignorant. He wanted to know about this box. He wanted to understand it. He didn't like to leave mysteries unsolved. It simply wasn't his nature.

He was reaching for his shoes when the phone rang. It would probably be somebody looking for Derek. Somebody was always looking for Derek. It was funny how Albert was always looking to avoid him.

He sat down on the bed and answered the phone.

"Is Albert there?"

It was a woman's voice, feminine, petite, pretty. "Speaking," he replied.

"Hi. This is Brandy. From Chem."

Albert stood up again, surprised. They exchanged numbers the first day of class in case either of them missed and needed notes, but he never expected her to use it. "Hi."

"Hey, did you find anything out about that box?"

"No. Not a thing." His heart sped up a notch when she told him who she was. Now it jumped again, shifting from second to third.

Brandy was quiet for so long that he began to think the line was disconnected, but before he could ask if she was still there she said, "There was something in my car when I left class today."

Fourth gear. He started walking across the room, pacing as he sometimes did when he was on the phone. "What did you get?"

Instead of answering, she said, "You're in Lumey, right?"

"That's right." Lumey Hall was the most expensive dormitory on campus. He'd spent the extra money for the semi-private bathroom and coed environment. From his first tour of the Hill he did not like the prison-like feel of the community halls elsewhere on campus, so he forked over nearly twice what other freshmen were paying in the Cube. Over here, two rooms made up a suite and a bathroom connected the two, so only four people shared facilities, instead of an entire floor. Also, unlike any other building, Lumey was entirely coed, hence the fact that there were girls living right across the hall from him. And since Lumey was usually reserved for students with a junior standing or higher, he was very fortunate to obtain his room. It turned out that the freshmen dormitories were overcrowded. In the next few years they would probably have to build a new one.

"What floor?"

"Second floor. Room two-fourteen."

"Meet me in the second floor lounge. I'll be there in about twenty minutes."

"Okay."

She hung up without saying goodbye and he stood staring at the dead phone, his mind a cyclone of thoughts. He was about to get information about the box. Maybe together they would figure out what it was and who gave it to him.

Chapter 2

Twenty minutes turned out to be twenty-five. Albert would be the first to agree that five minutes was hardly an eternity, but Brandy knew something about the box, something she was not willing to disclose over the phone. Now every minute passed like an hour as he sat in the second floor lounge of Lumey Hall, waiting to see what she knew.

There was something in my car when I left class today. Those words kept ringing in his ear. He remembered how he'd unlocked his car the previous evening and found the box sitting in the driver's seat. It was a frightening experience. He did not even see it until he opened the door. Brandy at least found her package in broad daylight, but it still must have been unnerving, perhaps even more so since whoever left it there was bold enough to get into her car in the middle of a busy school day.

The box had Brandy's name on it. Now Brandy had found something too, and in exactly the same way, no less. Perhaps it was no accident after all that he found himself in possession of the box.

At the other end of the room, two boys were playing table tennis. One was a skinny blond kid, his face a spattering of pimples. The other was of an average build with a red goatee that wasn't quite thick enough yet to completely cover his chin. Nearby, a skinny girl with raven black hair cut short enough to stand on end sat in one of the plush chairs watching them. She was close enough to them in such an empty room to indicate that she was with them, but her eyes kept drifting from the boys to the door to her watch and back again, suggesting that she, too, was waiting for someone.

The steady *plink-plunk* sound of the ping-pong ball could be annoying at times, but tonight Albert found it and the occasional outbursts of frustration and excitement from the boys relaxing, almost hypnotic. It was a perfect distraction for his senses. Too much silence made him think too much and just lately that made his head hurt.

He was sitting off to one side of the room, positioned so that he could see out of the lounge and down the hallway to the main doors. Lumey was built on the slope of a hill, so on the back side of the building the first floor was the ground floor, but on the front—the side he was facing now—the main doors led in on the second floor. The visitor parking lot and the meters were located on this side of the building. Therefore, he'd determined that this was the direction from which Brandy would most likely enter.

He spotted her as she was climbing the steps. She was wearing a dark shirt and jeans, different from the shorts and tank top she'd been wearing that morning in lab. She was clenching a black leather purse in her left hand and carried a cigarette in her right.

Albert thought that there was something stiff about her. She looked tense. He watched her as she paused at the ashtray outside the door. She drew one last time from the cigarette and then crushed it. As she did so, she turned and looked around, as though she expected someone to be watching her.

Of course there *was* someone watching her, but he didn't think that it was him she was looking around for.

Perhaps he was imagining it. Maybe she heard something somewhere, someone yelling or a car horn blaring. Maybe he was simply looking for things that weren't there. Puzzling over the box for so many hours had caused his imagination to run a little wild.

At last she opened the door and walked in. Almost immediately, her eyes found him. Albert stood up and greeted her and immediately the smell of her cigarette tickled his nose. He was not a smoker and did not like the smell of cigarettes, but his mother smoked and he was used to it enough that he was not really bothered by it. He always said it would have to be a pretty fine line between yes and no to turn down a date based on whether a girl smoked.

"Sorry I'm late," she said as she sat down.

"It's okay."

She did not relax at first. She held her purse in her lap and looked at him. Albert realized right away that there was something cold about her, as though he had done her some grave evil of which he was not yet aware. Her eyes were a soft and gorgeous shade of blue behind the gold-rimmed lenses of her small glasses, beautiful enough to be hypnotizing, but when she leaned forward they were focused so fiercely on him that it made him want to shrink away. "I'm just going to say right now that if this is some kind of practical joke I'm not going to be happy. There are laws against breaking into someone's car, you know."

Albert stared at her, his own dark eyes wide and shocked. Those words struck him like a hammer. He'd never even considered a practical joke. That cast a whole new light on the subject. What if someone was trying to pull something on him? What if someone somewhere was laughing his ass off at his silly obsession with that nonsense box? "If it's a practical joke," he said, almost numb with the realization of that possibility, "then we're two cheeks on the same butt of it."

Brandy watched his expression as he spoke, her eyes stony and piercing. Finally, after a moment, she laughed. It was a quick sound, a huff of air, almost a sigh. In an instant her features melted back into that sweet, ladylike girlishness that he'd seen so often in the classroom. She relaxed back into her chair, her posture slightly slouched, comfortable. She gazed at him through her glasses, her eyes once more soft and sweet. Her hair was very light blonde, a little past shoulder-length, straight and smooth with short bangs. She was wearing a simple, short-sleeved shirt, black with red patterns around the neck and sleeves. Albert couldn't stop himself from noticing the low neckline. She was not big-breasted, but neither was she shapeless. She was quite pretty, blessed with a girlish figure and a soft and delicate complexion.

Overall, she was a sharp contrast to him. Whereas her hair and eyes were light and fair, his were dark and deep. Her nose and chin were soft and round, while his were straight and pronounced, almost pointed. He was rather short, although still a couple inches taller than she, and a little stocky, and he appeared bulky compared to the soft curves of her petite figure.

"I'm sorry," said Brandy. "I don't mean to accuse you of anything. I wasn't trying to be a bitch."

"No, don't worry about it."

"It's just kind of scary, you know. Somebody got into my car while I was in class."

"I understand. I mean this is some pretty weird stuff."

"I almost threw it away. I didn't want it, really. It kind of gave me the creeps."

These words were like a slap in the face. She almost threw it away? "What did you get?"

She opened her purse and withdrew a small brown pouch. "I feel silly even bringing this to you, but I guess it sort of belongs to you." She opened the pouch, which appeared to be made of soft, aged leather, pulled closed with a simple piece of coarse twine, and then emptied it into her left hand. She turned her eyes up to his as she held it out to him. "It's a key."

Albert stared at it for a moment before taking it from her. It was a flat piece of brass with a simple ring for a grip and a single tooth on each side. Just looking at it, he could understand why he was unable to pick the lock with the pocketknife. Even though the key was flat instead of round or grooved, it still required teeth to work the tumblers inside the lock.

He reached out and took it from her warm palm. He felt a

million miles away, as though he were staring at it through a television set instead of holding it in his own fingers. It didn't feel real. He turned it over, almost mesmerized, and suddenly he was drawn back with a slap. Seven letters were scratched onto this side of the key, just like on one side of the box. But instead of B R A N D Y R, the key read A L B E R T C.

"Albert Cross?" Brandy guessed.

"Seeing as how you're the only Brandy R. I know and I'm probably the only Albert C. you know," he replied, "I'd say it's a pretty good bet."

"Do you think whoever gave us these things got them mixed up? Mine had your name and yours had mine?"

Albert shook his head. "But then we wouldn't know where to find the other half."

"Yeah. That's true." Brandy's eyes dropped to the backpack at Albert's feet. "Did you bring the box?"

"Yeah."

"Can I see it?"

"Of course." Albert unzipped the bag, removed the box and handed it to her. "After my American History class last night I walked out to my car and it was just waiting for me. I'm in there from six to nine. It was in the driver's seat. I always lock my doors."

Brandy held the box in her lap as she studied it. "My car was in the commuter lot next to Wuhr." The Daniel R. Wuhr Building was the science and math building on campus. It was where their Chemistry classrooms were located. "It was right there in my driver's seat after class today."

"Did you have your doors locked?"

Brandy shrugged, almost embarrassed. "They were locked when I came back out, but I have a bad habit of not locking my doors. Whoever put the bag there could've locked them."

Albert nodded. "I can't be a hundred percent sure of mine, either, actually. I say I always lock them, but every now and then..."

Brandy stared at the box as she held it in her lap, her eyes fixed on the letters of her name. "I didn't say anything earlier, but when you showed this to me the first time there was just something eerie about it. It gave me chills. I didn't even want to touch it." She turned it over in her hands, looking at each side. "I'm not sure I want to be holding it now."

Albert said nothing. He watched her expression for a moment and then followed her gaze to the box.

"Brandy R.," she read.

"Yeah. I guess we know for sure what that side means now."

"You haven't figured any of the other sides out?"

"Nope. Maybe they'll make sense once we open it." Albert looked down at the key he was holding. He could feel a cold tingle of excitement rising up his spine.

"Maybe." Brandy turned the box again, observing the other sides. "Well these are all Beatles songs."

Albert's eyes snapped from the key to the box. "What?"

"'Help', 'Come Together' and 'Yesterday' are all songs by the Beatles."

Albert stared at the words on the side of the box. "Are you sure?"

"Of course I'm sure." She glanced up at him, met his eyes for just a brief moment, then looked back down, as if she detected the hungry attention her revelation had drawn from him and was disturbed by it. "I like music. I listen to a lot of it. All different kinds. I don't know what 'G N J' means, though."

Albert felt numb. "The Beatles." He might have recognized country or pop titles, but The Beatles?

"That doesn't mean that's what these mean," Brandy explained. "It could just be a coincidence. But they *are* Beatles songs."

"Wow. I'm impressed."

Brandy looked up at him again. This time she smiled a little.

"Any clue about the other side?"

Brandy turned the box again and tried to read it. "Just looks like garbage to me."

Albert nodded. "Yeah. Me too."

"But these last two sides are a map, right?"

Albert nodded. "Yeah, but I don't know what it's a map of."

"Maybe it's inside."

"Maybe." He looked down at the key again. "Let's see."

Brandy looked up at him, but made no move to hand him the box. "Do you think we should?"

"What do you mean?"

Brandy shrugged. She looked extremely uncomfortable. "I'm just not sure about this. Somebody went to a lot of trouble to set this all up. Why?"

Albert stared back at her, unable to answer.

"I mean this thing still gives me the creeps. It's just too weird.

It's like something out of a... I don't know. An Alfred Hitchcock movie or... Or a Stephen King short story. It's just not *natural*, you know."

Albert looked down at the box. She was right. It was *very* unnatural. Inside, he'd understood that all along.

"I don't want to sound crazy, but there's a part of me that really thinks that maybe we should just throw it away. Forget about it."

This suggestion hit Albert like a punch in the gut. How could he just forget about it? That box had commanded his every thought since he first laid eyes on it. But then again, wasn't that reason enough to do just as she suggested? Perhaps she was right. Perhaps it *was* unhealthy, even dangerous.

The two of them sat there, each of them staring at the box.

"There's also a part of me," Brandy added, a little cautiously, "that still doesn't trust you."

Albert looked up at her, surprised.

"I mean I don't know anything about this. One day, out of the blue, you show up to class with this box with my name on it and say you found it in your car. After class I go to *my* car and find a key with your name on it. And I really don't know you."

Albert lowered his eyes all the way to the floor. She certainly made a point. "That's true." He nodded and looked back up at her. "I guess I really can't expect you to trust me. I really don't have reason to trust *you*."

Brandy started to say something, but she stopped herself.

"As far as I know, *you* could've left that box in my car. After all, I have no way of knowing whether you're telling me the truth about how you came by this key. For the same reason, you have no way of knowing how I came by that box or that I didn't put the key in your car."

"Yesterday you beat me to class and I left before you did…"

Albert was impressed. She'd really thought this through. "But I could've had an accomplice."

"Yeah."

He leaned back against the cushions of the couch and stared down at the key. Three more people had entered the room since Brandy arrived. Two were young men who were speaking a language he could not place and playing a game of chess. The third was a young woman with a huge mane of curly black hair and a surprisingly unattractive face. She was sitting alone by one of the windows with a Dean Koontz novel in her hand. The girl who was with the ping-pong players still seemed to be waiting on whoever it was she was expecting. "You don't really seem like the kind of person who would ever want to do me wrong," he said at last.

"Neither do you," said Brandy.

"But we don't know each other."

"Exactly."

Albert continued to stare at the key.

"But so what if we're both telling the truth?" Brandy asked after a moment. "Then what? *Somebody* sent these things. *Somebody* scratched our names into them. That person knows what cars we drive, what classes we have, when we're in class and God only knows what else. So then who was it? Why would they do something like this? I'd rather think that *you* were trying to prank me. The fact

371

that someone else out there is capable of this sort of stunt is way worse."

Albert could think of no reply for her. Come to think of it, how could anyone have known to leave that box in his car the previous night? It was the first time he'd ever driven to his night class. He didn't know until the previous weekend that the campus police stopped ticketing after five o'clock. *He* didn't even know he was going to drive until just before he left. He'd intended to drive only on rainy days, but he decided to see how much time it saved him.

That meant that someone must have been watching either him or his car that evening. The thought of a pair of eyes lurking unseen somewhere out there sent a shiver down his spine.

Two more students walked into the room together. One was a stout young man with short black hair and a thick, black goatee. The other was a rather plain-looking blonde girl with remarkably large breasts. The shorthaired girl stood up from the couch as they approached and greeted them both with a hug.

"So what do we do?" Brandy asked after a moment.

Albert held up the key. "I guess we open it," he replied. "We're both here. We have it. What can it hurt to open it and look inside? Maybe we'll figure out what it all means."

Brandy held onto the box, still not sure. She looked at the key for a moment, then looked up at Albert and said in a voice that was nearly a whisper, "What if it's a bomb or something?"

Albert hadn't considered a bomb. He stared down at the box, his thoughts whirling. Why would it be a bomb? But why not? Why crash airplanes into the World Trade Center? There was no end to the number of horrors that could be hidden in a box like this. He could almost imagine turning the key and watching it fly open as some hellish creature burst from within, its vicious jaws tearing the flesh from his body before he knew what was upon him.

He shook these thoughts away and met Brandy's eyes. "If it is," he decided at last, "we probably won't feel it."

Brandy's face paled at the thought of such an abrupt and brutal end. "I guess that's true," she said after a moment.

"With or without you," Albert said. "I think I have to open it. I have to know what's going on."

Brandy gazed back at him. "Why?"

"It's just who I am. I've always loved a good mystery. I read mysteries, I watch them, I can almost always figure out who did it." He looked down at the box. "This is the first *real* mystery I've ever come across. I guess I feel like, even if it's dangerous—stupid even—to open it, I want to." He shrugged and lowered his eyes. He felt foolish. "I feel like, above all else, I *want* this to be something real, you know?"

Brandy stared at him, surprised. "Yeah. I guess I do."

"I'm not saying we should. I don't know. Probably we shouldn't. I'm just saying I *want* to."

She nodded. "Okay." She moved the box closer to him, resting it on her knees, and then turned it so that the keyhole faced him. "I guess I do too."

He looked up at her, relieved that she understood him. He wanted to ask her if she was sure, but he didn't dare tempt her to reconsider. "Ready?"

Again, she nodded.

Slowly, Albert slid the key into the lock and began to turn it. For a moment he could feel the key searching for the slot—he still did not know which end was up—and then it fell into place and he felt the lock begin to turn. It moved sluggishly, as though stiff with age. When he had turned it a complete ninety degrees, a firm click announced that the lock was sprung and the key stopped in his fingers.

The two of them sat there for a moment, staring at the box. It was unlocked now, or at least they could only assume that it was, but they still didn't know how it was supposed to open.

"Now what?" Brandy asked, looking at Albert.

He did not know.

"I heard it unlock."

"So did I."

"So how does it open?"

He shook his head. "I don't know. I couldn't figure that out before when I was looking at it." He began to pull the key from the keyhole and after a moment of fumbling, the box began to open. It was now that it finally made sense to him. The box appeared seamless when he first examined it, except of course for those seams that one would expect to find in a wooden box, those where the wood was glued together. There were no hinges because the box did not have the kind of lid he'd been looking for. Instead, it consisted of two separate pieces, one inside the other. As he pulled the key out, the entire front side slid outward from the rest of the box.

"I see," Albert said. "It's like a drawer." It quickly became obvious that the box was lying on its side and he picked it up and turned it. Brandy's name was carved on the top of the box while part of the map made up the bottom.

"How'd you know to pull on the key like that?"

Albert glanced up at her. "I didn't. I was just trying to take it out."

She did not respond and Albert felt an odd sense of guilt. He could almost read her thoughts as she wondered if perhaps he'd been aware of how the box worked all along. "It's a really good fit," he observed, trying to keep her attention on the box itself. "You couldn't tell that the wood wasn't glued there, but it wasn't stuck closed, either." This was true. More true, in fact, than he cared to elaborate on. He pushed the box closed again for a moment and examined the seams. The fit was so perfect that there was not even the slightest movement when they were together, especially when the lock was turned. As he pulled it open again, he saw that there were small but formidable bolts on all four sides of the keyhole side of the inner box, and four no-doubt perfectly sized holes to receive the bolts in the outer box, like the deadbolt on a door, but four times as secure.

Still Brandy said nothing. Her silence felt like an accusation of some heinous crime for which he did not have an alibi.

Albert opened the box and peered inside. It would do no good to try to talk his way out of any suspicion. If she intended to blame him, there was nothing he could do to change her mind. The more he tried, the guiltier he would be perceived.

Besides, *he* knew he was innocent.

He hoped that opening the box would lead him to some

answers, but as he gazed in at the contents, he quickly realized that there were only more questions within.

Random junk was all he found. There was a flat piece of rusted metal, a small stone, a dull metal object that he realized after a moment's consideration was a brass button, a dirty black feather and a silver pocket watch that might have been an antique, but was corroded far beyond any real value.

"What is all that?" Brandy asked, leaning forward until their foreheads were almost touching. "Does it mean anything?"

Albert shook his head. He did not know. He reached in and removed the watch. Its lid was loose, but still intact. Carved into the front was an elegant letter G. It was dirty, as were all the objects in the box, as though they had been dropped in mud at some point, and he used his thumb to clean the dirt from the design. Did the "G" indicate the owner of the watch, he wondered, or the company that manufactured it? Maybe he would look it up on the Internet sometime. He opened the cover and was surprised to find that the glass was still intact. Except for its apparent age, it was in surprisingly good condition. He found the stem and tried to wind it, half expecting it to start working again, but the insides had apparently not aged as well as the rest. The hands would not turn.

"Is it broken?"

Albert nodded. "Yeah." He handed it to her so that she could see it and then removed the feather. There was nothing very special about it. It wasn't from a very large bird. It was dirty and rather ratty-looking, like it was simply plucked from the gutter somewhere and dropped into the box.

Brandy placed the watch back into the box and removed the button. There were no distinguishing markings on it. It appeared to be a simple, old-fashioned brass button.

Albert dropped the feather back into the box and withdrew the stone. It was dark gray in color, about an inch in length, semicylindrical, with a strange texture. There were small creases along the sides. He rubbed away the dirt with his thumb and forefinger and saw that both ends were rough, as though it had been broken from a larger object.

Brandy dropped the button back into the box. "Does this stuff make any sense to you?"

"Not a bit." Albert dropped the stone back into the box and removed the final object. After turning it over in his fingers several times he concluded that it was the broken tip from some sort of knife. It was large enough to be from a dagger or a sword and, looking at the condition it was in, it certainly wasn't stainless steel. The original blade could have been just about anything.

"It's just junk."

"I know." Albert dropped the blade piece back into the box and fished out the button. As he examined it, four more people entered the room and sat down at the card table by the window. He recognized them immediately as the residents of the suite down the hall from his own. One of them was already shuffling a deck of cards and soon they would be immersed in a game. Albert saw them here often. Hearts seemed to be their game of choice, but he had already seen them play everything from Spades to Poker.

The room would only get more crowded as the night went on.

By eight o'clock the only place that would be busier than the lounges was the computer room on the first floor. Albert tried to go there once just to check out the facilities, in case his own computer ever failed to meet his needs, and he was not even able to get in the door.

Brandy leaned back in the chair and looked sternly at Albert. "So what does it all mean then?"

"I don't know."

"Someone went to all the trouble of getting us together to open this fucking thing, so what are we supposed to get from it?"

Albert met her eyes for a moment and then dropped the button back into the box. He'd heard plenty of swearing in his life, as much from women as from men. Hell, his sister swore like a sailor when they were growing up. And he'd already heard Brandy swear plenty of times in the short time he'd been acquainted with her—she always seemed to be coming up with some delightfully creative expletive during their lab experiments—but it still surprised him somehow every time he heard something vulgar pass from her lips. She projected such a girlishly polite image that it was hard to imagine her as anything but young and innocent, virgin even. Of course, that wasn't to say that it was unattractive by any means. On the contrary, he actually found it to be something of a turn-on.

"I really don't know," he said after a moment. "You'd think there'd be something more."

Someone walked into the room and looked around, as though looking for someone. Albert glanced at her and recognized her as Gail from across the hall. He wondered vaguely if her presence here might indicate that Derek was no longer in her room. If so, he hoped he wasn't hanging out when he returned to *his* room. After a quick look around, Gail turned and left the lounge. Whoever she was looking for obviously wasn't here.

"This is ridiculous." Brandy closed the box, lifted it off her knees and dropped it into his lap. "I don't get it. I don't really care to get it." She grabbed her purse and stood up.

"What are you doing?"

"I'm leaving. You can keep all that. The key too. I'm not interested."

Albert stared at her, surprised. "You're not even curious?"

She half turned as she slipped the thin strap of her purse over her shoulder. For a moment she paused, as though struggling with herself. "Yes," she said at last, her eyes fixed on the door. "If you come up with anything, let me know tomorrow in lecture."

"Okay." He could not believe she was just walking away from this. How could she? It was such a delicious mystery. Sure, the lack of answers inside the box was discouraging, even aggravating, but it was also all the more intriguing. These new questions were even more alluring than the first. How could anyone just walk away from such an enigma? Perhaps she was only being the more mature one, even the smarter one, but to just drop it and walk away? The very ability to do such a thing seemed so alien to him.

"I just don't like it," she explained before she walked away, as though she could feel the weight of his eyes and read the questions inside his head. "It's just... I don't know. It's just too much. I don't want to be a part of something I don't know anything about."

Albert nodded. He understood. It was probably the right thing to do. Nonetheless, he was disappointed.

"Bye." Brandy walked out of the room as a very pretty redhead entered and dropped into one of the soft chairs with a textbook.

Albert watched her go without getting up. It felt surprisingly sad knowing that this mystery was once again his alone.

This is only the beginning!

Don't miss

THE TEMPLE OF THE BLIND

A horror-adventure, mystery and suspense series by

BRIAN HARMON

ABOUT THE AUTHOR

Brian Harmon grew up in rural Missouri and now lives in Southern Wisconsin with his wife, Guinevere, and their two children.

For more about Brian Harmon and his work, visit
www.HarmonUniverse.com